The Olive Tree

The Olive Tree

To Fenella
Best wishes

Andria Lawrence

ANDRIA LAWRENCE

© Andria Lawrence, 2015

Published by Andria Lawrence

A CIP catalogue record for this book is available from the British Library.

ISBN 978-0-9934222-0-1 (Hardback)
ISBN 978-0-9934222-1-8 (Paperback)

Book layout and cover design by Clare Brayshaw

Prepared and printed by:

York Publishing Services Ltd
64 Hallfield Road
Layerthorpe
York YO31 7ZQ

Tel: 01904 431213

Website: www.yps-publishing.co.uk

In memory of Heinz 1948-2003

~

For Roger

A talented author, historian and friend, whose support
and encouragement has enabled me to write this story.

This story is about triumph over adversity,
sacrifice and the power of love.
Also a reminder for those who do not play
by the rules, to be prepared to suffer the
consequences.

PREFACE

In 1861 the regional states of the Italian Peninsular Sardinia and Sicily were united under Victor Emmanuel the First. However, the industrial north was far more prosperous than the southern regions. Poverty was rife in the south, where life was hard and reliant on what produce the people were able to grow. This enabled a barter system to exist, making it possible for them to feed themselves with enough of the locally grown food to survive. Also payment in kind was another option, i.e. medical help from whoever was able to provide it. Quite often a local woman would help with childbirth in villages where no doctor was available.

It was quite common for grapes to be exchanged for eggs or milk, or if they cultivated olives these could be exchanged for wheat; a prime staple of their diet required to make pasta and bread. Such similar arrangements seemed to help with all the necessary requirements for the essentials of life.

The close relationship between families and neighbours made their lives possible to survive the hardship. This part of Italy was so beautiful with stunning scenery, which seemed to influence the passionate songs and the music that revealed something of their heritage, which came from the many early settlers from Greece, Arabia and further afield.

PROLOGUE

1880: *The village of Monte Verde in Campania, Southern Italy.*

Giancarlo Villarni sat on the old stone wall outside the school door. The view was so breathtaking he often sat there drinking in the blueness of the sea with its pride and joy Vesuvius, standing majestically in the distance. Even in his young life, having never seen anywhere except the local towns and villages, was certain there was nowhere in the world quite so beautiful.

He waited for Father Di Marco to join him as it was his last day at school, which would close for the summer months as the heat became intense in July and August. It was also the end of his school days. He was now expected to help his father; this being the norm as in every family the children especially the boys, who helped their parents in whatever was needed to feed the family. This mostly meant toiling the land.

In Giancarlo's family their father worked hard to provide for them by growing fruit and cultivating some olive and lemon trees and a few grape vines. These were supplemented by his skill as a carpenter. The knowledge of all these tasks he taught his two sons. Lucio at twenty was the eldest, and now Giancarlo who was expected to join them to provide the help needed to continue to cultivate their land. His daughter Patrizia was taught by her mother, Anna, to cook, sew and to cultivate other household skills, expected of another woman in the house.

The priest soon came and sat down beside him. He was so proud of Giancarlo, although pride was not what he would want to admit; but the boy had such a thirst for knowledge and in time had exhausted his entire collection of books. He realized that Giancarlo's future after leaving school; would be labouring in the fields when, with his intelligence and desire for learning, he could achieve so much more.

Father Di Marco had arrived in Monte Verde as a young man sent by the Vatican to tend his flock and provide the necessary duties of a priest; performing weddings, christenings and funerals for the departed.

He was not only the village priest. He, being popular, was their friend, their guide, and counselor as well as teaching the children the three 'R's.' As a man of principle there was always emphasis to play by the rules: be honest and compassionate to others and to keep the faith.

When he first arrived he was shocked to see the children running around barefoot and illiterate, as were the adults. Coming as he did from the more affluent north, knowing that education was now compulsory in the newly created provinces that formed the country of Italy, he was surprised to find it was still not implemented everywhere.

One of the first decisions he made was to open a school and teach the children how to read and write, and give the younger generation a chance to improve their quality of life. Without literacy they would never achieve anything but working on the land with no opportunity to provide a better quality of life for them and their families and community.

Father Di Marco had a plan; he would speak with his seniors in Rome first, and tell them about Giancarlo who he felt sure could achieve much if properly educated. This could eventually bring rewards to this beautiful, but poor village, his family-and possibly the church.

He would wait until he had contacted an old friend he had studied with in the seminary in Rome, who had progressed over the years to a senior position in the Vatican. He knew there were occasions when a clever young man could be given a scholarship. This would not necessarily be for the priesthood, as there were many requirements by the church for other roles. They needed lawyers, doctors and other professionals for the monumental task of running the church's role in the world.

He explained the circumstances to his friend of how he had taught a pupil who he was convinced had the ability to be anything in life with the right education. The reply came back that this could be possible. More details would follow on how to proceed. The moment had arrived at last when he could now approach the boy to ask him about his future. He looked at Gianni 'Its spectacular isn't it? he said smiling.

The boy looked back at him and said 'I think it must be the most beautiful in the world Father'.

'Now what are you going to do with your life?' Gianni didn't reply for a moment.

He paused then replied 'I don't know, help my father I suppose.'

Di Marco then broached the question he had longed to ask.

'If there was a chance to study in Rome for something that would help your family and maybe many others in Monte Verde, what would you say?'

Gianni, giving a little sigh, replied 'I don't know', wondering why such a question was even put to him.

The priest smiled knowing that with Gianni's handsome looks, the priesthood would definitely not be an option!

Gianni, now going along with this fantasy that might be a game, said 'I think a lawyer'.

Father Di Marco asked: 'And why a lawyer?'

Gianni replied: 'To help people with little money to know how to protect their rights.'

Di Marco, was surprised that the lad's reading had not been confined to the usual academic subjects. This convinced him that this was no coincidence, but destiny.

The priest was now convinced that God had given him the chance to teach this young man, who was compassionate and intelligent enough to use his gift for the benefit of others.

He then told Gianni of his plan and that, if his father agreed, it would be up to him to take up the opportunity. There was just one condition he wanted to apply: if he became successful in life he would never forget to help his family and the people of Monte Verde.

Gianni now had much to mull over, but within his heart he felt some kind of compulsion that he must listen to, if God had planned it, who was he to deny Him.

Father Di Marco was a popular man and over the years had become so much part of the community he found he was the centre of life and social gatherings in the village of Monte Verde. He was invited to all social events and celebrations and had become very close friends with many families.

One in particular was the Villarni family. He was often invited to their house to play Scopa, a very popular card game, with Salvatore the head of the family. On such a visit, the opportunity came for him to raise the subject of Giancarlo's future knowing full well the young lad would be expected to help support his father. Every hand was needed in the hope that they could help increase productivity, all of which was hard work in the hot weather.

So began the difficult task of explaining to Salvatore that his son was the brightest young boy he had ever known; how he absorbed the contents of books like a sponge absorbs water and could retain the information. Now he was no longer able to supply Gianni with the books and teaching that would enhance his knowledge, as realistically he had exhausted his library.

He believed that his gift was from God and that he could achieve something far more valuable for his family and his community if he was able to be educated properly. Gianni should go college and university, as he could become anything he put his mind to.

He understood that Salvatore would want Gianni to stay and work with him and his other son, but it would be wrong to deprive him of a chance to a better life. So, if God was willing to bless him with this opportunity, would his father allow him to go to college in Rome?

Salvatore himself was illiterate, as were most of the villagers of the region, that had been left behind for centuries. Nevertheless, he was intelligent and realized that this was a gift from God, however much he could do with another hand to help him; it was an opportunity that came once in a lifetime.

Salvatore paused for a moment and slowly nodded his head. Looking into Father Di Marco's eyes, he replied softly that he would not stand in his way.

The priest took his friend's hand. 'God bless you, Sal. Have faith, as things are sometimes sent to us for a reason. Don't worry, there is no hidden agenda for him to go into the priesthood; I think God has different plans for Giancarlo's future.'

He smiled and could see that his friend had an expression of slight relief.

'I asked you first, now I will speak with Giancarlo to assure him that you agree. 'The two men now poured a glass of the home made wine and Salvatore sighed: 'Now I have to tell his mother!'

CHAPTER ONE

1898 Helen and Giancarlo

It was fifteen years later when Giancarlo sat down at the table in his favourite trattoria, 'Luigi's' in a side street close to the Via Veneto. This was his usual lunchtime venue come rain or shine, where he would order his favorite dish. Luigi made the best lasagne in the world, except of course Gianni's mother's, but she was a long way away in his village, Monte Verde in Campania.

He had just returned to Rome after spending most of August in the hills surrounding his home, away from the searing heat of the city. Those that could escape did so to somewhere that offered respite in similar areas or to the sea. It was always a delight for him to go home, which he did as often as business would allow.

He felt such a feeling of satisfaction and joy that he had been able to bring so much help to his family and to the village. He was treated like the Second Coming every time he arrived there, so much so his days and nights were filled with invitations to everything. There was little opportunity to refuse or just laze around. Gianni had brought running water to their homes, a telephone line and electricity. Best of all was being able to help his father develop the vineyards, bringing a thriving business and employment for so many. The wine had proved to be excellent and was now sold all over Italy and abroad.

The olive grove had been enlarged covering many hectares, the oil bottled and sold all over Italy and also exported abroad. It seemed that the population of Monte Verde was at last enjoying the fruits of its labours.

Their children were educated and now had a future that held great promise.

Father Di Marco, now semi-retired, had been sent a young priest to ease the burden of duties and, as always was delighted to see Giancarlo and to hear about his life in Rome. He, in turn, always looked forward to seeing the old man whose joy was always expressed with such passion that he could see the tears welling up in his eyes. Gianni knew full well that the day would eventually arrive when news would come that would be hard to bear: that the priest had gone to his Maker.

If anyone deserved a place in Heaven it would be Father Antonio Di Marco, for everything Gianni had in life he owed to this wonderful man's faith in him.

Now at the beginning of September the days were full of blissful, gentle warmth that was so enjoyable and Gianni was now back to work after the summer break. Fratelli Donati Legali, the most eminent lawyers in Italy, thought a great deal of their junior partner. He had been with the firm since leaving university and, with the passes he had won on graduating, they had seized a great opportunity to nab a very clever young man. They did a great deal of work for the Vatican, and knowing the right people had secured the talent of a brilliant student.

It was Saturday, but he had popped into the office just streets away, to drop off some papers. Now he looked forward to the weekend doing whatever appealed to him.

Luigi, the proprietor came out, his apron secured in front with the tapes tied in a bow on his well-rounded stomach. He greeted Gianni with a big hug, as if he had not seen him for a long time. However, it was only yesterday but to Luigi time was of no consequence. Both men came from the south, and they shared a warmth and affection as they conversed in their native dialect, which was almost incomprehensible to those from the north.

Gianni was used to this affectionate greeting, which frequently brought a big smile to the other diners. Luigi said proudly: 'You know, not many achieve your success while so young.'

Gianni laughed; he knew Luigi loved having such a distinguished customer and made it impossible for his other customers not to hear. But he was right, as the partnership had come after only five years. Gianni had risen like a star to become a very successful and respected lawyer. He had decided to specialize in business and company law which, he believed, would bring the most benefit to those who had given so much for him to be here. For a young man he had already made a lot of money. Many clients, in appreciation of his help, had given him advice of where to invest and, with other opportunities that had come his way, he had acquired a small fortune. It was not because of greed, but to keep the promise he had made to Father Di Marco that he would help not only his own family, but the village of Monte Verde.

He finished his lunch and ordered a coffee when a young woman sat down at an adjacent table. She had fair hair and from what he could see of her face that was intensely buried in books and maps, she was quite beautiful. She was tut-tutting and biting her lip, when she turned and saw him looking at her. He took the opportunity to speak to her in Italian: 'Can I help you Signorina?'

She did not look up, as her host the Barone Di Sanro, a close friend of her father, had warned her to avoid young Italian men who were often looking for vulnerable foreign tourists.

She replied. 'I am sorry, I don't speak Italian,' not looking up and continued turning the pages of her pamphlets that were covering the table.

The voice spoke again this time in perfect English.

'You seem to be a little lost or unable to find what you are looking for.'

She turned and looked towards the voice. It belonged to the most handsome young man she had ever seen. He had dark wavy hair and smiling brown eyes. Taken by surprise she hesitated, taking time to think how she should react. However, before she had time to reply, Luigi who was a romantic at heart, could tell this might be a good moment to step in and help things along. He had seen Gianni accompanied by different young women, but no one special. This one was different, a beautiful young lady who obviously stood out as having class.

He quickly walked over to their tables and said 'Signorina, allow me to introduce my friend, Giancarlo Villarni, the youngest partner in Fratelli Donati Legali, the most famous law firm in Italy.'

She smiled and thought goodness, what a recommendation, feeling relief that this young man seemed respectable and surely could not be the type that went around trying to pick up tourists. She decided to take a chance: she was no shrinking violet and was quite strong-willed, her gentle manner belied her strength of character. She offered her hand to Gianni.

'I am Helen Davenport,' she said.

He took the proffered hand and replied: 'I am pleased to meet you Helen Davenport.' She looked at the eyes, the hair, the slightly bronzed skin, the way he was dressed in a light cotton suit which took away any hint of formal attire in the still warm weather.

'So, where is it you want to visit first? May I suggest you take time to see everything properly?' he said.

She answered 'There are so many places I have to see: the Coliseum, the Vatican, St Peter's.'

Before she could say another word he said, laughing: 'Not all in one day I hope, you need to take time to be able to enjoy each place. How long are you here for, a day?'

She smiles 'No, I am staying here a year to study art and the Italian language.'

'So, what's the rush? You have a year to see everything and many of the sites are not close together. I suggest you visit something near here to begin with, and if you would like me to show you around, I will be happy to escort you.'

She was quiet for a moment, so much wanting to accept his offer, but hesitating and trying to think before she leapt into the unknown. Before she could answer, Luigi witnessing this scene, interrupted.

'Signorina, this man has an excellent reputation, I know him well for many years, and you are quite safe with him.'

Helen answered: 'Well, it's very kind of you.'

She stopped, hesitating for a moment. She was already fascinated by this young man, so elegant, so handsome and so different to anyone she had ever met before; so she let her adventurous spirit throw caution to the wind and was not going to let the opportunity slip by.

Luigi was now happy that he had spoken for Gianni and was thoroughly enjoying playing matchmaker to this lovely young couple. Helen was already feeling at ease after Luigi's intervention and they all laughed.

They stayed chatting as if they had known each other far longer; whilst Luigi insisted on something tasty for Helen to eat and some wine for both of them 'on the house'.

After what seemed to have turned out a very long lunch they thanked their host and departed with lots of hugs between the two men, as was the custom, with promises to tell him of their sightseeing and to hurry back as soon as possible. Luigi watched them go, delighted that his helpful intervention had proved so successful and muttered to himself his satisfaction.

The next few weeks flew by and by the time the summer months had passed their sight seeing together had brought about a deepening of their friendship that had gradually become much more, as Helen and Gianni found themselves deeply in love.

The Barone began to be curious why Helen's friends were never available to come to the house. It was quite odd, as when she was not attending some class or other something was occupying all her time; which meant he always seemed to be dining alone. He did not intend to question her in a way that might make her defensive. The last thing he wanted was for her to feel he was interfering with her personal life, and recognized that Helen, although seeming very passive and sweet, certainly had a mind of her own.

However, it was his duty to protect her from any undesirable characters and he decided to have her followed when she left the house.

One early evening she set off on foot always declining an offer of an escort, saying she enjoyed the walk being inside most of the day at college and was not going far. One of his employees, a man that Helen did not know, followed her at a discreet distance. She had walked for about ten minutes and arrived at the busy part of the city and continuing down a street she stopped and entered a large building. He waited as she entered and then walked up to the entrance and read the sign on the wall. It read *FRATELLI DONATI LEGALI*.

He then quickly hurried to the corner of the street and waited in a doorway. About five minutes later Helen and a handsome young man came out of the building and walked to a parked motor vehicle that he recognized as being very expensive and one that only the wealthy could afford. It was one of the first automobiles produced by Fiat to be seen on the streets of Rome.

The employee watched them drive off and hurried back to report to the Barone who was totally surprised and puzzled as to just what Helen was doing at his lawyer's office and leaving the building with a handsome young man! The Barone realized he had to hear an explanation from Helen and could hardly wait until the opportunity arose. However, he didn't have to wait long as he was having dinner that evening with friends at a very exclusive restaurant.

On arriving there he was greeted by the maitre' d and led to the bar where arrangements had been made for him to join the party. They were shown to their table shortly afterwards, and glancing around the room, he saw sitting at a table in a discreet corner, Helen and a young man. This was surprising enough, but recognizing immediately who she was with was the biggest surprise of all: it was no other than Giancarlo Villarni, his lawyer!

The Barone wasn't noticed and decided that the much-needed explanation from Helen could wait until the morning, as it was Saturday and an ideal opportunity to discuss things and bring them out into the open. He was actually relieved and in a way delighted to know that she was with the most eligible young man in Rome, whose reputation and standing were exemplary. Giancarlo was also someone that he liked very much but how Lord Davenport would react was something else. He was a man set in old traditions, in which marrying into the right families was sacrosanct. If this situation was not a brief dalliance, as he feared, Davenport's reaction was not something he wished to think about.

It was after breakfast that he told Helen that before she rushed off somewhere, he would like to have a word and suggested that they go somewhere quiet. Helen looked slightly puzzled and wondered what on earth her host wished to talk to her about that was evidently so private.

She followed him out onto the terrace where he bade her sit and after a pause came to the point.

'Helen, I understand you are acquainted with Giancarlo Villarni.'

She was surprised and, not sure what to answer, took a deep breath and hesitated before answering 'Yes,' looking slightly uncomfortable, not knowing quite what was coming next.

The Barone, also not quite sure how to begin and not wanting it to sound like this was an inquisition, began to speak.

'Giancarlo is a fine young man, and as far as I am concerned the most eligible to be found anywhere. If this is a friendship or something much more, Helen, I am sure that you are aware that your father will not approve. As far as I am concerned, I am very fond of him and know that if it is more, you are a very lucky young woman, as I believe you could not find a more worthy one.' He paused for a moment then continued: 'I am sure you realize it will not be accepted by your father, but I can assure you it will not be me that would side with him.'

He stopped speaking and leaned forward and took her hand. Helen, not sure what to say, looked a little tearful. She was only too aware of the position that she and Gianni were in. He had already told her he wanted to marry her, but that he knew what he was up against.

She answered 'Thank you; I don't know what to do. I love him, Barone, and I am afraid if my father turns up he will drag me back. I don't want to go back, I love it here and I am determined to stay and marry Gianni.'

'In that case I will tell you something, I married for love a woman without social position and considered unsuitable and I was the happiest man in the world. Gossip and comments were of no avail and when she passed away, my life was empty.' He sighed, and continued, 'But life goes on and I live with memories that are precious and know I did the right thing' he smiled as if the past was here with him.

Helen, with tears in her eyes, went and hugged him, now aware she had a friend who understood everything that concerned her, as in his own life he had experienced the same dilemma.

He smiled and said: 'Invite him to dinner Helen and let's discuss what to do next.' He took her hand and Helen, knowing she had an ally, nodded.

'Yes, Gianni will be so relieved and happy to know you approve, thank you.'

He smiled and said 'Tonight if it's convenient?' She answered 'It will be!'

Now that they no longer had to hide anything as they had the approval of the Barone and had overcome one obstacle; and knowing they had a friend on the inside might prove very helpful?

Helen, more determined than ever, knew that the one thing that would decide matters would be if they eloped, because once she was married her father could do nothing about getting her back to England.

Once she belonged to her husband, her father would have no further jurisdiction over her, although with his connections he might possibly find a way.

She told Gianni: 'Why don't we go to your home during the holidays and be married by Father Di Marco? It would be wonderful Gianni and we could have our honeymoon there.'

'Are you sure Helen? It would alienate your father, perhaps forever, could you bear that?'

She looked at him and said: 'Gianni I love you and he will have to accept it or never see his grandchildren.' Gianni roared with laughter and replied, 'We are not even married and you're talking about grandchildren.'

'Well,' she answered 'We have to think ahead.'

She laughed as he took her in his arms and said 'Do you want to practice now?' She didn't answer, but raised her eyebrows and gave him a very provocative smile.

So plans were made that the first week in August they would go to Monte Verde, as hopefully it would be cooler there. Gianni notified everyone they were coming and specially Father Di Marco who, to all accounts, was overjoyed. This would be the wedding of the century in the village church, and the guests most likely would be the whole of Monte Verde and possibly further afield.

They had discussed the situation before about her visiting his family and Gianni explained that there things were very old-fashioned: a man taking a young woman home to his family meant they would have to be engaged and a wedding planned as soon as they arrived.

He said 'We have to be positive about our plans before we announce anything, as you have no idea my darling what a celebration will be prepared and you will be wined and dined and be the centre of attention, so be warned.' He knew that this was no exaggeration.

He smiled at the expression on her face, so obvious that she had no idea about weddings in his village, where none had to be formally invited as everyone just turned up.

As their plans for Christmas had to be decided another dilemma arose, as they would be married by then and would want to spend it together. The Barone suggested this was an opportunity for Helen to go home to her family. Perhaps she should stay for two weeks to give them all the positive news of how well she was doing with her studies; and tell them that she had to return for her final exams. This could help Gianni prepare the news to his family about the lovely young woman he had met.

They both agreed and saw that this might prevent her father deciding to turn up unexpectedly. Helen making the effort to spend Christmas with them would hopefully encourage her to complete her studies, so both of them knew he was talking sense.

However, as the time approached Helen felt she could not face the ordeal. She was worried that her father would prevent her returning to Rome and the plan to spend Christmas with her family became something she could not face alone.

All the attempted persuasions of both Gianni and the Barone were in vain and a tearful Helen found herself trying to find a reasonable excuse for her parents. One excuse was suggested that her best friend at college was getting married and wanted her to be bridesmaid and if her parents could forgive her she would visit as soon as possible after.

This had proved a possibility and when the summer months approached they had more or less planned everything. Helen had already told her father that when the she finished college she was taking the opportunity to travel around Italy, as she had not had the opportunity before whilst studying. This all sounded quite reasonable and this would give the newly married couple time to enjoy their honeymoon in the most beautiful place on earth, according to Gianni.

At the first opportunity they set off to Monte Verde, the Barone promising to join them a day or so before the wedding. They hoped for some respite before facing up to the inevitable revelations to Helen's father, without dreaming that he had other plans. This was that Lord Davenport had decided to make a surprise visit to see Helen and his old friend Christo Di Sanro and the opportunity to join Helen on a sightseeing trip together.

Fortunately, he had informed the Barone of his intentions and the Barone had immediately broke the news to the couple who were ready to depart to Monte Verde for their wedding preparations.

Panic ensued, but Christo being a diplomat handled the situation like the professional he was. Welcoming his old friend warmly said, with the appropriate form of disappointment, that Helen had already departed with some friends and at this point did not know where they wanted to go first, probably travelling from place to place. Naturally Charles Davenport was more than disappointed and only because Christo convinced him that if only he had let Helen know earlier, she would have changed her plans.

The poor man had found himself in a complicated situation and was very uncomfortable having to lie to his friend, but he knew that once on the road to deception it was difficult to undo. His attendance at the wedding was uncertain as he could not leave Davenport.

Fortunately, the wedding was not taking place until all their arrangements were completed to their satisfaction and they decided to set the day for a few weeks later. The Barone was not going to put Helen and Gianni in a panic and decided to wait for a day or two until Charles Davenport decided what he wished to do.

Meantime, Helen's father was entertained with great enthusiasm; meetings were arranged with old acquaintances and he found himself being overfed and watered. Finally he decided to go home. Disappointed, but accepting the situation and feeling slightly foolish for not giving notice of his intentions to Helen.

Helen's mother Anabel had not enthused about the prospect of travelling to Italy in high summer. It was the last thing she had wanted, and preferred to stay on their country estate in Hampshire. From the outset she thought her husband's plan had been badly thought out and was glad to hear he was coming home and wait for Helen's return from her travels.

The Barone knew that this situation could not continue indefinitely and after all the celebrations Helen and Gianni returned, deliriously happy. Their wedding had turned out to be the event of the year for Gianni's family and the whole village of Monte Verde.

They returned to Rome and settled into Gianni's very elegant apartment a few weeks later. Waiting until the appropriate moment Di Sanro confronted the couple with what he felt was the appropriate thing to do. They must go to England and face the music, as this situation was not solving anything and the longer it continued the more pain and heartache would be the outcome. He reminded Helen that her father and mother were no longer young and wanted to see their offspring happily settled with spouses suitable for their backgrounds; and in Charles Davenport's eyes preferably not to foreigners.

When things settled and they had time to contemplate their position they took his advice, knowing the visit was never going to be an easy one. There was a certain amount of distance between father and daughter due to her long absence and so little information received to her whereabouts. Helen was sure that Gianni would make a good impression, particularly so with her mother, who had no such prejudices as her husband. She would probably think he was the nicest young man, handsome and able to support her daughter in comfort. Hopefully, she would see Helen's choice had been an excellent one.

Helen's one regret was that she had been unable to confide in her mother. Although they were very close, it was a risk she could not take. When she recalled how her parents had met, their love story had been like a twist of fate. Except for the saving grace of her mother's distinguished ancestry, which was impressive for anyone, however grand, she might have been considered unsuitable.

Lady Anabel Bourke, was the daughter of an impoverished Irish earl, but was nevertheless brought to London when she was eighteen for her 'coming out' and to be presented at Court. She was a descendant of Irish Kings and royal blood flowed through her veins. Her parents had taken a house for the season and a splendid Ball arranged for the beautiful Anabel to be seen by the most eligible young men.

Lord Davenport was a handsome dashing young cavalry officer and he was among the guests. He had been led to believe that breeding and wealth, rather than love were of primary importance in marriage. However, all that went out of the window when introduced to Lady Anabel, for he soon found himself in love and as luck would have it, the beautiful Anabel had also fallen for Charles.

Within a suitable time frame they were married and lived on the family estate in Hampshire and in Chelsea for their London home. Helen was their first-born and was followed a few years later by a son, so the family title was protected. Charles always a slightly pompous man, an inherited feature of many of his class and probably aided by his position in the army. Although unaware of it, he was not the power behind the throne. Usually, Anabel in her gentle Irish way, was quietly able to persuade Charles to accommodate most of what she felt was needed, without the man even realizing it. He, still very much in love with his beautiful wife, considered himself the most fortunate of men.

The problem now was Helen who being the apple of his eye had great plans for her to marry well. Yet being the man he was, his old fashioned ideas were stuck in tradition. Now there was no more putting off the necessity for both Helen and Gianni to go to England and face what they both knew would be an ordeal of gigantic proportions.

Helen had sent a wire to her mother breaking the news, as she couldn't bear to turn up without preparing her with for what was going to be one of the hardest things she would ever have to do. Gianni constantly comforted and supported her, reminding her they would face the outcome together.

Her mother, pre-warned of their arrival, had everything prepared and was secretly very excited to see this man who had won her daughter's heart to the extent that she had followed her own wishes. Knowing that a storm was expected over the horizon, she had suggested they arrive when Charles was not at home, giving them time to prepare for the inevitable.

Anabel greeted them with affection and approval, overjoyed to meet at long last this gorgeous young Italian her daughter had chosen. The love between them shone out; not only was he successful, wealthy and well established in Italy, Anabel's romantic Irish blood made her plan to make their happiness succeed whatever it took.

Anabel suggested to Helen that she should just hurry up and have a child, and she would then see her father would be a changed man. She smiled and kissed her daughter's cheek. Helen felt maybe it would not be very long for that event to take place, as she began to feel her clothes were a little tight around her middle. She giggled as she prayed it was what she suspected.

The explosion that everyone expected did not happen. Instead Charles Davenport found himself inexplicably busy avoiding any kind of social contact with his daughter and her husband. Anabel, though, made it her business to show her disapproval of his behaviour. She just let him get on with his ridiculous childish sulking and entertained Helen and Gianni the best she could, knowing they had her approval. She made sure their Christmas was a very happy one, and was quietly confident knowing that the one who would be miserable was her husband.

They had visited all the places that had been just names to Gianni; had dined in the famous restaurants, gone to the opera, the theatre, and seen all the historical sights, Westminster Abbey and St Paul's. Anabel had been a wonderful hostess and when it was time to leave, told them that she would visit them, with or without Charles. She knew he was beginning to feel the freeze, but was too arrogant to come down off his high horse, much to her amusement.

Both Helen and Gianni were relieved that their visit hadn't been a confrontational disaster and realized that her father had probably suffered by his own unreasonable behaviour. Gianni told Helen if he hadn't already been in love with her it would have been with her mother! She laughed, 'I don't blame you.'

He took her in his arms and said 'What about that grandchild then? She looked at him and said, laughing, 'Well you never know.'

The following year had passed quickly and Gianni had bought a villa in the Parioli, the most prestigious location in Rome, as he felt that the space would be more suitable for them to raise a family. Helen had guessed correctly and it was confirmed she was pregnant and within the year gave birth to a son they named Carlo.

On a visit to Monte Verde for Gianni's parents to see their grandson, they knew they were going to need a nanny. The young widow Rosa from a large family that Gianni had known for years, seemed to be the ideal candidate as she had helped to raise her many younger siblings.

Rosa, at only nineteen, had lost her young husband in an accident and her prospects were not the best for a life in the village. She leapt at the chance to look after Carlo and returned with them to Rome and a life beyond her dreams. They all seemed to bond straight away and baby Carlo, from the beginning, was treated as if he were her own.

Anabel had eventually brought Charles around to consider a visit to see the baby and made it clear she was intending to go with or without him. She knew that he was dying to see his grandson and it was just stubbornness on his part at playing the decision maker. Naturally, Anabel had already made plans and just waited quietly for her husband to convince himself that it had been his idea.

When they arrived and were given a warm welcome, it was plain as a pike staff that Charles Davenport was more than impressed by the villa and all the beautiful marble bathrooms and elegant furnishings of the rooms. Helen greeted her father as if there had never been any difficulties and Gianni politely shook his hand.

A splendid lunch had been arranged and, as is the norm, rooms were arranged for them to rest and have a siesta. Helen explained that Carlo was having his nap and they would see him after they all had rested.

Charles had insisted they stay at the Excelsior Hotel on the Via Veneto the most prestigious hotel in Rome, but Anabel had a suspicion that their luggage may be sent for later.

Charles awoke after his siesta feeling rested, and glanced across at Anabel who was still sleeping. He decided to explore a little and quietly leaving the room, he began walking down a corridor that had several doors.

Suddenly, one of them opened and there stood Rosa holding the baby. She stepped in front of him and gently pushed Carlo into his arms. Surprised and without any chance to refuse, he took the gurgling infant from her. Rosa said something in Italian and disappeared down the corridor. The smiling child held up his tiny hand toward his grandfather's face and Charles Davenport, filled with emotion, could not control the tears that began to fall down his face. Rosa watched from a discreet distance and smiled as she knew that she had done the right thing, and that now everything would be different.

Christo Di Sanro, with a very influential position in the Italian Foreign Office, had a long-term plan. Helen was not quite sure exactly what the plan was, as it was never openly discussed, but she knew his position was important and his name was well-known and respected.

When young men of exceptional ability, well educated and with unblemished reputations got to be recognized by the hierarchy, they were often snapped up. Di Sanro thought he had the solution to heal the heartache that he knew his friend Davenport was suffering.

Now that Gianni had a family the importance of his future was recognized by the Barone. His intervention, by a suggestion and recommendation in high places, could be the answer.

If the Barone could secure him a position in the Italian Foreign Office it might in time lead to an opportunity, that once again with a little word in the right ears, lead to a post in their Embassy in London. As in most cases these things are arranged by those who have the most sway.

Gianni had risen to the top of the tree with Fratelli Donati and this new challenge certainly had its appeal. If he and Helen were willing this would be the answer to everything. So when the offer was made, a positive answer came from Gianni. He then began working for the diplomatic Service.

He enjoyed his new career and it was when Carlo was seven years old the long awaited opportunity arose for him to be posted abroad, as a place had become available in London.

Gianni never knew just how much the Barone had to do with it and he wasn't going to ask, but realised that a great deal of 'who you know' was behind it.

They moved to London and would, for the time being, live with Charles and Anabel. With their grandson Carlo there to love and spoil, all old wounds were healed.

Eventually Helen's parents, appreciating more and more the quieter life away from the city, decided to move to their estate in Hampshire. They left Gianni, Helen, Carlo and their nanny to reside in the house in Chelsea close to the river, away from the crowded streets of Mayfair with fresher air, an area that had grown in popularity in recent years.

CHAPTER TWO

London's East End 1898

Molly Carter, only half awake, slowly opened here eyes. Consciousness slowly overcame the comfortable world of dreams that was her preference to reality. Now as the wakefulness took over completely, so too did the annoyance she felt with herself. It was Sunday and only six o'clock in the morning on the one day of the week when she could sleep late. She had been so tired and had forgotten to draw the curtains and now the sun had drenched the bedroom with sunlight and for Molly, the end of her slumbers. She knew she could not go back to sleep now, but lay there contemplating the ceiling; not that the ceiling had any real fascination for her but gave her time to decide whether to risk getting up with this bad mood.

Her father Henry forbade any disturbance before 10.30am; the one day of rest after a busy week running his business. This consisted of successful ladies' outfitters of two shops, and soon a third for men's apparel. The noise he objected to came from Molly's younger siblings; twins of six years old, a boy and a girl that, to put it mildly, were a handful. Any disturbance resulted in a threat of death by whatever means seemed the most appropriate. This usually meant no visit to the park, no ice cream and house arrest for the whole of Sunday afternoon.

At first when the threat was implemented after a particularly disturbing morning which Molly thought was sheer bedlam, her father, furious at being woken up at seven o'clock, got up, separated the twins and locked one in one room and one in another. After a lot of screaming and crying to no avail, silence reigned, and a lesson learned. Now Sunday mornings were sacrosanct and peaceful. Molly, although appreciating the result, had felt a little sorry to see the children chastised in this manner. However, knowing her father was never cruel and usually spoilt his offspring, in this case something had to be done, and it was achieved successfully.

Molly was a strikingly pretty girl with dark hair and bright blue eyes, the dark hair from her mother and the blue eyes of her father. She was quiet and there was something quite elegant about her, although unaware of the fine impression she gave of a gentleness that belied her inner strength. However, when she made her mind up her determination usually won the day.

Her mother Annie had come over from Ireland as a seventeen year old to find work. She was a talented seamstress and felt that England might provide better opportunities to earn a decent living, as Ireland was suffering the worst famine in its history. Molly's father Henry had done quite well with his ladies' clothing shops in the East End and it was whilst working in one of his shops they had met and married. They had seven children, of whom Molly was the second eldest girl. With her father's successful business and her mother's dressmaking skills, the family were well fed and, of course, fashionably dressed. They lived in an impressively large house, one of many properties Henry owned.

Henry Carter was a charming and lovable character, but the one thing that could sometimes effect their lifestyle was his love of gambling. At times their quality of life was influenced as to whether the horses complied by winning or not, although they never seemed to go short of the essentials. When luck was kind they did very well, as Henry was generous to his family and friends. That he was often regarded as a wealthy man, was partly due to their mother's additional income. With her many private customers and her business acumen, there had been one or two occasions when the reigns were tightened which slightly influenced some cutting back on the luxuries the family were used to.

Molly was a quiet girl and had always gone to school regularly and learned her three R's, plus a love of literature. She would spend hours reading if she could and at sixteen began to read the romantic penny farthing sheets as often as she could acquire them. She loved romantic novels best and when possible the classics; among her favourites were the Bronte sisters and Charles Dickens.

Two years previously tragedy had come to the family when Annie, Molly's mother had fallen sick with some strange unpronounceable

THE OLIVE TREE

illness that eventually took her from the world at forty-five years old. This left three children younger than Molly without a mother. From then everything changed.

Gone forever were the carefree days that had been hers in the past, full of romantic thoughts of meeting her Prince Charming, and running off into the sunset and living happy ever after, because now she had to carry a huge burden.

With the loss of his wife, her father Henry not only gambled, but turned to the bottle for consolation. Now poor Molly was forced to become mother, nursemaid and chief bottle washer to her younger siblings. The two oldest in the family, one a boy, had the spirit of adventure in his blood and went off to sea much to Henry's dismay. Being his oldest son he would have been expected to learn the business and run it when Henry was no longer able to do so.

Her older sister Annie had eloped with a young man, the full story to which Molly was not privy. Questions were quickly discouraged making the mystery more intriguing than ever. Either way, neither was there to help to care for Louise, who was named Lou Lou for short, and Richard, called Dickey Boy. It seemed all of them had shortened names in the family, but Molly as the eldest found herself with a responsibility which required a great deal of care and guidance.

The last baby of the family was premature and did not survive. Her younger sister Lizzie now fifteen going on sixteen was of little help, as she was now the next eldest after Molly who was still at home and available for helping her father in one of his shops.

Molly loved her father, but felt that if she were ever be able to free herself before the best years of her life had passed her by she needed to escape. She knew she just had to get away unless she wanted to finish up an old maid. Her problem was she did not know how or where to go.

It was more than two years since her mother's passing and she was now more than ever determined to find a way to free herself from this daily grind because she was not cut out to be a children's nanny. What her father needed was a woman in his life, to marry again and hopefully find happiness that might curb the need for his addictions. It would of course have to be a kind woman who loved children and would help raise her brothers and sisters, for whom Molly felt she had done enough.

Her departure would have to wait until the right moment and when she had made sure that the right opportunity arose; probably a Sunday morning when the house was still asleep.

If it wasn't for her close friend Lottie there seemed to be no respite for her from what she considered a daily drudge. The two girls had devised a plan for Molly to escape and join her friend, who had made the choice to do the same, but for different reasons.

Lottie wanted to help her mother to free herself from her violent drunken husband, and to earn enough money to pay for her mother's escape to her sister in Scotland. Lottie had already found a position as a maid in South London and had convinced Molly they could manage to find something for her too. The two girls planned carefully how this was to be done and celebrated their secret with an ice cream.

Molly felt that if she didn't get away soon, her chances of making a life for herself would ebb away and she began to prepare for her departure. She had carefully planned everything weeks before and at last the day came when she realized that her only choice was to leave as soon as possible, probably on a Sunday, and decided at the very first opportunity she would pack her bag and go.

Lottie had found herself a position in a house she termed the 'posh house' belonging to a very wealthy family who lived in Chelsea.

This actually was as a scullery maid, but as she said confidently, it was a step in the right direction and may lead to other opportunities, although Molly was not quite sure what those might be.

Although with Lottie's pretty face and happy-go-lucky personality it could certainly be a possibility, but only time would tell.

Her childhood had been hard and the family poor and with such an abusive father Molly had often wondered how Lottie was such a strong and positive girl.

There were several times that she had turned up on their doorstep with suspicious bruises here and there, and Henry would invite her to stay until things settled down, but she usually returned the next morning to make sure her mother was safe.

She had run away as soon as she could but it was too late and it wasn't long before her mother's life of poverty as well as the cruelty that she had endured most of her life with Lottie's father, had proved too much she went to what Lottie believed was a better place. Her greatest regret was that it had been too late as she had not been able to change her Mother's destiny and sad demise. She was now more than ever determined that her own life would not end in such a tragic way.

Molly and her younger sister Lizzie, were as different as chalk and cheese. Lizzie was full of exuberance and cheeky with it, she had her mother's dressmaking skills, which had been taught to both daughters, but Lizzie had taken to it like a duck to water. She also had the gift of the gab. Her father would say 'that child could talk the hind legs off a donkey' and he began to feel that she could turn out to be an asset in one of his shops. Probably the nearest one in the local high street where not only her dressmaking skills would be valuable, but also to polish up her chatty approach into a skilled sales ability.

Henry sold smart ladies attire and hats of the latest fashion, and on his better days, planned to increase his stock to include menswear. More sales assistants would be needed eventually, but for the time being, who better than his own daughter now that his son and heir had departed.

This of course was all very well, Lizzie being over the moon at the prospect. Molly however, was trapped with not even proper help from her sister who now felt she was above domestic duties after a 'day in the shop' and was quite exhausted and unable to lift a finger. Molly, more fed up than ever was determined to keep to her plan to escape.

One day fate seemed to intervene with a surprising turn of events.

Lizzie had a best friend at school, a Jewish girl named Bella, Bella Bernstein. Her father Morris and his brother Irving ran the Kosher Butcher shop in the High Street, one of several that the family owned. They were what were often termed as being 'very comfortable', which was quite evident by the large house that they owned. They were a very nice family and as Bella's best friend, Lizzie had been invited to their house on several occasions. She was not sure if she appreciated their style of furnishings and decoration, lots of gold tassels and brocade, a little overdone as far as she was concerned.

However, she enjoyed Mrs Bernstein's culinary skills and begged her to teach her how to make some of her favourite dishes. Mrs Bernstein delighted to have such admiration, said to Lizzie 'Are you sure you don't have Jewish blood dear?'

Lizzie was fairly confident that she didn't and replied 'I don't think so, my mother was Irish.'

'Well my dear, there are Jewish folk in Ireland you know, what about on your Father's side?' she added. 'No, I was told my father's line came from the Huguenots.'

Stella looked at Lizzie. She was not sure whether she knew anything about Huguenots or whether they could be Jewish, anyway she decided not to pursue this avenue of conversation any further.

She smiled and said 'I see' although Lizzie was not convinced she did.

The added interest Lizzie had was that Bella had a brother who had also been at their school and Lizzie liked him. He was also named Morris, Morrie for short, and he also liked Lizzie a lot. Of course this was not made obvious to his parents, as getting involved and possibly wanting to marry a Shiksa (non-Jewish) was not acceptable. Bella made sure that her friendship with Lizzie was a good reason for her being invited to their home as there was nothing wrong with the girls being friends.

Morrie as almost a year older than Lizzie and was working in his father's butcher's shop. They had become closer than ever and their friendship had begun to develop along romantic lines. Once again the family history had parallels. Morrie being the only boy, it was his father's intention to get him into the family business. However, it seemed that Morrie had other ideas. At first he had succumbed to his father's wishes, but not only was he not keen on the idea, in fact it now revolted him. The thought of cutting up dead animals all day and in particular the grisly method of preparing them for their destiny on the dinner plate did not appeal one bit! He didn't mind eating meat, but handling dead carcasses was definitely not his cup of tea.

Morrie junior was in fact a very bright young man and decided to confide in his mother his secret that he did not want to be a butcher, but wanted to be a doctor. Mind you, he did not want to be a surgeon either, as cutting up people was just as unappealing as being a butcher and was definitely not on his agenda. Being very close to his mother, he one day took the opportunity when they were alone in the kitchen to open his heart to her.

Stella was preparing dinner as usual when he told her mother of his feelings. Her mouth opened wide with a combination of surprise and disbelief and for a moment or two she did not speak. Then with a look of nothing less than admiration when the words had sunk in, exclaimed.

'My Morrie a doctor?'

The words had emerged slowly, together with a look of surprised admiration in her eyes. This was obviously beyond her wildest dreams, in a Jewish family a doctor, lawyer or rabbi was the best thing that could happen to a son. The idea was indeed wonderful, but she knew how the news would affect Morris senior and had no idea how she would break it to him.

She looked at her son and asked 'When are you going to tell your father? You realize that you will have to go to college for years and it will be expensive. Without his approval financing will be a problem.'

Morrie looked at her with eyes that almost pleaded for her approval and help.

'I know, Mama, but I will have to find a way, maybe a scholarship? I don't know, or work as well.'

She knew her son and could read the desperation in his eyes. It would be cruel to see such a clever brain like that of Morrie wasted; he deserved far better than being a butcher, even a wealthy one when he inherited his share of the business.

Stella Bernstein was a handsome woman; tall with black wavy hair that framed her olive skin making her quite striking and drew attention to the brown eyes that revealed the warmth and kindness within. Her cousin had become a doctor, and had come from a family of merchants, and to mention their son was a doctor was tantamount to saying he was one of the chosen; a rabbi even! She would talk her husband round and make him see that this would raise the family's esteem in the community. She put her arms around Morrie and assured him she would do her best when the subject could be broached at the best opportunity, if there was one!

Of course for the moment there were certain advantages for Morrie to be working in the family butchers, as after work he would head off to the high street and wait for Lizzie to finish work. Tucked under his arm was a parcel containing his precious offerings, the best he could manage at the moment, wrapped up in paper. It's a wonder Henry did not question where the leg of lamb came from or the top side of beef. His only comment was the meat wasn't so juicy these days. Lizzie knew the meat was Kosher, but didn't know if that had anything to do with it because they were always the best cuts, so she did not reply.

'Nothing was the same these days,' he would mutter 'uhm' and go on chomping away. Half the time it was after he had already had a few generous tipples. He then soon fell asleep in the kitchen armchair. Juicy or not was soon a distant memory.

One day Henry made a comment: 'You know Lizzie, the next time you go shopping, what about a nice piece of pork with a bit of crackling?' Lizzie looked at Molly and mumbled something about it was always sold out quickly; she then made a hasty exit, winking at Molly as she went.

Then an unexpected calamity befell the Bernstein's: Morris senior was cutting up a carcass and the knife slipped and cut a large wound in his arm. He was rushed to hospital, but somehow his arm became infected. The doctors thought it may have been the animal's blood had caused the poisoning, whatever the cause; he developed septicaemia and died within a few days.

Stella, Morrie and his sister Bella were in deep mourning and soon their relations came from everywhere and performed what Lizzie learned was to sit and perform the Shiva.

In the evenings the rabbi would come and they would say prayers for the next seven days. She had become so close to the family she was invited to join this important ritual of the Jewish faith. With all this going on Henry seemed to only see Lizzie in the shop and the family did not see much of her either.

Henry finally spoke to his daughter. 'I know you have become very friendly with Bella and I want to ask you a question. Are they trying to convert you to becoming Jewish?'

Lizzie, feigning shock replied: 'Don't be silly Daddy, it's just that now Mr Bernstein has died they are all devastated and it's a time that all the family and friends come together for this tradition.'

A week or so went by and Molly realized the plans for her departure would have to be put on hold. How could she leave at this time? It would be heartless and cruel. She would have to put up with this situation until the sadness, that seemed to have pervaded even into their house, had eased. Now that Lizzie was spending so much time at Mrs Bernstein's, it was not going to help the situation and she could not desert the ship now.

Molly knew that she and Morrie were close. Bella was even party to the conspiracy and loved the idea that her best friend and her brother were 'seeing each other.'

One late Sunday afternoon the door bell rang. Molly called Lizzie who happened by chance to be hovering in the hallway looking very smart, to go and answer the door. Quite surprisingly she couldn't get to the front door quickly enough and if Molly hadn't been so tired she would have soon put two and two together, particularly as Lizzie had on her best dress. Molly was just about to sit down and rest her aching feet after preparing lunch and trying to train the twins to clear up and wash and dry the dishes, without a catastrophe of broken plates.

Lizzie rushed to the front door and opened it to see Mrs Bernstein and Bella standing there.

'Oh what a lovely surprise' she said with such conviction that Molly who was close by, thought 'an actress, not only my friend, now my sister' Molly realizing who this unexpected visitor was, had to admire her sister's performance.

'Oh please come in Mrs Bernstein,' she said, smiling at Bella, who smiled back with a look that didn't fool Molly for a minute. She looked at her younger sister with an expression on her face that said she was well aware that this was no surprise call.

Molly said to Lizzie: 'You had better tell father he has a visitor,' knowing full well this might not be what her father would want on a Sunday afternoon!

Henry was more than surprised, he was irritated at being disturbed from his afternoon nap and for a moment had to gather his wits about him. The last thing he wanted on a Sunday afternoon was to meet this woman who had somehow entered into his life and influenced his daughter without even having met her.

He stood up. Now fully awake and feeling slightly grumpy he walked into the scullery and splashed some cold water on his face muttering all the time about it being Sunday, etc.

Lizzie accompanied her father to the front parlour, so rarely used except for visitors and kept pristine from lack of use. Molly followed on behind not wishing to miss what might be the highlight of her day!

Stella was sitting on the sofa with Bella and when Henry entered the room she stood up. Holding out her gloved hand, she smiled and stood for a long time just looking at him. He moved towards her and took her hand as if he never wanted to let it go. He looked at her for what the two girls thought seemed like an eternity.

'Henry, is it you?' she asked, her eyes wide with surprised curiosity. Her father continued holding the gloved hand and said with what was undisguised emotion in his voice.

'Stella, Stella Cohen?' never taking his eyes from her face. She laughed recognizing the blue eyes she remembered from so long ago, and replied

'Not any more Henry, it's Bernstein now'

The two sisters looked at each other and bit their lips both thinking alike, well if manna had come down from Heaven this could not have been a better scenario.

'I could never forget that beautiful smile; it must be more than twenty years' he said. Stella seemed as delighted to see Henry as he was to see her; the smile he had never forgotten had lit up her face.

'I could never forget your blue eyes Henry, you were the best looking boy in the class; if only you had been Jewish, who knows' she said. Both girls looked at each other and winked.

'Please excuse me Mrs Bernstein,' Molly said, 'I have to see what the twins are up to,' and she slipped out of the door.

Lizzie followed her saying 'I will bring some tea father' and hurried after her. 'I will help too,' Bella added, rushing after them.

It seemed that after all that time they had lived only a mile and a half or so away from each other and never knew the other was so close.

Now Molly with a big sigh murmured quietly to herself, 'Oh thank you God, thank you, thank you for answering my prayers.'

Meanwhile, Lizzie was thinking something similar. Was this the answer, wais this their lucky day? 'Oi Ve', she said in Yiddish.

Molly laughed as the three of them hugged and danced around the table together. Now of course she realized this was a well-orchestrated conspiracy. The best thing of all was that they had not known Henry and Stella had been school friends and, even better, sweethearts.

It seemed that the friendship between them hadn't gone unnoticed by Stella's parents. Suddenly, quite out of the blue, her father declared the family was moving to North London; Golders Green to be exact, miles away from where they were living.

Manny Cohen was not going to let his Stella become involved with a gentile; he had already made plans for her match with the son of his friend Joseph Bernstein. She would marry well and the family ties would be cemented. There had already been discussions between Manny and the Bernsteins, so Stella, at seventeen had no say in the matter. Removing her from this neighbourhood would ensure the couple would soon forget each other.

But they had not forgotten each other and now the two of them sitting in the front parlour, were able to remenisce and tell each other about their lives. Henry had found the woman that he had been in love with all those years ago. This surprise meeting, out of the blue, made him suddenly feel alive again. The empty feeling that had flooded his every moment since his Annie had departed had suddenly become less painful. He almost had a feeling of contentment, even anticipation as he looked at Stella.

Had destiny brought them together again, when there was no one to interfere or bring objections to their friendship? A lot of water had passed under the bridge since, and now things were different. Stella had made the best of her life with Morris who had been a good husband and she had never wanted for anything, but her first love had never been forgotten.

The strange thing was that Henry had been given the greatest possible help in his life was from a Jewish man called Jacob Finkelstein. Jacob had a garment factory, making women's clothes, which he sold to the very up-market stores in the West End. Well-known in the Schmatter business was that the material for the making of the garments was supplied and paid for by the stores. This meant there were times when yards of material were left over, commonly known as 'cabbage' in the trade; the non-edible kind.

Jacob was a widower and his beloved wife had died giving birth to their one and only child and neither had survived. He never married again although everyone in their community had tried to marry their women off to Jacob, who was a wealthy man. But never flinching he remained single for the rest of his life.

One day the then young seventeen year old Henry, was wandering around Petticoat Lane, the famous street in the East End that sold everything from cats and dogs to clothing at bargain prices. The weekends attracted people from everywhere, north, south and west as Londoners flocked there in their hundreds to buy and be entertained.

Henry was always fascinated and intrigued by the stall holders' gift of attracting the passers by; their sales chat, so often amusing and entertaining, that drew in the customers. Jacob was really good at his trade and Henry hung around until business finished for the day.

He sauntered over to Jacob and said 'I like the way you get people to listen to you, would you teach me how to do it?'

Jacob looked Henry up and down and said 'I don't know if you got the talent my boy.'

'Well if you don't try me, you'll never know will you?' He said.

Jacob smiled at him and replied, 'Well maybe you have got the chutzpa, come along tomorrow and we can see how you do'.

He could certainly do with someone to work the stall whilst he attended to his shop business. Now he had to divide his day between both, because the stall could be very profitable and he liked the look of Henry. He most certainly didn't look Jewish, but Jacob was not about to enquire about that now as he thought the lad had an outgoing personality which was exactly what was needed for this job.

'Alright,' said Henry, who really needed work. Experience in anything that would earn him some money was a good idea.

Jacob said if he did well he would get commission on his sales and after a bit of haggling, which Jacob thought even more encouraging, they settled on a modest sum to increase if Henry was good at selling.

It didn't take long before Jacob could soon see a great deal of potential in Henry, who seemed to be a 'natural'. He had made a success of selling the garments made from the 'cabbage' sold on his market stall. This sideline was always very profitable. So, before long, Jacob gave Henry more opportunities to increase business and, with no one to hinder his choice, took Henry under his wing.

Jacob rented another shop and Henry was given the opportunity to run it. As time went by business grew and grew and, there being no heir, Henry was made a partner.

As the years passed by Jacob, not so young anymore, had made enough to retire comfortably. He arranged with Henry that for a small settlement the business was his. What is more, when Jacob died he left everything to Henry who had been like a son to him. The irony was that if things had turned out differently, with Stella's parents not whipping her away to north

London, he would have been able to have provided for her very well. More than twenty years had passed and the weeks and months seemed to fly by since their reunion.

After a suitable time had passed, Henry's family and Stella's spent more and more time intermingling. It was Stella's idea that as the tradition of Friday night dinner became a permanent invitation to the Carter family. The only problem was that someone had to look after the twins, and that person was always Molly. So Stella suggested that it would be more practical if Henry would let her cook at the Carter household and the family could all be together.

Molly thought that at last this was going in the right direction. At least she wasn't left at home just being the babysitter. Plans for her escape were put on hold for the time being to await the outcome of the reunion. However, after the Friday night arrangement had proved successful, things seemed to have slowed down and no further progress was made to cement the relationship between Stella and Henry. Of course, if there was to be any permanent solution, her father and Stella had to get married, allowing suitable time for mourning after Irving's passing.

Fortunately, Stella loved the children and made a fuss of them. They liked her too, so Molly knew that she might have to take things into her own hands and play her trump card. She would leave and force the issue.

CHAPTER 3

Lavender Street

Molly began to plan her getaway again and this time with great precision. She found her old valise and would depart before the family woke up. She thought that the ideal day was Sunday, as she knew everyone else would rise later than usual. The youngsters were forbidden to leave their beds too early and wake their father. He had declared peace and quiet until after ten thirty am.

The morning came at last, it was still very early, but the excitement and trepidation of what she was about to embark upon had made it impossible to lie there just looking at the ceiling, which seemed to be a habit when Molly experienced indecision.

She had prepared everything to take with her, now all she needed was the courage to slip out of the house as quietly as possible. She had written a note to her father, but now the moment had come the tears welled up and the inevitable sadness that followed.

She told him she was sorry, but, full of mixed emotions, she knew she could no longer stay as she felt completely trapped. She wanted to go out into the world and find whatever was beyond this house, this street, this neighbourhood and being a nursemaid to her siblings. Also if she continued in this situation, she might miss out on what was supposed to be the best years of her life. She hoped he would marry Mrs Bernstein and hoped they both would be very happy. She promised to contact him when she got settled, signed it and added several kisses.

She decended the stairs without her boots and headed towards the front door quietly exited and ran silently down the front path. The street was very quiet, which was fortunate, as she didn't want to bump into any neighbours, who were likely to stop and ask her where she was off to with her valise. Fortunately, no one was to be seen, except an old tramp asleep in a doorway. She hurried past him as quickly as she could, thanking heaven the streets were dry, as she did not want to have dirty wet feet and have to clean them on her petticoat.

She came to a small wall and sat on it and put on her boots. She had some difficulty doing up the little buttons without the hook she knew she had put somewhere, along with the money that she had saved. This took several minutes but at last she found it and got the boots secured and headed for the tram stop, which was where she would begin her journey to south London where Lottie lived. They had been friends since their school days and were as close as sisters. Lottie had given her all the relevant information of how to get there; which tram to take to the city centre and then the different means of transport to south of the river.

Lottie did not live in the 'posh house' because there was not enough room to accommodate all the servants. It was arranged by her employers, the Courtney Browns, that she could stay in a rented room close by. This would be paid for by them until other arrangements could be made. Lottie had a room in a house in Lavender Street, a mile or so over the river from Chelsea where their house was situated. According to Lottie, her employers lived in the grandest house she had ever seen and it overlooked the River Thames.

Molly headed toward her destination, never having seen this part of London. She found it fascinating to see the river so close and the many trees that lined the edge of the park. It was so different to anywhere she had been before and as she had crossed over the bridge, more beautiful than where she had lived all her life. The air seemed fresher so close to the river, and the houses that lined the street quite grand.

She continued walk along the road, which Lottie had explained led the way to the house where she was to stay. Lottie said this would help her to get to know the area. As she walked further on, the architecture changed and was almost like another world, the houses were small and terraced and bunched together, no posh carriages here. Oh well, she didn't expect to find Lottie lodging in a palace! At least this was a start and that's all that mattered. She was now free to explore whatever life had in store for her. They had kept in regular touch, usually on Sunday, when it was Lottie's day off. She went to see her mother who lived a few streets from Molly's home. It was also the one day Henry would take the twins out if they had behaved well enough to deserve the treat.

The two friends would take a walk together in the afternoon in the park nearby and exchange girlie gossip, not to mention a glance or two at the young men passing by. Lottie was such an outrageous flirt that Molly wished she had the confidence of her friend, for she was far too shy to be so adventurous, but greatly admired her friend's boldness. It certainly seemed to work, as the young men, with any further encouragement, certainly would have approached them. At this point Lottie would lift her chin high in the air and march ahead without a second glance behind her, of course this would make them both collapse in a fit of giggles.

Most of the gossip supplied by Lottie was regarding the goings on at her employers' house. She was such a cheerful, pretty, young woman that she seemed to get on well with them and apparently with most of those that knew her. When Lottie heard Molly's plan to run away she was delighted to have her dearest friend to stay at her modest dwelling. She assured Molly that she could stay with her and share the double bed or sleep on an old sofa in her bedroom until she got established.

They didn't go hungry either, as Lottie always seemed to be able to scrounge some food to bring back for their supper. They laughed a lot like the two young girls they were. Molly was at last enjoying the greatest adventure of her life, and was gaining confidence with the help of her friend.

The little house was very simple and nothing like the home she had come from, but it was freedom at last and to Molly that was the most important thing. They had to share the kitchen with an old lady whose name was Gladys, a widow.

She spent most of her time keeping the place clean and tidy. She liked the company of the young girls and did her best to keep the privy at the end of the garden clean, although it could hardly be called a garden as it was just an overgrown concrete path to the convenience. Neither did it deserve to be called a convenience, as in winter it was cold as the Arctic according to Lottie! A chamber pot was more of a convenience in the circumstances.

It was only two days later that Lottie came back to their room quite excited with the news that she had overheard her employers talking to the vicar, who was a frequent visitor with his wife to the house. It seemed that they were looking for a young woman to help Violet their housekeeper-cook. Violet was not getting any younger, but whose talent in the kitchen was widely appreciated by the vicar and his wife, not to mention all those who had, had the privilege of being invited to dine with them.

Lottie's experience of vicars had not been extensive, but influenced by the rather ancient gentleman who preached at their local church. His sermons seemed to be full of fire and brimstone, which put Lottie completely off her venerations. Nevertheless, this might provide an opportunity not to be missed. She told Molly the location of the vicarage, giving her the address and instructions how to get there.

'Go on see if they will take you on, there is nothing to lose,' she said in her usual cheerful way. She was told to ask for the Reverend Stone or his wife.

The next morning Molly took extra care with her appearance, after having washed in the scullery with the coldest water she had ever experienced. She put on her best frock and, satisfied she had done her best with her appearance by putting her long hair up in a chignon, stepped out into the sunshine. She thanked God it was not raining and hoped to arrive looking as neat and tidy as when she left the house.

She set out to walk the mile or so to the vicarage, stopping now and again to glance at Lottie's directions. It was fairly easy to find as there were not any twists and turns. Molly found the walk quite lovely, with the park one side of the road and the bridge crossing the river straight ahead. This was easy as it was the same way she had walked the previous day. There was just one turn and she found herself in a road with large houses either side. She could not miss the church and the rectory next door.

The house exterior was pretty with pink wisteria climbing the walls, although she could not put a name to the plant, but thought that it made the house look beautiful and inviting.

Molly rang the bell and waited, and waited. She pulled harder on the ring dangling on the wall, but no sooner had she dropped the thing, than the door was opened by a puffing and panting middle-aged woman, who was quite rotund. She looked at Molly with an air of impatience and said, quite out of breath, 'Whatever is it? Give a person a chance to climb the stairs; if you are selling something, then not today thank you.'

The woman began to make as though closing the front door. Molly was a bit nonplussed by this greeting and thinking it was quite presumptuous, replied hesitantly: 'No, I am not selling anything, I was wondering if the vicar was needing some domestic help. I am young, strong, willing, and experienced.' She stopped speaking, afraid she may appear to be overdoing it and seeming too desperate.

She gave a little smile at the woman, hoping it might soften her attitude, and waited for a response. Little did Molly know just how much Mrs. Violet Burridge wanted and prayed for some help. What with cooking, cleaning, and up and down those blooming stairs, and not getting any younger, it was all becoming too much for her.

Added to those duties, there was arranging the hospitality, so often part of the Stones' busy lifestyle. She prayed for the vicar to employ some help as her old legs were beginning to feel the strain.

The Reverend John Stone and his wife, Clara, were very popular. What with weddings, funerals, and he being a compassionate man who would listen to the woes of his parishioners, he found himself much in demand socially.

Violet said: 'You had better come in.' Her tone had slightly softened and, looking Molly up and down and appearing thoughtful, her attitude seemed to change for the better. Molly followed her down the stairs to the kitchen.

'I'm just about to make some tea if you would like a cup; sit down and tell me about yourself. The vicar is just about finishing his morning services, and will be back soon, so it will save much time if you begin telling me your name and your experience.'

Molly thanked her and accepted the offer of some tea, and sat at the large wooden table in the centre of the kitchen and began to give Violet a convoluted and highly-edited version of her experience. She left out any negative items, instead putting a great deal of emphasis on having raised her siblings practically single-handedly since her mother's death.

She reeled out her accomplishments, her ability to clean, cook and iron and all the other desirable requirements that might be needed to make a very suitable domestic help.

Violet seemed pleased with what she was hearing and began to warm to this pretty young thing, with her blue eyes, long dark hair and a neat and tidy appearance.

'Well, write down your name and address. You can read and write I presume?

'Oh yes, very well,' Molly replied.

Violet gave her a questioning look and said 'Alright? I will speak to the vicar and if I have anything to do with it, I may well recommend he give you a try. He should be back soon and, if you care to wait here in the kitchen I will speak to him and see if he has time to see you.'

Molly couldn't believe her luck, liking what she had seen, although Violet seemed a little peeved at having to answer the door, which was taking her away from important duties in the kitchen.

Molly did sympathize with the poor woman. Apparently Violet's greatest talent consisted of making pies and preparing other delicious edibles, and by the look of her comely figure, sampling the results appeared to be an essential part of her employment.

Violet could not believe her luck either: someone who would clean the grates, change the linen, answer the door and climb all those stairs. What's more, to have someone bright and intelligent around, could be the answer to her prayers? Indeed so.

Molly sipped her tea and ate the biscuit that was offered, whilst Violet chatted on about this and that until at last there were sounds of the vicar's arrival in the hall upstairs. The bell rang and Violet, mumbling away about him wanting his tea and biscuits, turned to Molly and said: 'I will serve his cup of tea and tell him his lunch will be, as usual, at one o'clock. Meanwhile, I will suggest he sees you when he has had time to draw breath.' With that she hurried up the stairs with a china teapot and cup and saucer to match, all sitting neatly on a tray.

After about ten minutes the bell rang and Violet told Molly to go up stairs and the vicar would see her in the front parlour. Molly knocked on the door and waited until she was bid enter. Mr Stone looked over the rims of his spectacles and beckoned her to come into the room. He put down the paper he was reading and asked her to sit in the chair nearest to him. Molly was surprised to see such a young man. She thought that he was probably in his late thirties. He had a cheerful disposition and a kind face.

After listening to Molly repeating the information she had given to Violet, he had to admit this young girl did seem to have the necessary requirements to fill the position of a much needed help for Violet. In fact he was quite impressed with Molly and thought to himself that it would be quite pleasant to have a pretty young woman to help out. She was bright, intelligent and presentable and, most importantly, would make a good impression to all the parishioners who came to the vicarage.

She skipped her way back to tell Lottie the news when she arrived home. Of course her ambitions did go beyond those of being in long-term domestic service, but it would do for now. They didn't need her to live in. This suited Molly, as she was to receive a little more money which would help her pay her way and stay with Lottie.

She had been at the vicarage for several months and enjoyed her job. Nothing seemed too strenuous for her young body: in fact her duties were not heavy at all; cleaning the grates in the mornings was the worst and having to wait for the freshly lit fires to give out some warmth during the winter months. Violet always had some hot tea and toast waiting after that chore was done. In fact, Molly got on very well with Violet, who had taken her under her wing like a mother hen. She always gave her tips about this and that and, as for food, Molly thought before long she might begin to attain a girth similar to Violet's. What with her contribution of food for Molly to take home and Lottie's from the posh house, Molly and Lottie both agreed they would never go hungry.

One regular delivery that came regularly was the coal by horse and cart. Fred Grey was the young man who drove the horses; two mares named Bonnie and Bess. Molly loved to spoil them with some carrots, which Violet always seemed to have abundance in her kitchen. She thought Fred the most handsome young man and began to ask Violet if he and his mate might have a cup of tea and a taste of one of her pies, because theirs was a very thirsty job.

Violet could read Molly like a book and said she could tell the two lads that they could come to the kitchen door for some tea and a bite of her delicious pies.

Mr Stone and his wife were as kind and generous as they could afford, with the fairly limited stipend from the church. With so many charities and other things that Mrs Stone was involved in, she was able to help Molly with items of clothing donated for good causes and gave her whatever came her way in hand-me-downs, that were in good condition and of quality. These were very much appreciated by Molly. Thankfully, her maid's uniform saved the wear and tear of her own clothes as she did not have enough money to buy new ones. No longer able to have the luxury of the clothes from her father's shop, she was too proud and embarrassed to let him know her circumstances, and had to make do with whatever came her way. She did like to look her best and this enabled her to afford her rent at Lavender Street. Now that she had her own room, this allowed her to be able to save something for a rainy day and other necessities.

The year had passed quickly and she loved working for the Stones. It had been such a happy time. After several months, Fred asked Molly to walk out with him on Sunday afternoons when she had time off. Then the day arrived when Fred proposed. Molly, having always planned to marry a man who could give her as a comfortable life as the one she came from, hadn't bargained for falling in love with a man who delivered coal.

Although Fred was not rich, but he was handsome and a hard worker and a good man who adored her. She loved him with all her heart, so day dreams were soon forgotten.

They were to be married in the church next to the vicarage by Mr Stone. Fred thought it would be lovely a surprise if he could persuade old Barney to let him drive the horses to take Molly to the church on the front seat of the cart. He would dress the horses with garlands of flowers and decorate the cart with colourful bunting. He thought how beautiful Molly would look sitting in the front with his beautiful Bonnie and Bess clip-clopping through the streets, dressed up for all and sundry to admire as they drove to the church.

He would scrub that old cart until it shone, not a speck of coal dust anywhere to be seen. A fresh coat of paint was applied to complete the work. What a day this would be thought old Barney. There maybe one of 'them photographer fellows' there. It would really be a treat if he could have a picture, which would be a wonderful souvenir and a reminder for him always of this special day.

Of course Fred could not accompany Molly on the driver's seat: he had to join her at the altar as tradition demanded. Molly was overjoyed to ride on the cart and let Fred's mate be the driver. They arrived at the church and she was helped down by her father, who much to Molly's amazement, was there ready for the photographer to take a picture of them all in their finery. How had he learned of the wedding, she wondered? She had been afraid to tell him that her intended spouse was a coalman.

He helped her down and kissed her cheek and said 'I would not have missed my beautiful daughter's wedding, for anything. The past is forgotten, my dear. All I want is your happiness and that you have chosen a good man.'

Actually, her leaving had been the best thing that could have happened as it helped him to realize his priorities and furthermore, he had very quietly married Mrs Bernstein, who had made conditions before they married; no gambling or hitting the bottle. At last Henry had found a new lease of life.

Her father hugged her and with tears in his eyes, kissed her forehead, Molly was near to tears with happiness. There waiting on the steps of the church were her whole family; brothers, sisters and the new Mrs Carter, who in turn hugged Molly as if she had always been one of her own children. Lottie, who was waiting with them, ran to Molly and put her arms around her.

'Forgive me Moll, I told your Dad,' she said, smiling. Molly looked at her friend and said: 'Oh Lottie, thank you; I just didn't have the courage, but now it's the happiest day of my life'.

Fred was waiting inside as she walked down the aisle on her father's arm. He thought she was the most beautiful vision he had ever seen. He had actually been in on the plot to tell her father and knew it would make Molly so very happy.

The service taken by Mr Stone was perfect and, on top of this, they had arranged for everyone to enjoy a wedding breakfast in the garden of the vicarage, all prepared by Violet. The garden was in full bloom, the rich colours of the flowers radiant in the July sun. Molly could once again hardly hold back the tears of happiness. This really was the happiest day of her life.

Fred and Molly moved into Lavender Street, but rented another room so that they could have a bedroom and a sitting room. Lottie still kept a room there, but had moved to another smaller one so that Fred and Molly could have more space. She had progressed to trainee parlour maid and now lived in at the 'posh house'. Lottie being Lottie with a sensible head on her shoulders thought that if she ever found herself without a roof over her head, she had somewhere to go and where better in a crisis than with her best friend.

CHAPTER 4

Lottie and William 1907

Lottie always believed that working at the 'posh house' could lead to a possibility of meeting a nice young gentleman with 'opportunities', as she put it.

Being pretty, intelligent, full of personality, and being the vibrant young woman she was, had enchanted a young man whose name was William Cavanaugh. To him she was so unlike the usual young women to whom he was encouraged to become acquainted and who he found shallow and vain and obsessed with fripperies, to him Lottie was like a breath of fresh air.

William had made a point of volunteering to accompany Mr Jenkins a man that had been with the law firm for years, as a solicitor with Messrs Frampton, Frampton and Grimes, who came to the house for everyday legal dealings with the family. Usually a big law firm would expect their client's to go to them, but Sir Lionel being a very important and wealthy client, his solicitors sent their employees to see him.

Mr. Jenkins was good at his job; however he tended to waffle on for ever with all the minor details of this and that, in prolonged detail. This not only irritated Sir Lionel, who had better things to do than listen quite un-necessarily to the finer points of the law explained to him, but also for his employers, who needed him back at the office.

Mr Grimes one of the senior partners decided that Mr Jenkins needed to be accompanied and brought back to the office in Lincoln's Inn as soon as possible and this hopefully could be achieved, by William accompanying him and driving him in the company car.

The first occasion William had been sent to accompany Jenkins turned out to be the first time he saw Lottie. From then she would always greet him with a smile, as as she led them to the drawing room.

'Mr Cavanaugh, would Mr Jenkins and yourself like some refreshment, tea perhaps?' she would ask in her poshest accent. William smiled back and replied, 'That would be very nice, Lottie, thank you.'

He watched her leave the room to bring the tea. She did a little wiggle as she went and, turning coyly, smiled again at William, who smiled back.

The tea arrived promptly on a silver tray containing what looked to William like the best china. Naturally, there were some sweet biscuits to accompany the tea.

'Thank you very much, Lottie' he said with a grin.

She replied 'You're most welcome, Mr Cavanaugh,' with a little curtsy.

Each visit William found himself becoming more and more fascinated with Lottie. Each time he saw her he began to wonder how he might suggest taking her to tea on her day off. More to the point was how to handle the situation with diplomacy and discretion for all parties. He was aware that the Courtney Browns would not take well to fraternization between their maid and the gentlemen from Frampton, Frampton and Grimes, and at worst Lottie might lose her job.

He didn't care that Lottie dropped her H's and said 'What' when she wanted to hear something repeated.

His imagination, now running wild, inspired his determination to meet the challenge to try and teach her the requirement for her to feel comfortable in his world. This was necessary if there were any chance to be a success. For William it was worth a try; as this became more and more important to him, for now he was totally besotted and for the moment, all common sense had gone out of the window.

William knew that these visits with Jenkins to the Courtney Browns were going to end at some point, even be quite soon. The purpose of these visits was for the signing of urgent contracts, as Sir Lionel Courtney Brown was a land owner in the West Indies and owned other properties here in London. He had inherited the family fortune, which he had managed to increase sufficiently to provide for the lavish lifestyle he and Clarissa enjoyed.

However, Clarissa was no oil painting and Lottie thought was slightly dizzy. She had however, come from a titled family with a history that went back to the Domesday Book. Sir Lionel had only been knighted, but being a frightful snob, had, by marrying Clarissa the daughter of an earl, risen in society. Her father, not blessed with a beautiful or brainy daughter, had began to wonder if he would ever find someone to marry her, although they were no longer rich, their heritage was a gateway into top society. By marrying her off to Sir Lionel achieved more than he ever dared hope. Of course in the circumstances, the Courtney Browns were a very important client that had been with Frampton, Frampton and Grimes for many years and were therefore treated with veneration.

An opportunity came, when least expected, for William to speak with Lottie and ask her to have tea with him. Jenkins was off with an attack of gout or something, and on arriving in the office in Lincolns Inn William was immediately summoned to see Mr Grimes, a senior partner.

'Good morning William, I understand you are familiar with our clients the Courtney Browns and I would like you to take some papers for signature. It's urgent and these papers have to be dispatched to arrive immediately after the Easter holiday. So get them signed and bring them back to the office. You may take the office car and be as quick as you can.'

'Yes Mr. Grimes,' he replied, thinking how fortunate and at last the opportunity he had been waiting for, to see Lottie, hopefully alone!

'Good, then collect the papers and set off, you will be expected as close to ten o'clock as possible. Don't be all day.' With that Mr. Grimes dismissed him from his presence.

William couldn't help feeling thrilled as now, with a bit of luck; he might be able to speak with Lottie alone; well, hopefully, if she would be opening the front door. He picked up the documents and placed them in his briefcase and set off to the car parked at the back of the office.

He drove to Chelsea and, as usual, parked the car round the corner as he knew that Frampton, Frampton and Grimes had always instructed them not to park outside a client's house. He could hardly wait to knock at the door, praying that Lottie would be there.

Little did he know that hearing that, on someone was coming from the family solicitors for an important meeting before the Easter Holiday, when her employees would be going away for a few days to the country, Lottie, persuaded Betty that she would stand in for her.

Betty's various duties included dressing Lady Clarissa's hair, so this would also require a stand-in. Being spared this frightening and dreaded part of her employment brought huge relief, as she really did not look forward to it. Always terrified of the curling tongs knowing that any mistake, such as burning the hair, would result in Heaven knows what retribution, let alone a screaming outburst from her ladyship!

Betty was more than relieved to know that, for the moment, she was no longer required to carry out this terrifying ordeal and hoped Lottie would be able to deal with her mistress's tantrums. So when Lottie came to the rescue and actually volunteered to take her place, it resulted in the two young women becoming firm friends. Of course this had to be with the permission of Lady Courtney Porown, and Lottie was going to make sure she was on her best behavior and paid attention to detail, to impress her ladyship.

William knocked at the polished oak front door. A minute after, Lottie was there to open it, both so pleased to see the other. With no-one in sight, William took Lottie's hand smiled, and before she could catch her breath he said. He said: 'Lottie please may I take you to tea when you have time off?'

She smiled back at him and replied 'I would be delighted Mr Cavanaugh' William, overjoyed, said 'When?' trying not to show his anxiety.

'The master and mistress are away for Easter, so maybe Saturday afternoon?' she replied.

He smiled at her 'That would be perfect Lottie, where shall we meet?' Lottie thought that it would be safer not too near the house. 'I know,' she replied. 'Over the other side of the bridge there is a tea room in the square, at four o'clock?'

William was over the moon. 'I will be there Lottie, now I have to get these papers signed and be back to the office, no time for tea today,' he said.

'That's alright, we will have time on Saturday,' she replied and, beaming her best smile, she showed him to the study.

William almost skipped back to the car. He had already decided to try to start, very gently, to give her some tips that would help her to learn a little etiquette as soon as possible. This was, of course, if she allowed it. From her attempts to be ladylike in his company he thought she would be agreeable and find the whole thing quite comical.

In fact William had quite radical views on social reform and was what one might regard as quite left-wing, much to the disapproval of his father who was as decidedly a right-wing. However, besotted as he was, he also realized that if he was ever going to make her a permanent part of his life, he would have to coach Lottie in the ways of the well-to-do. His father had big plans for William, therefore a great deal of caution, and avoidance of his intentions becoming known, was paramount at this stage.

Thus started the romance that Lottie had dreamed of. She had not wasted her time whilst being a scullery maid, she watched and listened and worked her way up to helping when needed as an extra parlour maid. Then an amazing turn of good fortune happened one afternoon when Lady Clarissa, due to attend a supper with her husband, found she was without her usual helper and personal maid, Betty, who was still rather poorly. Lottie, now warned of the dire consequences of accidently crisping her ladyship's tresses, was prepared when called upon to bring the curling tongs.

Lady Clarissa, unused to fiddling with such things, was making a bit of a mess of her coiffeur. Lottie watched her frustration.

'Excuse me my lady, may I assist you, you have such beautiful hair and perhaps I could help dress it for you,' she said smiling.

Clarissa looked at Lottie and had noticed her striking red hair which Lottie had always taken great care of.

'Well, as you couldn't make a worse mess of it than me, or that silly girl, then you had better do it.'

Lottie picked up the hairbrush that her employer had thrown on the floor in a temper. She proceeded to brush the fair hair that was as straight as any she had ever seen, it was long and had been quite shiny until the tongs had been applied, nearly causing a disaster to its condition.

'Have you got some hair oil my lady?'

'Yes,' Lady Clarissa answered grumpily as anything 'Over there in the cupboard.' she answered.

Lottie took the bottle and applied a small amount in her hands and rubbing them together so no surplus was to be seen, she ran her hands through the hair, immediately improving the texture.

'Have you some decorative combs in your dressing table?' Lottie asked. Clarissa opened a drawer where there were at least a dozen in many colours with matching stones, as well as some that looked to Lottie like they may have been real, perhaps diamonds, although she had never seen a real diamond except on her ladyship's fingers.

'May I ask you what colour dress you will be wearing?'

'The blue chiffon,' came the reply.

Lottie saw a beautiful dark blue comb with little white stones set in the top. She took it out and placed it on the dressing table. She then took a handful of hair and twisted it into a neat roll pinning it in a design that was elegant and flattering, and secured the finished coiffeur with the comb. The whole effect was beautiful and quite professional.

Lady Clarissa was delighted; so delighted she turned to Lottie 'My dear girl you are wasted downstairs I am going to make you my personal hairdresser. Are you as talented with the art of make up?' Lottie knew she could certainly make a better job of it than Clarissa, who sometimes overdid the rouge and lipstick, not to mention what looked like a flour bag on the cheeks.

She replied, 'Well, why don't I try?'

So out came all sorts of facial adornments, rather pink powder, red rouge and lip colours, that would not have looked out of place in Shepherds Market.

Lottie was enjoying herself and did her best with the economically endowed looks of her mistress and proceeded to make the best of what she had to work with. Clarissa looked at herself in the mirror and realized that she actually looked younger than she had for years. She stood up and hugged Lottie.

'You are a very clever girl,' she exclaimed continually looking at herself in the mirror, all the time prancing up and down with delight.

'I will make sure you have an increase in your wages, but you must be prepared to help with some other duties if needed, she added 'No longer in the kitchen.'

Lottie overjoyed replied 'Oh thank you my lady, thank you.'

Clarissa went to her purse and took out a coin and handed it to Lottie, it was a sixpence, 'And there will be a little extra when I am extremely pleased.' she added

Lottie couldn't wait to tell Molly of her good fortune, and of course, William, who already recognized that his Lottie was a rose in a garden of weeds.

William, it turned out was the son of a lawyer himself, but he was not like the usual snobs of his class. He did care that the underprivileged found it difficult to lift themselves out of poverty. He believed that everyone should be educated sufficiently to find work and afford a decent life. He hated the lack of opportunity for many and if he had anything to do with it, he would try to change things for the better, if he could, and he would start with his beautiful Lottie.

When William was a young boy, his father, busy with his law practice, had very little time for him. Every time he looked at the boy it reminded him of his Susan, who had passed away leaving him with a young son to bring up.

As was the norm, William was sent away to boarding school at seven years old. This was soon after he had lost his mother. His father was always busy and quite often away, which left William to entertain himself during the holidays.

Sir James Cavanaugh was not fond of having lots of staff running all over the house. As there was only himself and William, and neither of them there all the time, he kept his retainers to a minimum.

Fortunately, Davis, who had been with the family since he was a young lad, as his father had been their coachman, was now Sir James's 'man of all things'. He had also become more like a father to young William.

In the holidays, unbeknown to his father, Davis would take William on little excursions to areas of London he would never have seen. He took him to working class districts in the East End, to the markets with their lively atmosphere that William found so exciting and colourful.

The stallholders would always give him an apple or a sweet. Davis would hold his hand as they walked together and explored the crowded streets chatting to all and sundry. They were always cheerful and friendly, and which William regarded this as a real adventure.

Davis would buy him ice cream. To William this was a side of life he would have never experienced. It affected him deeply and made a deep impression that it stayed with him all his life.

He loved these outings so much and would always ask when they could go again.

Davis would reply: 'Whatever you do William, you had better not tell your father, it might get me the sack.'

William answered 'It's our secret Davis, I promise,' and he would keep it forever!

Now the treasured memories came back to him as he assured Lottie that he was not ashamed of her, or her cockney accent. He explained that he wanted her to be comfortable in any social circle. In his work he would have to present her to people who were important and he wanted her to feel like a queen, 'his queen.'

He taught her to say pardon, not 'Aye' or 'what?' and gave her other little tips in etiquette. Lottie loved the way he taught her and thought the whole thing hilarious and always teasing him. Sometimes shewould do it all wrong on purpose just to see his face, and then plant a kiss on his lips.

She showed him that she had been joking and that she was becoming quite accomplished at learning to be a lady.

Actually, they both found the whole process highly amusing, along with William's determination to achieve success, but he still had not found the courage to tell Lottie who his father was. He felt this was better kept quiet until it became essential. William was not looking forward to that event and preferred to let things be.

The day came when she shocked him rigid when holding her nose high in the air, said in a voice in an unrecognisably haughty voice that he had never heard from her lips.

'Would you mind please sir, helping me into my carriage.'

William put his arms around her and kissed her cheek.

'Good Lord, I will make a lady of you yet.'

They both collapsed with laughter, but little did Lottie know that William's reason for all this was in the hope he would finally be able to explain to his father that he wanted to marry her. There was no way that he would give her up whatever happened. However, the mere thought of Lottie being presented to his father, concerned him greatly, but made William laugh until his side ached.

There was also another challenge ahead, as Lottie was neither aware who William's father was, nor that he lived in his father's house only four streets away from the 'posh house'; nor did he share accommodation in Lincoln's Inn with another employee, as he had told her. This would no doubt need some explaining.

However, fate had given William a good turn; he had passed all his law exams and progressed to being a full-blown lawyer, much to his father's delight.

'You know, William, there may be an opportunity for you to carry out your career in the diplomatic service,' said his father. I was talking to Sir John Travers and this could lead to very privileged assignments. They always prefer legal experts in this field and with your knowledge and an interest in international affairs it could be the making of a brilliant career,' he said.

William was taken by surprise: his father, now a prominent judge, seemed to move in all the highest circles.

'Oh Father, I don't know if I am ready for that,' he said, thinking how this would affect his plans for himself and Lottie.

His plan had always been to be a lawyer who would become involved in helping the disadvantaged and underunprivileged working class in London, or for that matter elsewhere. He was determined to put his professional knowledge to good use. The diplomatic service had not been the direction he had envisaged going. Then William had a brilliant idea. Perhaps being sent to some far off country would be the perfect answer. It could provide an opportunity for Lottie to be coached longer and to become acquainted with the do's and don'ts; a good opportunity to refine her language skills.

This might be an excuse to use this as a good reason to be a little shy in company, and hopefully would not be under the intense scrutiny of English society, although the very thought of a shy Lottie made him laugh.

He was confronted by his father who continued to carry on with this topic of conversation, which was by this time no longer having William's full attention.

'Nonsense, you have the right assets my boy, I have every confidence in you, and you might well become an ambassador for your country.'

Oh Lord, thought William, how am I going to get round this one!

William excused himself as quickly as he could saying that he had a lot of work to do. He needed time to think. Lottie had certainly done very well with her education and elocution lessons, but there was still some work to do.

She was a born actress and put on the airs and graces of a lady as if born to it. However, if in a situation where this was to be a carried out for any length of time, William had grave concerns. Should they get married and keep it quiet. Should he confess to his father? No, perhaps not yet anyway. This really needed some deep thought.

Sure enough an interview was arranged for William to see Sir John Travers at the foreign office

'Delighted to see you William, I heard the good news from your father about how well you have done with your career so far. Now, my boy, it is my great pleasure to tell you that we can offer you a post in Sweden as the Third Secretary at the Consulate, but it has to be taken up within the next three months.'

William tried to smile and would have been more than pleased had circumstances been different. He knew that this had been something to do with his father and the old pals' connection. How was he to get Lottie there without marrying her? And if he did marry her first, how complicated would that get?

He knew the day would soon come when he had to tell Lottie that he may have to go abroad. He needed to decide on the right moment ideally at Lavender Street. This had now become a haven for them to meet in private, when Molly and Fred would plan on going out. Lottie always offered to baby-sit to give both couples freedom to enjoy their time together. Particularly for Molly and Fred, as they would enjoy going for a walk or to the music hall.

William broke his father's news as gently as he could, but Lottie took it badly. There had been no talk of a future and now a sudden need for this conversation had shocked her and had convinced her that his intentions had been all along just to seduce her. They had been alone a few times and things had been passionate and both of them had found it difficult to stop matters going further. Now she turned tearfully on him and with heart rendering sobs exclaimed: 'I now know the truth, you just wanted to get into me drawers. You thought just cos I am not like you and from some la-de-da family I'm not good enough. Well William Cavanaugh you made a big mistake, I'm a good girl!'

The tears still flowing, William, shocked at her outburst, was lost for words.

He had never told her who his father was and began to deeply regret his reluctance to tell her the truth. He realized that she would now distrust his intentions. Of course she realized he was well-educated. And he being in a law firm had to be clever. That was one thing, but the rest was a shock.

He had never found the right moment to tell her everything and realized he should have been more open and told her the truth. It now seemed that everything had gone wrong.

He took her in his arms, kissing her cheeks and trying to stop her the heart-breaking sobs.

'Listen my darling Lottie; I know there are things I should have told you, but I was afraid to.'

She stopped crying 'What do you mean? You're not married are you?'

'No nothing like that, I have never lied to you,' he hesitated, 'just not told you everything!'

She looked at him with such a stern face he knew now he had to tell her everything.

'Well, you had better start now then,' she said firmly.

William didn't really know where to start and his hesitation convinced her more than ever he was hiding something. She turned on him 'I'm right you are just…' He interrupted her.

'Of course I want to get into your drawers, what man wouldn't? You're beautiful and fun, you make me laugh, and Lottie I love you and I want to marry you, and I will tell you everything.'

'Now,' she said as firmly as she could manage.

He took her in his arms and kissed her with such tenderness that all the fight went out of her. He held her arm as he sat her down on the couch and proceeded to tell her everything. She sat there trying to take it all in, as he left nothing out including his father's intentions regarding his future and the predicament he had found himself in.

Lottie was silent, she was no fool and she realized that this man she loved had difficult choices to make in every direction.

'Look William, it's you who must decide what to do, it isn't for me to know the answers, I love you and I will not try to interfere as you would always resent me.'

William looked at this woman whom he found so incredible, so sensible, so determined to improve herself, and now one he respected so highly for saying that she would step aside if this was what he wanted.

William was more than ever determined that she was going to stay in his life, come what may. He would face the consequences with her at his side, as he again took her in his arms and said 'Will you be my wife and one day become Lady Cavanaugh?'

She looked at him and exclaimed, 'Bloody hell!'

They both laughed, and laughed as now they were both relieved the truth was finally out.

Within days fate took another hand in their lives when William's father became unwell and had a stroke. William was broken-hearted. His father was unable to be able to communicate properly and was partially paralysed. The opportunity to take the Swedish post was put on hold and he found himself spending as much time as possible at his father's bedside.

Sir James has been a widower for so many years and his housekeeper, Doris, had run his house and saw to his every comfort. She now made sure he had constant attention for his every need and, with a private nurse in attendance, he had the best care possible. His father survived briefly, but finally his heart failed and he passed away in his sleep. William's relationship with his father had not been an easy one. Nevertheless he loved and respected him, but he knew that, when his mother had died, his father had never overcome his loss and had just buried himself in his work and remained solitary.

CHAPTER 5

The Partings

William was taking two month's grace from the Prime Minister before taking up his position in Sweden. During that time he and Lottie, who was his rock through the heartache, made William more determined than ever to marry her as soon was respectably possible. He would take the post offered to him and take Lottie with him as his wife.

They planned a discreet wedding in a quiet country village in Surrey that Davis had found for them. Molly was to be maid of honour and Fred, Best Man. Neither, Molly nor Fred could believe such an honour being bestowed on them and were thrilled to bits. When the brand new Rolls arrived at Lavender Street, with Lottie and William inside, they knew it was going to be a very special day in all their lives.

'Hop in,' said William after they parked outside the house.

Fred thought this was as unconventional a wedding as his and Molly's with the horses and the painted cart, except this was the posh version. A chauffeured Rolls-Royce and a secret shared with their very special friends.

They had arrived at a little village in Surrey named Richmond; the church was in the centre by the village green, not far from the river. How lovely, Molly thought, how beautiful it all was, and the sun was shining just like on her own wedding day.

The whole thing had been arranged with the height of discretion by Davis, who had always been the one to rely on. Their friendship had become closer than ever and William had always regarded Davis as his other father.

Lottie looked wonderful in what Molly thought was the most beautiful dress of chiffon and lace. She didn't even try to guess what it had cost. She knew about clothes and how expensive the material must have been even without the making. Lottie looked like a titled lady and no one would have ever guessed the truth of her humble beginnings.

Their celebrations were tinged with sadness, very soon Lottie and William would be leaving as he was to take up the post in Sweden which had been put on hold. They had decided to take their honeymoon visiting the fjords in Norway and to see other parts of Sweden before William started his role in the embassy.

Molly knew she was going to miss Lottie dreadfully. So many years spent together since girls was almost like losing a part of herself and Lottie also knew how much she would miss Molly. Both dreaded the goodbyes, but tried keeping from crying and promising all the time they would keep in constant touch by letter. There was an assurance that there would be times when they would return.

Fred and Molly had settled into married life and she had continued working at the vicarage and Fred continued working for old Barney. A year or two later their first child was born, a boy they named Albert. Molly worried that because of her confinement and having to stay off work she would lose her job at the vicarage, for this would mean a big loss of income for them. But within a short time Fred's mother became a widow and it was decided that she would move in with them and would look after the baby. Things seemed to be working out for them, because gradually another room at Lavender Street became vacant and as Fred's mother had a little money put aside from her husband, she was able to contribute to the rent and Molly was be able to continue working.

Fred's mother, Martha, was a nice gentle woman and got on well with Molly. They say 'never live with your mother-in-law', but nothing could be more from the truth with this family. She didn't interfere in their lives and loved little Albert to bits. Molly just hoped she would not spoil him too much. She also made sure that Fred had a dinner prepared and this saved Molly having to cook after a long day at the vicarage, as she still tired easily after the birth.

Albert was growing up and remained their only child for some time. She had miscarried several times and both she and Fred felt that fate had decreed that it was meant to be. When least expected, Molly fell pregnant again and this time carried the baby full-term and gave birth to a healthy girl.

They called her Emma; she was the image of Molly, dark hair and beautiful blue eyes. Fred thought she was the most beautiful child he had ever seen; he called her his little princess and would sing lullabies to her.

He would joke to Molly, 'She doesn't look like me; she must be the coalman's,' he grinned.

Molly would laugh and hug Fred. 'I think you must be right, are you jealous?' she asked.

He kissed her cheek, 'not half' he said, still loving her as much as the day they married.

Emma was seven years old when Fred started coughing and growing thin, the doctors said it was the coal dust. Whatever it was, Fred was only thirty-five years old and was in his grave by the age of thirty-seven.

Molly was broken-hearted and cried her heart out for what seemed forever. It was only when she realized how distressed Emma was that she knew she had to pull herself together. It was only the previous year that Fred's mother had passed away, at the age of eighty, quite peacefully in her sleep. So now Mollie had no help with Emma as Fred's mother had always been there.

When young Albert, Molly's first born was nearly fifteen, he had a job delivering laundry to the Tower of London and this helped towards their expenses. Little Emma loved to hear the stories when Albert would talk about the Beefeaters and the ravens. He didn't care much for the ravens, 'them big black crows, didn't want them flying near me,' he would say.

Still, he got a halfpenny a day which would buy a penny's worth of fish and potatoes for the family on a Saturday night, a treat that they eagerly awaited. By the time it arrived it was nearly cold because Albert would walk all the way from Battersea to Chelsea and back with his packet of fish wrapped in newspaper. When he arrived home Molly would put them on top of the range to warm up. The crispiness had gone, but that didn't matter, they still enjoyed this treat enormously. Now, however much she tried, the memories of the past kept coming back to haunt her and were too painful to bear.

One thing that warmed her heart was when the Reverend and Mrs Stone had a baby daughter they named Tessa, who had been born at nearly the same time as Emma. Clara had been a teacher at a private school in Berkshire before marrying Mr Stone and she decided to teach Tessa at home as she felt that she was qualified to give her the best education in her early years. Knowing how fond they were of Molly, and had known her for so long, they understood how difficult life was for her with no bread winner and no one to look after Emma.

One day Clara said to Molly: 'I have an idea, as I am going to teach Tessa at home and she and Emma are the same age, why if I am teaching one child, can I not teach two? They could learn together, would you agree to it?'

Molly could not believe the words she was hearing. 'Oh thank you Mrs Stone, you cannot believe how grateful I am, you are always so kind to me I don't know what to say.'

Molly smiled happily as her Emma was to have a private tutor. What more could she ask?

'Listen, my dear Molly, the truth is we don't want to lose you. Neither does Violet, who as you well know, is happy just to potter in the kitchen making her pies and preparing those wonderful dinners,' she said with a little smile.

'Children work better together and they need playmates, so you will be doing us a good deed, as both children know each other from babies and always played well together. So is it decided then?'

Molly gave her a hug and the two women were happy to have found a perfect solution.

Clara kissed Molly's cheek and said 'Shall we start on Monday then?'

'Oh yes,' she replied, feeling relieved and happier than she had been in a long time.

Molly knew the only way to try and go on with her life was to keep busy and to provide an income for her family. It all depended on her to hide her heartache for the children's sake. They missed their father so much, although Albert would put on a brave face realizing that now he was the man of the house and must play his role confidently.

Emma, who loved her father, could still not understand and why he had been taken to Heaven, as Molly had often told her. She would say that the really good people went there and he would be happy and out of pain. Somehow Emma was hard to convince and would have bouts of crying not really understanding anything, except her daddy was no longer there to cuddle and play little games with her.

A week after the funeral, Molly started back working at the vicarage, taking Emma with her. Clara had set up a room suitable for a classroom: two little tables and chairs facing a larger desk from where Clara would teach the girls. The walls were pale pink and painted with coloured pictures of animals, mostly exotic: elephants, lions, parrots and other different species. There were birds of every description and on another wall creatures that Emma had never seen before. She thought it was lovely.

So began a period in Molly's life that again gave her hope and helped her to ease the pain of losing Fred. She began to realize that Emma was receiving a private education, and that was something beyond her wildest dreams. When Emma arrived home full of knowledge of things that were quite beyond Molly's experience, she couldn't help thanking God for her good fortune. As Fred would say, 'When one door closes another opens.'

Molly had loved to read and could do so well, but the things that Emma was learning were subject a world away from just the three R's.

Emma was learning French and mathematics and geography and history and her favourite subject, English literature, in so much depth that Molly could not keep up with it all.

But soon another blow was to strike Molly's heart. The war between England and Germany had broken out in 1914 and things had changed in every way. By the following year so many young men had been called up to fight and Molly, glad that Albert was still under age and was safe. However, the day came when Albert said determinedly, 'I must fight for my country, Mum, and they need every man.' She pleaded with him to change his mind, but to no avail.

Molly cried to herself 'Oh God, how many times can a heart be broken?'

She sobbed and prayed that he would change his mind, but without success. How he ever managed to fool the recruitment office she couldn't imagine. They were supposed to be seventeen years old to join up, but what she didn't know was the authorities were very aware of these young volunteers being under age. They were so desperate for soldiers to join up, they turned a blind eye.

Albert loved horses and had learned how to look after them, groom and feed them, like his father, after working with Bess and Bonnie and with

Jenkin's laundry horse. He had somehow managed to join a cavalry unit as an unlisted man. Molly, with so much heartache, seemed to lose the will to live. Her health had become a worry for some time and now she seemed to be deteriorating more by the week.

When she looked at Albert it was like looking at young Fred all over again and the memories were like a knife penetrating her heart. It was so long ago, but seemed just like yesterday.

Life had become more difficult and depressing. Nothing seemed to relieve the hardship they and many others were suffering.

News from Albert was sparse and took weeks to arrive, if at all. They had received the odd letter from him and it was never good. He was in the trenches somewhere in France; he was never too explicit, maybe for reasons of security. They never knew, but his experiences were something that sounded horrific, always cold and wet and forced to spend hours never knowing if it was their last. The horses had to be cared for and when they were lost in battle it broke Albert's heart. He said that he may ask for a transfer to another unit, but this was not considered as every man was needed for the front line. He had found himself in hand to hand combat with the enemy, had been wounded in his face and been sewn up without anything to kill the pain.

The final blow was when the telegram came through the front door. Molly opened it with fear in her heart, as she knew the way the War Office delivered bad news.

Even when she had read Albert's letters, Molly had cried for hours, 'What is my child doing in this war, he is still a minor; why on earth did they take him?' Emma had cuddled her and tried to explain the need for everyone, no matter their age, to fight. Emma realized this was the final turning point as Molly no longer seemed to have any interest in anything. Eating was something that failed to have importance, in fact nothing did, and Emma became more concerned every day.

Finally, since the dreaded news had arrived, saying their beloved son and brother had been killed, her mother's deterioration both mentally and physically was no longer in doubt, the will to live seem to have gone.

Molly had been forced to scrub floors and take in washing and sewing to keep a roof over her and Emma's head. They had to pay a few shillings a week rent for the old house in Lavender Street, which meant there was little left for food or clothes. The clothes they wore were hand-me-downs from wherever they could be found. Molly would have loved to return to work for the Stones again, but their circumstances had changed. It was now the height of the war, which took all the men to fight the Germans. Mr Stone had been called to serve his country as he was to care for the soldier's spiritual well-being.

Mrs Stone went to help nurse wounded soldiers, and Tessa had been sent to boarding school. The need for a housemaid was no longer necessary. Violet was semi-retired but remained to keep an eye on the vicarage, and for any replacement for Mr Stone who might become available.

Molly, no longer able to help support them, suffered with her lungs and was prone to infections. Emma noticed that her memory had also started to fail. At first it was little things like losing a key to the front door, progressing slowly to all sorts of odd things. She could no longer sew, which meant that the money they relied on had been reduced to what Emma could bring in, with some sewing and taking in ironing.

Molly seemed to live in the past and was always reminiscing about when she and Fred were young; when they went to Brighton for the day, or the park with a picnic, and always Fred and Albert there. But something that happened only an hour before was forgotten and Emma was now afraid to leave her.

If it hadn't been for the local grocer, who had known them for years and was aware that they were in need of help, would always have some vegetables and apples dropped round by his lad. Emma was very grateful as without this help they would have starved. She would collect bits of old wood when she could, to burn in the range. In winter the house was so cold and they would cuddle up in the old bed with coats and anything that she could find to throw on the top to give some warmth.

The biggest worry for Emma was that the privy was at the end of the backyard and she was no longer able to get Molly there. They had a potty, as everyone did for their night needs, but this was only a temporary solution. She knew she had to try to acquire a commode, but where was the money coming from?

She was desperately trying to think what she could sell and where and how to get out to look for one, as now she was afraid to leave her mother alone. Then she remembered there was something she could sell that could bring enough money for her to buy a commode. Her mother had given her a gold bracelet that her mother had given her on her sixteenth birthday. Annie had been given it by her grandmother on her sixteenth birthday; something that been handed down in the family for years. Emma cried at the thought of what she must do, but it was the only thing of value she had and it was more important for her mother to be able to manage her needs in the house. She was also aware that Molly would never know and, if she took it to the pawnbrokers in the High Street, maybe she could somehow try to retrieve it later.

She would have to ask their neighbour, Mrs Biggins, if she could possible stay with Molly for an hour or so while she went out. Mrs Biggins, being a kind woman who understood the circumstances, agreed to mind Molly for as long as she was needed.

Emma remembered that there was a shop that sold second hand furniture and collectables, where she might find a commode. So she quickly went to the hiding place and retrieved the bracelet. It was gold and pretty with delicate filigree work. She had no idea how much it was worth, but it must be more than enough for a commode, with maybe some left over for coal for the range.

With the bracelet safe in her purse, she headed to the shops as fast as she could go. She went to the second hand shop first, where the proprietor already stood hovering. He spoke as she entered the door and asked her if there was anything in particular she required. It seemed she was in luck as sure enough, in the back, in a corner was a brown mahogany commode.

Emma was delighted and asked the price. The shop owner, keen to get the most money possible, said 'Well this is an antique you know,' rubbing his chin. Emma stared at him, worried at this response. She knew well enough to show disinterest before the man answered. Emma began to wander away and look at other bits and pieces.

The man, following her, said 'Of course if you really like it I am sure we can work out something agreeable.'

Emma looked at him. She did not like the way he eyed her up and down, with a look that made her uncomfortable. She certainly had not been prepared for this reaction, which had something unpleasant in its delivery.

She decided to play her part of being no longer interested and started to walk away.

The man, then realized he had played the wrong card, said: 'For you, my dear, I will make it a bargain; thirty shillings.'

This sounded a lot, she paused, and now a little wiser to his game, said: 'I'll think about it.'

The man quickly responded: 'I wouldn't wait too long there has been quite a bit of interest. It only came in this morning.'

Emma thought 'what a liar' and replied: 'Well, I will have to chance it then, won't I.'

With that the man said: 'Alright, as you are so pretty, twenty five shillings and I will deliver it.'

'I will be back in a short time and will let you know then,' she replied.

With that she walked out of the shop knowing full well he was desperate to sell and she may even get it cheaper. She headed off to the pawnbrokers with a heavy heart, but knowing this was something she had to do.

She asked the man behind the counter 'Can you tell me how much you will give me for this gold bracelet?' taking it out of her purse.

'Is it real gold? I will have to test it' he said.

Emma thought any fool can see its real gold, but said nothing.

He got out some scales and weighed it.

'Um, looks alright, I'll give you one pound.'

Emma knew it was worth more than that and thought is everyone so greedy that they are trying to rob me. She looked at the man and let the tears fill her eyes.

'I need more, my mother is dying and I need medicine.'

It took the man by surprise, not expecting a tearful customer and being a little more aware that this could be true, said: 'Alright, I'll give you two pounds and that's it.'

Emma knew this would give her enough for the commode and enough left over for some coal and food. She took the receipt and remembering the words the man had said. 'Keep it safe,' as the date on it meant if she wanted to, she could pay to reclaim it.

She took the money and hurried back to the second hand shop. Now feeling more confident, she addressed the shop owner with the remark 'I have seen another in better condition, so I am not sure whether it would be a better buy.'

She turned away as if to go, but the shop owner, deciding to grab the sale, said: 'Alright, £1.'

Emma retorted, 'And deliver?'

He looked as if he had lost a fortune, but agreed.

She gave him the address and said it was needed today and she would pay him half now and half on delivery. She wasn't going to give this slippery customer any opportunity to rob her!

Feeling that she had done quite well in the circumstances, she hurried back to Lavender Street stopping to buy some bones from the butcher to make some soup. The butcher made sure their was plenty of meat on the bones, and Emma was eternally grateful for his compassion and generosity.

She hurried back to the house and as she approached she was aware the street door was ajar. She wondered why on earth it was left open. She entered into the hallway and found a tearful Mrs Biggins. Hardly able to talk in between sobs, she pointed to the bedroom. A feeling of dread filled Emma's body as she dropped the shopping on the floor. She entered the room. Standing by the bed was Doctor Murphy, who had been so kind to them in the past; giving them medicine, probably paid for out of his own pocket. Accompanying him was a policeman taking notes, both nodded and added their condolences.

Emma hardly noticed as her worst fears had been realized. She now felt full of remorse and heartache for being too late.

Her mother was lying still with eyes closed and Emma knew immediately that she was no longer living. The shock had taken away all means of speech.

Mrs Biggins, still hardly able to speak herself, muttered words that meant nothing.

'I thought she was asleep, I left her and sat in the other room awhile and when I went in to see if she needed anything, I could see she was gone,' she sobbed. 'I got Pete, my son, to get the Doctor and he brought Sergeant Jennings.'

With past experience of the need to get the authorities as soon as possible in these circumstances, she added tearfully 'I hope I did the right thing.'

Emma managed 'Yes, thank you, Mrs Biggins, you did the right thing.'

Emma was almost blaming herself. What if she had been there and called for help? But she knew in her heart it would have made no difference. She went to her mother and kissed her, but was shocked to find she was already cold.

Mrs Biggins sat with her for a long time, until Emma was ready to inform the doctor and policeman and they could take over. Now was the awful task of burying Molly with little money to pay for it. For years her mother had paid a penny a week to what they called the funeral man to save for a burial, but now Emma wasn't sure if there would be enough. She would have to deal with that tomorrow. That money and some she had left from pawning the bracelet would have to suffice.

The man delivered the commode much to Mollie's shock as she had forgotten it was being delivered. She asked if she could cancel the sale and get back her deposit, but the man would have none of it so she now had a commode. At least she would not have to go out in the yard in the middle of the night.

However, the funeral took nearly all her money and the knowledge that it was to be a pauper's grave with no head-stone, left her with a heart broken in tiny pieces, that she believed would never mend.

CHAPTER 6

Emma

It was 1925, the war long over, and Emma was now alone. Her mother having died from what turned out to be complications of pneumonia. Emma realised it was when the news came that Albert had been killed in France that Molly, broken-hearted, seemed to have given up the fight to live. Emma was at a loss what to do and how to survive with no one left to turn to, at least this was as far as she knew as the family seemed to have all gone.

She was bright and intelligent and had learned much from the excellent teaching of Mrs Stone. However, she had no professional training for any employment. She knew that she must do something to earn a living.

If she could help it, she would never work as a domestic servant.

What Emma did have was beauty. Her long dark hair and striking blue eyes denoted a mixture of Irish and perhaps something a little more exotic somewhere in her ancestry. Emma was not conceited. She realized that her looks were an asset and, if she could afford to keep herself looking presentable, she might have a chance to achieve that better life she was so determined to make for herself.

Since the war had ended life had begun to return to a different England: a country at last at peace and with an atmosphere that screamed for carefree rejoicing. But for many life was still hard and jobs were scarce and not well-paid.

Emma, still desperate for money, wondered where to start looking for a job to help her survive.

She had no-one to turn to and found herself alone in the world. Everyone that she loved had gone. Even her grandfather and Stella had passed on.

Lizzie and Morrie had gone to America. Morrie had become a qualified doctor, specializing in something Emma couldn't remember the name of. Even her aunt and uncles seem to have vanished from her life.

Then she remembered Lottie, who had been her mother's best friend and was her Godmother; who had been abroad for many years and whose husband William had become not only a fully fledged lawyer, but a foreign diplomat.

Emma knew her mother missed Lottie a great deal, and they had kept in touch by letter as much as they could. But it had become more difficult to do so as frequently as they had wished, due to the war and slow and difficult communication. Recently they had lost touch, although now Emma began to wonder if her mother had heard anything and had just not remembered. She had certainly stopped talking about her friend for some time. Molly had told her that Lottie and William were in some country far away but couldn't remember where. Now it was peacetime again and Emma must try to find her and tell her that her beloved friend had gone to her Maker. Just thinking about it brought tears to her eyes.

She did not know how to start, but perhaps she could find something in her mother's belongings; a letter with an address or something that would help her. She knew Lottie had lived over the river in Chelsea, quite near what her mother had always called the 'posh house', but she could not remember where that was either.

She began her search in cupboards and drawers. Finally her persistence proved successful as, tucked away in a drawer was an old embroidered bag filled with letters and cards secured by coloured ribbons. Sitting on the bed she began to look through them and was surprised to find some from far off places, mostly un-opened. Among those few that were opened were some from Lottie. It seemed her mother had been so far from reality that even the memory of her best friend had been locked in her heart.

It took some hours as there were so many things that Emma wanted to look at and read. Old photographs and cards with flowers and words of love from her father to her mother. She could hardly read them for the tears that filled her eyes. She wiped them away and continued until she found an envelope with an address in Chelsea. It looked like 39 Cheyne Walk but the last digit was smudged. She now remembered when she was quite young being taken by her mother to a grand house near the river to see Lottie, but she could not remember the proper address.

She decided to walk to Albert Bridge: she could go by tram, but every penny she had left was precious and so she thought better of it.

She had to walk quite a while to find 39, but it didn't look familiar. She wandered further down the street and eventually arrived outside the very imposing exterior of a large house. Something about it looked familiar and memories of her last visit began to return. She vaguely remembered Lottie; how lovely she was, and the grandeur of the house, and how impressed she was with the beautiful drawing room with its rich furnishings.

She had never seen such luxury in her young life. Even at that age she noticed everything. She pulled the door bell and after a few minutes a young girl in a maid's uniform came to the door.

'Oh excuse me, does Lottie still live here?' Emma could not remember the last name.

The maid said 'I am afraid not.' The maid was new and had no idea who 'Lottie' was. Emma did not know what to say, she stood there, the disappointment so acute she could hardly hide her tears.

'You see I must find her, she was my mother's best friend and she has died. Lottie is my godmother but I have not seen her since I was little,' she said. 'Who lives here then, are they at home, maybe they might know something?'

The young maid stood there, not quite knowing how to deal with this situation.

'I am afraid Sir William and Lady Cavanaugh are abroad and will not be back for some time' she said.

Then a voice came from the hallway: 'Who is at the door Lilly?'

'I don't know a young woman is asking for Lottie,' she replied.

The voice came to the front door; it revealed a tall lady dressed in a smart black dress, at her neck she had a white lace collar to match the cuffs on her sleeves. Emma thought she looked quite important, maybe a governess. She looked at Emma, something familiar about her, she thought.

'What is your name?' she asked.

'It's Emma,' she replied, 'Lottie used to live here and she is my godmother and my mother's closest friend.' she repeated.

The woman said 'Run along Lilly' to the young maid.

'Come in Emma, maybe you don't remember me? I am Sarah and I met you when you were very young, when you came to the house with your mother. Molly isn't it?' she said.

'But the maid said Lottie does not live here.'

'Well, my dear you could not have known that your Lottie is Lady Cavanaugh. We call her Lady Charlotte.'

Emma couldn't believe her ears. Her mother had never told her Lottie was a titled lady. The tears had stopped because now, at last, she had renewed hope. She repeated what she had told the young maid.

'My mother died and I thought Lottie, I mean Lady Charlotte, would want to know.'

Sarah gently took Emma's arm and said 'Come and sit down and tell me everything whilst we have some tea.'

She guided her to the drawing room and bid her to sit down on the couch. She rang a bell and the young maid Lilly arrived and was told to bring them a variety of sandwiches, tea and pastries. Sarah thought Emma looked thin and tired and that there could be a lot more to her story that she needed to know.

Emma was so glad to find such a lovely kind lady as Sarah, who listened intently to all that had happened.

Emma paused to eat as she was quite ravenous; it had been a very long time since food had touched her lips. Sarah waited patiently while Emma demolished the sandwiches and a couple of pastries. Poor thing, she thought. Her heart went out to Emma and she wondered if she had enough money to buy food. Sarah waited until she had finished almost everything on the plate, then they talked for quite a while as Emma explained some of what had befallen them. Sarah listened with tears in her eyes, but trying very hard to hide how the story had affected her and knowing that Lottie would be horrified to hear what had become of her friend and goddaughter.

Eventually when Emma said she must get home before dark, Sarah said 'Emma, I won't be a moment I am arranging for Davis, Sir William's chauffeur to drop you home.'

'Oh no Sarah,' she said, swallowing the last mouthful of a strawberry tart, 'I couldn't. I mean, I could not impose or take up his time.'

'His 'time' is to keep me happy and him busy whilst his employers are away. He is my husband,' she said smiling.

Sarah was away a few minutes and Emma decided that the one remaining strawberry tart looked a bit lonely and ate it.

When she returned she was holding an envelope in her hands.

'Now, Emma, take this home and open it there. You will find our telephone number inside, and if you need anything, anything at all, please telephone me and as soon as Lady …' she hesitated.

'When Lottie returns home I know she will want to see you.'

With that she kissed Emma's cheek, gave her a hug, and said 'Now where shall I tell her you live?'

Emma replied 'Just tell her 'Lavender Street.'

Davis dropped Emma outside the house and escorted her to the front door. Oh, Lord she thought I wonder if the neighbours saw me arrive in the old Rolls-Royce, the age of which was not important. She felt so good that at last her spirits had been lifted in a very long time.

She bid good bye to Davis and thanked him what seemed a dozen times. She ran to her room and, remembering the envelope, opened it. Inside was a short note confirming everything Sarah had said, plus folded in half, were five crisp pound notes.

The note read:

Take this Emma and pay your rent and buy food and things you need, it will help you until you find some employment, which I am sure will not take too long. I know Lottie would never forgive me if I did not help you in every way I can. If you need to, you can phone anytime and come and see me when you like and hopefully Lottie will be back soon.
God Bless you.

The letter was signed Sarah with the phone number.

Now Emma could not contain the tears, 'Oh thank you God, and thank you'.

She had never seen so much money at one time in her life!

The next day Emma rose early and the first thing she did was to head to the pawn brokers and retrieve the bracelet. She had to part with more money than she had imagined, but with new hope and enthusiasm she would write to Sarah and thank her and ask God to bless her and Davis for their kindness.

She decided to walk to the High Street and start her search. She didn't really know where she would find work.

She certainly was literate and had good handwriting, and general knowledge, so feeling more confident she set off. She looked in the shop windows and after two hours had not found anything. Perhaps if she went to the library she could look through the newspapers and see if there was anything in the classified columns.

Eventually, she began to feel a little hungry and weary, and decided that with her new found wealth she could afford to buy a sandwich and a cup of tea. There was a tea room she had passed earlier. She began to walk back down the street until she found it.

She entered the door and as she did so she saw a notice in the window.

A position for an experienced waitress available, apply within.

THE MONTE VERDE RESTAURANT AND TEA ROOMS.

Emma sat at a table for two near the door. She noticed the room was almost full with gentlemen and ladies partaking of some kind of refreshment. It certainly appeared to be a very popular establishment, nicely decorated with warm pastel colours that gave the room a cosy feel.

Within a minute or so a small rather plumpish man came to her table. 'Good day madam would you like to see the menu?' he said.

Emma not used to being addressed as madam, hesitated for a moment.

'Um, she murmured 'Yes please, but I would love a pot of tea to begin with.'

The jovial man spoke with a foreign accent 'Certainly Madam', handing her the menu.

This was quite an adventure for Emma, but she tried to look as though this was her usual custom, having tea and whatever took her fancy. She studied the menu with great care. Some of the dishes she had never heard of and certainly did not know how to pronounce them.

LASAGNE AL FORNO, whatever could that be? Then the next dish was SPAGHETTI BOLOGNESE; she didn't know that either!

She moved on swiftly to the opposite page. Oh thank goodness, they had homemade individual steak and kidney pies. She knew what they were because her mother had made them rather well when they could afford the ingredients. When the little man returned to take her order, she gave it confidently.

'Good choice' he said proudly, with a smile, 'my wife makes them herself.'

Emma smiled back, thinking what a nice friendly man and such a kind face.

She tucked into the pie which was delicious, and drank the whole pot of tea She noticed the room was almost empty now. She asked the man, whose name turned out to be Giuseppe, if the vacancy for the waitress had been filled.

He looked at her thinking that she seemed like the kind of young lady that might be a secretary or teacher, not a waitress. She was certainly very beautiful and tidy.

He asked her 'Have you experience as a waitress?'

She replied 'Well, not in a restaurant or tea room, but I learned to lay table with silver service and serve the guests at the vicarage, and I was educated there.'

Well, he thought, this is my lucky day; this young woman would certainly be a great asset to the business. Having to do the waiting on the tables himself he was anxious to find suitable help.

'I will give you a try, when can you start?'

She laughed and said 'Tomorrow if you like.' She didn't even ask about wages, but he said she could have ten shillings a week, plus tips, and lunch.

Emma was delighted and shook his hand.

'Oh, by the way, I don't know your name, everyone calls me Joe, and what is yours?' he asked.

She replied 'Emma, Emma Grey' and gave him a big smile.

He liked this young lady and felt that they would get on well.

'You had better come and meet my wife, Maria,' and he led her to the kitchen. There she made the acquaintance of a rather plump lady who reminded her of Violet, and who obviously had the same leanings when it came to cooking and eating the end product.

'I loved your steak and kidney pie,' she said.

'Ah,' said Maria, 'no doubt you will have to try some other things like my Italian dishes, e molto buono.'

'Emma replied 'I will look forward to it, thank you, Maria.'

Not really exactly understanding the Italian words, she got the gist of them. Wishing them both good afternoon, she promised to be there at eight o'clock the following morning.

Emma felt really happy, she obviously was hoping to find something a little more elevated than being a waitress, but for the moment she had a job, with food and tips whatever they might be and these people seemed so cheerful and kind. She felt relieved and happy. As a quick learner she began to enjoy meeting the customers and soon became very efficient at her job.

Many of the customers were regulars. Some came for a morning coffee or tea, some business-men came for lunch; and ladies would meet their friends for tea and pastries. She also discovered the reward of a tip, which was usually placed under a saucer as the customers left.

The gentlemen were the best tippers. A little smile when they placed their orders often produced the best tips. Some of them would flirt with her and suggest that they might meet on her day off, but Emma became quite accomplished at politely declining with some excuse or other.

Joe was delighted at what appeared to be a surge in customers to the Monte Verde tea rooms and was thrilled to see the way Emma managed to decline the gentlemen's approaches in such a way that they did not feel rejected.

He would say to Maria 'That girl is worth her weight in gold.'

Maria would laugh and agree 'You know Joe, if we had been lucky enough to have had children, I would have wanted a daughter like Emma.' She had a tear in her eye as she spoke.

Joe cuddled her, 'I know Cara; yes a daughter like her would have been a blessing.'

The months went by and Emma had almost become part of the family. On Sundays the tea rooms were closed as it was a special day for Maria and Joe Bennedetti because in Italian families a big Sunday lunch with all the family and various invited friends was a tradition.

Now, Emma found herself included in these gatherings, much to her delight. She had never seen so much food, the variety of which she still had to learn the names; but she had grown to love Italian cuisine.

Maria took great pride in showing her their preparation and would say that one day she would have to cook some of these dishes herself.

They were also teaching her Italian. She loved the language, which she found so beautiful, so romantic, and so passionate and especially her newly found love of opera discovered through the records that Joe played on their latest acquisition, a 'gramophone'.

One day, before the rush started, a man came to the tea rooms. He was tall and well-dressed. Emma noticed something about him that she could not really describe. He was the most distinguished man she had ever seen. She took the menu and hurried towards him; he had taken off his hat and coat and hung them on the stand by the door. As she approached she thought he was quite handsome, with dark wavy hair and smiling brown eyes.

'Hello, are you new here? I haven't been here for a while,' he said.

'Yes, well quite a few weeks now,' she replied.

He continued to smile at her and she noticed the twinkle in his eyes

'What's your name?' he asked.

'Emma.' She replied.

'Well, Emma, can you tell Joe, Carlo is here?'

'Oh yes', she replied, 'I will get him, he is in the kitchen with Maria.'

She realised that he must be known to them as he spoke quite confidently. She thought he seemed important and wondered who he was as she handed him the menu.

'We have one of Maria's special Italian dishes today,' pointing to the item on the menu; 'it's LASAG-NI; I've seen already in the kitchen and it looks really good.'

He looked where she had pointed and replied, 'Well Emma. I don't think I could manage LASAG-NI today as I have a business lunch.'

'Maybe next time.'

He handed her back the menu, keeping a straight face and not wanting to any way embarrass this charming young waitress, who obviously had never heard of Lasagne, which happened to be one of his favourite dishes.

Emma hurried to the kitchen and told Joe that a Mr Carlo was here to see him. A big smile spread over his face. Before hurrying out he told Emma to ask Maria to make the special Italian coffee and a variety of some small tasty things to accompany it.

Joe sat at the table with Carlo and they spoke in Italian. By now Emma was beginning to understand some of the language, but only when it was spoken slowly. However, they were talking fast and it seemed to be regarding business of some kind. Emma could not help wanting to know who this man was and thought she might inquire politely when he had gone. Meantime, she wandered into the kitchen to chat to Maria. Before long she did not really have to ask very much at all. Maria was full of information about Carlo, singing his praises and telling her how fond she was of him.

It seemed that he, Carlo, was a relative of Joe's, their fathers having been something like cousins twice removed, whatever that was. Carlo's father had helped them to acquire the Monte Verde café when they arrived from Italy twenty five years ago. They had all come from the same village originally, except Carlo's father had been very clever and became a lawyer and diplomat. He had met and married an English girl who had been studying Italian in Rome. They fell in love and married.

Carlo was born in Italy, but when his father was posted to London, when Carlo was seven, he went to school here and stayed on to go to university. That is why he was fluent in both languages.

'Now he and Joe have some business interests together and he pops in when he can. He has a lovely wife, Flora, and a son, Robert. His name is really Roberto, but he doesn't like it and prefers the English name.' Emma listened intently as Maria chatted on, and wondered why he didn't like the name Roberto as she thought it was nice and, for her, unusual. Emma found out more about Carlo and the family without even having to ask.

'How old is Roberto?' Emma asked.

'I think he is about seventeen, now,' said Maria. 'You will meet them when we have our family gatherings, Easter, Christmas, birthdays and any other excuses. You know what Italian families are like,' she laughed.

'They must have married young,' said Emma.

'Yes,' said Maria, 'their parents knew each other and I believe encouraged the match, which I believe is a very happy one.'

Emma thought it might not be appropriate to ask too many questions about Carlo, but for her there was something about him that was so different. Her experience of men was rather limited, but she thought his manner and how well he was dressed completely fascinating and could not help wanting to know more. She could have gone on asking Maria questions about him all day.

Emma said: 'I had better go and see if they would like some more coffee.'

'That's a good idea, we must look after these men,' Maria replied, laughing, and went back to her pie making.

They had finished their meeting and Carlo was ready to leave.

He turned to Emma. 'It was nice to meet you, Emma,' he smiled, and was about to rise from the table.

He looked at her with that same twinkle in his eyes and said 'Maybe next time, if I am lucky, I could try the LASAG-NI.' He rose, still smiling and leaving something under the saucer.

Emma cleared the table and underneath the saucer was a shilling. She could not believe her eyes, and Joe saw the expression on her face.

'Joe, I think Mr Carlo made a mistake.'

'Joe said: 'No mistake, Emma, that is your tip.' He walked away with a big grin on his face.

CHAPTER SEVEN

Maria, Joe and Carlo

It was two months later when Joe decided to have one of his big Italian lunches on Easter Sunday. It seemed that he and Maria knew half the Italian population in London and the surrounding counties.

The amount of meat, vegetables and fruit ordered would feed an army.

A week before the big day Maria said to her. 'Are you happy here Emma?'

'Am I happy? She replied 'I cannot remember when I was happier.'

She hugged Maria, which was not too easy, as there was quite a lot of her.

The next day Emma did not feel well, she was sneezing and her throat was sore, but she was not going to let Maria and Joe down, anyway she could not tell them she couldn't work that day as the nearest telephone was streets away, so she might just as well walk to work. The weather was awful, raining and cold. She put on her warmest clothes and headed off.

When she arrived the cold and damp had made her feel worse, sneezing and shivering, which was being noticed by Maria and Joe.

'Good heavens Emma, you should be in bed, you foolish girl, not coming to work.'

Emma was feeling quite unwell, when Maria said 'Joe, send for a taxi cab and send her to the house and tell Gina to put her to bed in the pink bedroom.'

'Oh. Maria, I am sorry, I can go home.'

'No, you must be looked after darlin', and we will tell Gina to give you some soup until we get home.'

Emma did not argue, she felt dreadful and the thought of the lovely warm house was very appealing.

'But how will you manage?' she asked.

Joe said, smiling, 'Like before you came.'

Emma spent two days at their house and with so much care and attention from Maria, Joe and Gina, their help, she soon felt better and returned to work on the third day, when the cold had nearly gone.

'Well, darlin',' said Maria, who always left off the 'g' at the end of such words, 'Joe and I was thinkin', we don't like to see you goin' back to that cold house all alone, payin' rent and everythin', because we have become very fond of you. Come and live with us in our house, you can have your own room, your freedom to come and go, and some comfort and company when you want it; and if you are not well you will be looked after.' She stopped for breath and put her arm around Emma's shoulder.

Emma looked at Maria and suddenly the tears flowed freely down her cheeks.

Maria looked concerned 'You don't want?'

'Oh Maria, I do, I love you both so much you are both so wonderfully kind to me.' She sniffed a bit and wiped the tears.

'You know, Joe and I wanted children very much, but it didn't happen. I said to Joe if we had a daughter I would want her to be like you.' She kissed Emma on the cheek and gave her a motherly hug. 'So we will arrange for your things to be brought to the house and prepare a lovely room for you.'

When Emma got home that night a note had been put through the door. It was from Lottie.

'Where are you Emma? Please phone me I am longing to see you. Lots of love Lottie xx.'

Emma was overjoyed, she found some change and remembered there was a telephone box some streets away. Lottie had written the number down again in case she lost it. She dialled the number and Sarah answered and asked her how she was before Lottie came to the phone.

'Emma my dearest, I came to the house twice, but you were not at home and I was worried about you.'

Emma explained where she had been and why.

'Well, you had better come for supper and tell me all your news. I will send Davis to get you.'

Emma was so excited to meet Lottie and said she would love to see her. It was arranged for Davis to collect her in forty minutes, time for her to freshen up and change into her best dress.

Now, at last, things really did seem to be going so well that Emma was afraid that it was all too good to be true. She quickly made herself clean and tidy, put on her one best dress and waited for the knock at the door. She hurried to open it and almost immediately saw Davis standing there ready to escort her to the car.

Emma felt like a queen. Who would have guessed that she was being taken out in a Rolls-Royce? She giggled to herself at the prospect of being invited to dinner at this wonderful house with servants and to see Lottie again after so many years. She wondered if she would recognize her, as some memories grow dim.

Davis stopped the car outside the house and came round to open the door. He smiled as he gave her his arm to help her out of the car, and thanking him, she smiled back. She liked Davis very much and could see immediately that he was a kind and helpful man. She thought that he and Sarah were an ideal match, and realized they were two very special people who were trusted by Lottie and William to take care of everything in their absence.

They reached the front door and Emma could hardly believe that Lottie herself opened it and immediately put her arms around Emma, hugging her tightly before standing back and looking at what she felt was a young Molly standing before her. The tears welled up in her eyes as she said 'What a beautiful young woman you have grown up to be.' It was like turning the clock back.' She sighed, and tried to put on a smile that would hide the emotion she felt.

Now Emma remembered her so well, her lovely hair and her cheerful friendly disposition.

'Come, let's go and have something nice to drink whilst we wait for William to join us when he gets home. He is looking forward very much to seeing you Emma. He remembers you as a baby and we used to mind you whilst Molly and Fred went for a walk.'

Emma laughed. 'I don't remember.'

'Just as well dear.' Lottie laughed, and squeezed Emma's hand.

'Tell me Emma how did it happen, was she ill a long time?' Lottie now with sadness in her eyes needed to ask what had happened to her beloved friend.

'Yes, she slowly became very forgetful and did not remember things from one moment to another as if the only things that she could remember happened years ago. Finally the doctor said it was pneumonia that took her.' Emma could see that Lottie was near to tears. She tried to hide them and said' 'Where is she, Emma?

Now it was Emma who could not hold back the heartbreak she felt and whispered 'I had little money', and hesitating to control her feelings said, 'She is buried in a pauper's grave,' but she could not go on and Lottie, taking her in her arms, they sobbed together.

'We can change that, I will see to it, I promise.' The look in Emma's eyes was enough for Lottie to see the unspoken gratitude. This helped her through the painful moment they both shared.

After a while they regained their composure and, with a drink or two to help, began to catch up, telling each other about their lives. The evening was full of all the good memories and the stories that Lottie could tell about their escapades, when she and Molly were young girls. It gave Emma so much pleasure to hear Lottie talking so warmly about her mother; it was easy to see how much the two women had cared for each other.

Lottie said: 'Perhaps we should stop reminiscing for a while, as I can hear William is home. He will be so delighted to see you, Emma.'

They met William in the hall and he and Lottie exchanged a kiss. It pleased Emma so much as it was plain to see that these two people adored each other and looked forward to being together.

The evening was wonderful: the food and wine, which had gone to her head, had lightened everything and bad times had for now gone away. Emma couldn't remember being so happy since she was a child.

Of course it wasn't that she did not drink wine with dinner at Maria and Joe's, but this seemed stronger than she was used to and the result was she giggled a lot. She was what her father would have called slightly tidily, as were they all.

On leaving they arranged that Lottie would come to the Monte Verde Tea rooms and meet Joe and Maria. Lottie was keen to see the couple who had become so close to her god-daughter.

The next morning Emma arrived at the tea rooms full of happy anticipation of Lottie's visit. She had not told Maria and Joe any details about Lottie, except that her godmother was coming to meet them that morning.

About eleven some customers arrived in for their morning tea or coffee and both Joe and Emma were busy preparing the tables for lunch when the Rolls-Royce arrived outside the door. It was hard to miss and heads turned to see through the glass windows. Who this might be? Joe turned to Emma and said: 'My goodness don't tell me royalty's coming for elevenses,' with a little laugh.

At that moment Davis opened the door of the Rolls and Lottie swept out as though she were at least a duchess.

'Oh no Joe, that's my godmother, Lady Charlotte Cavanaugh. She has come to meet you and Maria,' said Emma.

Joe's mouth was opening and closing like a fish as words would not come out.

'I always told Maria that you were too good to be a waitress.' he said

'Don't be silly Joe, we all come from humble beginnings, its what you are inside that matters, I know you will love Lottie and she will love you.'

Lottie kissed Emma on the cheek, and then Joe, greeting Lottie with a small bow, said 'Good morning my lady, I am very pleased to meet you. Please take a seat.'

Joe took her gloved hand and informal old fashioned gesture, brought it a few inches from his lips.

Lottie smiled and thought, 'oh, so Italian.' She was already warming to this nice little man.

Emma observed the interaction between these people who meant so much to her. She thought it would not be long before they all felt comfortable in each others company.

Maria came out of the kitchen and, with the same polite formalities, introduced herself and laid a tray of assorted small sandwiches and pastries, along with their best china teapot.

Before long Lottie asked Joe to sit a while if he could spare a few moments to talk about themselves. She understood that they had invited Emma to stay at their home. In fact she felt happy with what she had observed of this lovely couple and maybe Emma had made the right choice to stay with them. She could see the fondness between them, and was a firm believer that if something seems right, don't change it. She was certain that they would take good care of Emma, and she would make it her purpose in life to keep in constant touch with Emma and make sure she was never in need of money or affection.

She would have insisted Emma live with her and William if they were permanently in London. However, as they were posted here and there it would not have been the ideal situation. If Emma felt happy to stay with these nice people then they had her blessing.

Lottie told her that wherever William was posted she would write and phone and return periodically for visits to London when possible. She stayed talking with them all until the lunch customers arrived. Apologizing for having to refuse their offer to stay for lunch, she promised to accept when the opportunity arose.

Joe and Maria invited her and William to come to one of their Sunday lunches whenever they were free. With fond farewells, and a kiss on the cheek for Emma, Lottie said she would send Davis to collect her belongings from Lavender Street and take them to Joe and Maria's. It was arranged that the next morning she would be ready for Davis to carry everything heavy and drive her to her new home.

Emma was ready and packed by eight and, as she waited for Davis to arrive, suddenly felt pangs of sadness. Lavender Street had meant so much to Lottie, her mother and father and herself. It was the end of an era and what if she found herself without a home? There would not be a place to run to. Little did she know that Lottie had bought the house and planned to have it modernized. She would keep it in case anyone she cared for had need of it.

It was Easter Sunday and the house was a buzz with preparations for the feast. Emma watched Maria's artistry with the varied dishes and Gina, their maid and helper who had come with them from Italy, playing kitchen porter. With all the preparations it was no wonder that lunch on this occasion was served at three o'clock, giving everyone time to attend church and to gather their families together without rushing. Of course, lunch would go on and on until whenever the last straggler departed. Monday was a holiday and so no one was in a hurry. Emma loved to see how these dishes were prepared and Maria let her participate and learn from the best of teachers.

She even learned how to pronounce Lasagne and felt so silly when she thought of the time she asked Carlo if he would like some LASAG-NI. He was so polite and did not attempt to correct her pronunciation for fear of embarrassing her, but she now realized how difficult it must have been to hide his amusement.

Maria would not tell her exactly how many or who were coming. Nearer to two o'clock she told Emma to go and get ready, as she may have to greet guests at the door with Joe. Near enough to three o'clock the guests began to arrive.

Emma had never met the first arrivals before and was introduced to cousins, aunts, grandmothers, and friends galore. Then Carlo and Flora arrived with their son, Roberto. Emma was so pleased to at least to have met Carlo, and now to meet his lovely wife Flora and their son. Emma was not sure what to make of Roberto: he did not seem to be particularly interested in anything and had a bored expression from the moment he stepped through the door. Emma thought it may be a boy 'thing', but then her brother Albert was the opposite and always cheerful and full of pranks.

More people arrived and Emma thought what a good thing the house was big, with a large dining room and a huge table to accommodate everyone in comfort. Then just as Emma thought most of the guests had arrived, the doorbell rang again, and standing there were Lottie and William. Emma had never been so happy, as she knew how little time they had in London, and yet they had made it their priority to be here with her and her new friends.

The meal was a great success. The guests who had not met before introduced themselves, and found in some cases they had a great deal in common. It was a great surprise that William's father had known Carlo's when he had been a diplomat at the Italian Consulate in London, so they got on like a house on fire. They had so many acquaintances in common and, they had both been at Oxford, at different times as William was older than Carlo.

Emma found herself talking to Carlo's wife, Flora. She was very interested to hear how much Emma enjoyed reading and music and could converse well on many subjects. It was with great surprise to her that Emma had not wished to work in some other capacity than a waitress.

'You know Emma, Carlo has to go away on business quite frequently, maybe you would like to accompany me to the opera at Covent Garden sometime.'

Emma could hardly believe her ears. 'What a lovely thought Flora, I would really love to,' she said.

'Well, we will arrange it soon,' she smiled. Emma liked Flora very much and thought what a beautiful woman she was. She could see she had a very kind heart, and there was something almost ethereal about her, something very special. No wonder Carlo had married her.

With her love of opera Emma had learned a great deal about the famous composers and loved to listen to the records that Joe had in his collection. Now it seemed that Carlo and Flora had an enormous collection of the greatest opera singers, including Caruso, Gigli and many others. They also loved literature and Emma found they had a liking for similar books and authors.

Before the end of the evening they had arranged to meet soon, Flora promising to contact Emma, also giving her their telephone number.

It seemed that the Easter Sunday lunch had been such a great success: new friendships had been made and a firm assurance between William and Carlo to get together when commitments allowed. Emma was so happy about the way the day had turned out and told Maria and Joe what wonderful hosts they were, giving them both a hug in turn.

It came about quite soon when the two women began to meet more frequently, not only for their trips to the opera, but also when Flora invited Emma to the house. Then they talked about their lives, which had been so different, both of them intrigued by the other's childhood and the events that led up to the present day. Their friendship grew over the next year or so. They appeared to have so many interests in common and both enjoyed each other's company.

It had been nearly three years since a young and rather shy Emma began working at the Monte Verde tea rooms. Business had grown and Joe, with Carlo's encouragement and investment; expanded into the shop next door, which had become vacant.

Over the years, Emma had received a great deal of attention from many gentlemen, young and old, who wished to court her. She had accepted some invitations to tea, playing safe, she thought.

However, no one swept Emma off her feet. She would receive a little encouragement from everyone to pursue friendships, but Emma knew that she could never marry except for love. For her that meant knowing from day one there was an attraction that made her want to get to know the man. Then, perhaps, she would find love, but so far she had found them all rather dull; even those who Flora said would give her a very comfortable life.

A number of young men had been introduced to her by Flora when they were invited to her friends and acquaintances for tea. It seemed that not only Joe and Maria, but Flora too, would make hints on the same subject. They began to worry that she was not finding a man she liked enough to fall in love with and marry. Not that anyone wanted to lose her, but they did not want her to miss out in life.

After a while they seemed to give up the match-making and Emma, although knowing their intentions were good, was glad to have some peace from the little hints. Her mother had married for love and never regretted it for a moment, even though fate had handed her so many cruel and heartbreaking times.

Lottie had also married for love, but thought her life had been like a fairy story. Well, Emma knew she would have to take her chances and let destiny decide. Meanwhile, she was perfectly happy the way she was.

CHAPTER EIGHT

Three Years Later

The work at the tearooms was carried out and the alterations were done with professionalism and taste. More staff was taken on for what became a very successful, flourishing business. Emma, now manageress, took some of the pressure off Joe. They had also employed an additional chef and kitchen staff to help Maria, who now spent less time in the kitchen, having trained them in the way things were done.

The opening night of the grander and newly named 'Monte Verde Restaurant' was a night to remember. Not only all their friends and relatives were there but many of their regular customers, too. So many guests arrived they had to send for more tables and chairs. When they ran out of seats they stood at the bar or went into the new extension in the garden on warm days and evenings.

Naturally, Carlo and Flora were there, but Lottie and William were now living in Rome, William was now Third Secretary of the British Embassy.

Lottie assured Emma that they would be back from time to time and that she hoped that if the opportunity arose a visit to Italy might be arranged. Emma could not imagine ever being able to go to Italy. Nevertheless, she hoped she would have the opportunity. She had heard so much about it and how beautiful it was. For the moment it remained only a dream.

Time seemed to pass so quickly and it was after another two years that one day Maria and Joe said they were beginning to feel very tired. Maria was also suffering from aches and pains in her legs. Doctors had diagnosed arthritis, probably due to the climate in England.

They now felt it was time for them to retire. It had always been their intention to return to Italy in their old age and they had a hard decision to make, for them it concerned Emma.

One evening after they returned home Maria said: 'Listen darlin', you can come with us, but what would you do in a village? No young man with prospects; no Emma, it is far better for you to stay here and you are very welcome to come and stay whenever you can.'

Emma could hardly take in what this meant. Her lovely Maria and Joe were leaving; no longer there to be in her life – well not closely, as Italy was a long way away. Tears filled her eyes. She did not want them to see her crying, but this was a shock, although she knew that one day they would have to retire as they were not getting any younger and had worked hard all their lives. Now, hopefully, they would have many years left to enjoy a good, long life together.

Maria could see that this was a shock for Emma so she quickly added what she felt might solve the problem.

'But I have some good news, darlin',' Maria said. 'You are very fond of Flora, si?'

'Yes,' replied Emma looking at both of them.

'Well, Flora would like you to be her companion: you know Carlo has so much business to attend to and he worries about Flora being alone. So they would very much like it if you would agree to accept. It would mean you would live as part of the family, not as an employee, as Flora regards you as a friend and would hope you would be happy with them. Emma, you would have a wonderful life and would be mixing with the cream of society.'

'They have a lovely housekeeper, Rosa, as you know, so you would not be expected to do anything more than be a companion to Flora.'

Emma took time to take this in. The sorrow that had been so paramount only two minutes before had now lessened as she realized that Maria was right. What would she do in a village? She was still young and maybe what she needed was the opportunity to mix with the kind of people that were the friends and acquaintances of Flora and Carlo. Perhaps she would find her destiny somewhere here, in her own country.

So it was decided, and Emma telephoned Flora, thanked her from the bottom of her heart for her and Carlo's kindness, and said she would come to them as soon as she had helped Maria and Joe move twenty years of their lives to Italy. The Monte Verde was sold: the buyer had offered a good price, which had been accepted, and preparations were made for their departure.

So many happy times had flown by and had filled Emma's life with affection and kindness. It was soon to change yet again, but the last remaining few months before their departure were as perfect as any, if not more so than ever before. Living with Maria and Joe had been the beginning of a new life for her and now two more people were taking her into their lives and their family.

Flora and Emma had become very close over many long evenings in winter, sitting in front of the fire, reading, listening to music; and when Carlo was home the three of them playing cards together. They taught her bridge and rummy and even poker, much to the amusement of both when she failed to win.

When they entertained they did it in style and, with Rosa's expertise in the kitchen, their friends and acquaintances who came to the house were entertained to the best culinary delights, not only from Italy, but from far and wide.

The guests were always interesting; and from many countries and walks of life and Emma enjoyed those times so much and she learned a great deal about people and the different cultures from where they came.

The only time there was a different atmosphere in the house was when Robert came home for the holidays. Emma could not understand what it was about him that seemed to affect everyone in the house, except Flora, who seemed to be oblivious to it. He had an attitude that Emma failed to understand. Coldness, almost an arrogance, which was so difficult for her to comprehend. So different to his parents and she wondered where he had got it from. Fortunately, he was away at college most of the time, as his presence always seemed to bring some sort of cloud to the house. She knew she didn't imagine it as it seemed to affect even Rosa, who avoided him as much as possible.

Emma often noticed him looking at her; the look was hard to read but it made her feel very uncomfortable. She had to be polite, being a guest in the house and never treated like an employee, she felt it to be her duty. Even Carlo seemed different and not his usual joking and teasing self when Robert was home.

Things came to a head one evening when Flora and Emma sat in the garden. It was one of those balmy August evenings when they could sit outside and enjoy the fresh air whilst engaged in their *tête-à-têtes*, when Flora suggested they might indulge in a glass of wine.

Emma said she would go the kitchen and bring a bottle and three glasses, as Carlo might like to join them after he finished some business in his study.

She opened the door and began to walk toward the kitchen when she heard raised voices. She stepped back into the little passageway that lead to the hall and realized it was Carlo and Roberto. Their conversation was such that Emma thought better than to intrude.

It seemed that Carlo had planned a surprise for them and they were to go to Italy for a holiday and stay with Maria and Joe. This was beyond Emma's wildest dreams; she was so excited at the prospect that at last her dream was about to come true. She had only seen the sea once when Fred had taken them to Brighton one day when she was a child. Although it had been a little cold it didn't matter, she had paddled in the sea and loved every minute of it, but swimming in the warm Mediterranean was something she had only heard about!

She now stood rooted to the spot and heard Roberto say to his father 'Oh, you're taking the staff as well.'

Carlo was angry. From what she could gather the conversation was about of her. He was so furious, his voice was as cold as steel. She had never heard him so angry and stern.

'No, I am taking your mother and Emma.' he replied.

'That's what I mean,' said Roberto

Carlo, now raising his voice, said 'Emma is not staff. She has been a blessing to this house and has been like a sister to your mother and looked after her when I have had to be away on business, in order for you to live with every privilege going: Eton and Oxford, never wanting for anything, but giving nothing, except a miserable and sullen face as soon as you enter this house.'

Emma stood very quietly in the recess afraid to move, but not wanting to hear more. The tears were now welling up in her eyes, which she was unable to stop.

She was forced to continue to stand there, as she could not go back to Flora without her realizing something was wrong. Neither did she want to have to confront this altercation between father and son.

'You will not be going to Italy; you can spend the rest of your holiday where you please. You do that anyway when it suits you. In any case in September you will start university so it would not be appropriate to be on holiday then. Now this conversation is over, good night sir.'

Carlo dismissing Robert from his presence began to walk toward the little passageway to the study and garden.

Emma was frozen where she stood, the tears unstoppable, she heard Roberto march out of the kitchen. Carlo had started toward the door when he saw her. He looked at her with a look of concern and said softly 'You heard that, I am so sorry, please don't cry.' He placed his hands on her arms and comforted her. He took a red silk kerchief from the top pocket of his jacket and lifting her chin he gently dabbed her eyes. She took the kerchief from his hand and tried to hold back the tears.

'Thank you.'

Still hardly able to speak she said 'This is your favourite pocket kerchief; I will launder it for you.'

He smiled at her and said gently 'Don't worry about that, you must not let Flora see you have been crying. Go and powder your nose and we will join her in the garden.'

'I was looking for Rosa to bring us some wine,' she said.

He stopped and turned back and said 'You know, Emma it's a terrible thing to admit, but I do not like my own son and it's all my fault.' He paused and looking at her, continued. 'I have to tell you, Emma, when Flora was a child she caught scarlet fever and it's a miracle she survived. Many women do not survive childbirth and Robert had a twin brother, but they were premature and he died. It was a very difficult birth and it has left Flora with a weak heart. That's why you are such a blessing, because I know she is in good hands, knowing how much you care for her and her for you. I could not leave her and go away without knowing she could not be in safer hands.'

He smiled and took her by the shoulders guiding her toward the stairs where he indicated she should go.

'Unfortunately, Robert has been over-indulged. I did not have the heart to exercise any discipline with him and stop it. He has grown up with the best of everything, but now thinks of no one but himself. Fortunately Flora does not see it and he plays his cards to his advantage and she doesn't realize.'

He stopped speaking and Emma could see how deeply he was affected by the confrontation that had transpired.

'But why does he resent me?' she asked.

'Maybe he is jealous of you,' he said'

'But why? I don't understand,' she replied.

Carlo looked at her and said quietly 'Maybe it's because he can see how fond we are of you and the closeness you have with his mother. Whatever the reason, nothing can justify his attitude or his behaviour.'

Emma did not have any real concept of envy or jealousy, or the destructiveness that could ensue from such a psychological problem. However, she was upset by the unpleasantness and unable to think of an explanation for Robert's behaviour as it had never dawned on her that this could be the reason for his animosity.

'Don't let this upset you Emma. I promise you I will not allow any further episodes of this nature to be repeated.'

He gently lifted her chin and softly said 'Now dry your eyes and let me see you smile, and let's take the wine and join Flora in the garden before she thinks everyone has left home.' He smiled and was back to the Carlo she knew.

He put his arm around her shoulders and guided her toward the stairs, gesturing that she should go up and wipe any traces of the tears and come back with a smile.

'You know, Emma, there is something my father told me when I was very young that is very important to remember in life. If we don't play by the rules we must suffer the consequences, which sometimes are far-reaching and can often cause others, who are innocent, to suffer. Its like when a pebble is thrown into a lake; the ripples go further and further and spread far and wide and no-one can tell where they will stop.'

She looked at him and said 'You are quite a philosopher, Carlo.'

'No, just a lawyer, but I so often see the suffering of the victims of those who don't think things through; who do what they want regardless of the pain they cause to others.'

He gently squeezed her arm and, with a little nod as he guided her toward the staircase, he walked in the direction of the kitchen.

With not a sign of Rosa in sight, he headed toward the wine cellar to choose a bottle for that much-needed drink. He stood for a moment leaning against the cellar wall and ran his hands through his hair, sighed and began searching for the best wine he could find.

The next few weeks seemed to fly by and the episode with Roberto was put out of their minds. Fortunately for Emma, and no doubt Carlo, he had decided to spend the rest of his holiday with college friends. Evidently they planned to hit Paris and no doubt in Emma's mind, Paris could do well without them. She hoped they would be spared having to meet him whilst they were there for a quick visit to see the sights, as they had planned.

A surprise came when Carlo announced that his cousin's son was coming to stay with them for a few weeks and would travel back with them to Italy. It seemed that it had become a family tradition for the men to study law and quite often with the same firm in Rome. Paolo wanted to brush up his English and Carlo thought it would be nice for the four of them to travel together. They intended to see as much of Paris as they could in their flying visit, although it would be done in comfort for Flora's and Emma's benefit.

Paolo, it seemed, was a very nice young man and Carlo assured Emma they would get on well. Actually she had met him once before when she first joined Maria and Joe. Carlo had forgotten he had been a guest at their house for a week or so when he was younger. Now Emma remembered him as being friendly and fun. She had thought at the time that he had the similar looks that seemed to run in the family: dark hair and brown eyes that were warm and friendly. Then he did not speak much English and Emma wondered if his grasp of it had improved as he was now in the legal field. Maybe his intended visit would prove beneficial.

They shopped for suitable clothes and the imminent arrival of their guest kept the whole house busy. When Paolo arrived all the stops were pulled out and the house was alive with laughter. For Emma the happiness was so apparent for all of them.

Paolo now spoke English and she was surprised to hear just how good it was. She and longed to be able to speak Italian as well as he spoke English.

Flora was fluent and she would encourage Emma to converse with her and Carlo. He of course would sometimes play jokes and tease her and she would pretend to be offended until he would believed she was upset. Then she would laugh. Now she could practise with Paolo who did not know her well enough to tease her. In fact Paolo was charming, a real gentleman and Emma enjoyed his company. He was very attentive and would ask her to show him the interesting places to visit in London.

When Carlo was at home, Flora insisted that she accompany him, which made Emma start to suspect that there may have been a slight hint of match-making again. For Emma this was no more likely than 'pigs might fly', as her mother would say. Nevertheless, he was nice, very polite and she was glad that he would accompany them to Italy. To have two gentlemen with them would be fun and helpful with the luggage and arrangements.

As the time grew closer to their departure they had settled into a very contented phase of enjoying such a happy atmosphere. At last their day of departure arrived. They set out to catch the train to Paris where they would stay for two days, partly to enjoy the spirit of the city, the food and to show Emma and Paolo the sights, as neither of them had been there before. Emma had never been so excited since she was a child when Fred had taken them to Brighton for the day.

Carlo had booked them into the George V Hotel; Emma was unable to express her thanks and just walked into her room lost for words. All she could think of what it was costing Carlo and she wanted to hug him, but she was afraid that it might be perceived as not quite the thing to do. So, instead she just smiled and whispered 'Thank you' afraid she might cry. He looked at her and in his usual teasing way asked, 'Do you think it will do?'

He broke the spell and she laughed, and replied 'I think so.'

She went to Flora and hugged her instead, Flora hugged her back; the closeness of the two women apparent to all.

Paris was wonderful. As for the new and different cuisine she tried, Emma was not quite so sure. Encouraged to try frog's legs and oysters was not a success. She took one oyster squeezed the lemon with a little pepper, as she had been instructed and swallowed whilst everyone watched.

Emma thought she was going to be sick and hurriedly took her napkin to her mouth.

Flora said 'Oh Emma, if you hate it spit it out,' trying to hide a grin that she and both men found impossible to disguise.

Emma got up, excused herself and hurried to the ladies' room where she expelled the offending oyster. Taking her time and making sure she appeared to be in control of her stomach, she powdered her nose and returned to the table.

Now Carlo, sympathetic, asked: 'Are you feeling better Emma? I am sorry, we did not realise that it would be such an unpleasant experience for you.'

'That's alright, I am fine now, but I never want to taste another oyster, thank you.'

Then Carlo with his dry sense of humour had a look that Emma suspected was slightly mischievous. 'What about trying some escargot?' he said with a grin.

'Actually, it is my aim in life to perpetuate the longevity of the garden snail,' she said in her haughtiest voice with a serious look on her face. Everyone stopped eating and looked at her with nothing less than surprise.

'Well I never, what a truly noble endeavour Emma,' said Carlo, with an equally serious expression on his face; but she knew only too well that he was joking, as indeed she was.

She burst out laughing and replied: 'You should see your faces,' and with that the four of them were laughing so much they could eat no more of escargot.

Their visit to Paris ended too soon, but they saw a great deal in two days and even managed a ride in an open-topped horse-drawn carriage to see the famous landmarks, including Notre Dame and the artists' quarter, also a cruise on River Seine where they had dined, seeing the lights of Paris by night. Emma for the most part, was speechless: this was like a fairy story come true.

The next day they boarded their night- sleeper to Rome where they were to meet up with Lottie and William who had promised them wonderful hospitality and a glorious escorted tour of the ancient city. Their busy itinerary had been planned with care by Carlo. Flora had managed quite well in Paris: he made sure that she did not have to walk too much and they enjoyed frequent stops for refreshments. Now, once settled on the train after a light meal, they retired to their compartments and looked forward to a good night's sleep, which was certainly achieved by Emma. She slept like a log.

Rome was another wonderful city, even more so than Paris for Emma. She loved the history of ancient Rome, and Lottie and William had laid on a wonderful sightseeing adventure in luxurious style. Emma, now an addict for Italian cuisine, was in her element. Both Carlo and Paolo felt at home and learned of the places to go, not just the everyday tourist attractions. Paolo, studying there, knew where to take them for the best restaurants and even gave Lottie and William fresh ideas of where to dine, where only the locals went.

After two days in Rome they headed off to Monte Verde where Maria and Joe had prepared a big welcome for them. Paolo had another few days left before he had to prepare for his law exams and came with them. William had kindly laid on a chauffeur-driven car for them and so they enjoyed everything in comfort.

CHAPTER NINE

The Village of Monte Verde

It was late afternoon when they arrived and what a welcome was awaiting. Emma jumped out of the car first and ran through the open doorway to the entrance hall of the villa. She just could not wait a minute longer to see them. Her lovely Maria and Joe: she had missed them both so much.

'Hello!' she called out and within seconds Maria was there, arms outstretched 'Carissima, Carissima,' she cried, hugging and kissing Emma; then came Joe, kissing both her cheeks.

'How we have missed you,' he said.

'Oh Joe, Maria, I can't believe I am here with you. I know why you wanted to come back here. It's so beautiful,' she sighed

'You haven't seen anything yet darlin',' Maria said, still with her arms around Emma.

Emma was quite overcome with happy anticipation and joy at last being here in Italy that she had heard so much about.

'Tomorrow you will really see why Monte Verde is so special,' Maria said, smiling.

Having alighted from the car, the others joined them and, with much hugging and kissing in this joyful reunion, they eventually were invited to freshen themselves up, led to their rooms and told that when they were ready supper would be served on the terrace, where in fact the party really began.

It had been a long day, but somehow it was such a wonderful reunion that everyone found enough energy to last quite well. Even Flora managed to stay up longer than usual and when, at last, they succumbed to the inevitable need for sleep, it was with happy reluctance. Tomorrow would bring them so much that they had looked forward to.

The next morning Emma woke early, the sun seeping through cracks in the shutters. She jumped out of bed and went to the window, opened the wooden slats and leaned out, breathing in the fresh air enriched with the scent of the wild herbs and flowers so abundant in the hills around the villa. She breathed deeply and became intoxicated with the scent and the view.

She washed hurriedly in the little closet adjoining her room which had surprisingly up-to-date plumbing. The water was tepid, not cold, but Maria had told her there would be a large jug of hot water waiting outside her door if she preferred.

She opened the door and sure enough there it was, although at this time of year most houses did not heat the water in summer. In fact it was a relief to be able to cool down. She hurriedly dressed in one of her new cotton blouses and skirt, which Flora had helped her choose as being the coolest things to wear. She was anxious to be able to chat with Maria and Joe. They had so much to catch up on, as it had been more than a year since they had left.

Maria was busy in the kitchen and when she saw Emma she hurried towards her and gave her a big hug.

'You look beautiful darlin', and so happy,' she said with her arms firmly holding her tightly; Emma could hardly breathe.

'Yes, I am very happy. Flora and Carlo are wonderful and treat me as if I have always been a member of the family.'

Maria nodded and beamed her satisfaction on hearing those words. She thought Emma looked even more beautiful than she remembered. It must be because time had dimmed her memory; or was it that she now had become more confident and had acquired the elegance of a woman? The shy young girl they first met had gone forever.

Emma kissed Maria on the cheek. 'Is Flora awake and where are the boys?' she asked.

'Flora is still asleep and the boys have gone to the village to get some fresh bread,' said Maria. 'I did not have time to make it, they also wanted to inspect the vines and the fruit.'

'Oh, I will go and explore a little, if I may?' said Emma, 'I thought I could hear a donkey, At least I thought it was a donkey.'

Maria laughed, 'Yes, that's Pippo; Joe has gone to let him out of his stable for some exercise.'

'Oh I must see him,' Emma squealed with excitement and rushed out of the kitchen and onto the path that led upward where she could see Pippo. Joe was walking along a path and holding a little rope tied to his head collar.

'Oh, Joe, isn't he beautiful?' She approached the donkey slowly and immediately fell in love with his big brown eyes and his wonderful pointed ears. She slowly touched his soft velvety coat, then his forehead, and then, getting more courage, she stroked his ears gently. His coat was the colour of several shades of silver and the experience of being so close to this kind of animal for the first time in her life was wonderful for Emma.

Pippo was quite delighted with the attention and voiced his approval with a few 'hee-haws'.

'Can we give him some carrots, Joe?' she asked.

'Maybe later Emma, after he has had his exercise. Maria or I sometimes ride him to the village to bring whatever we need, although of course, I sometimes take the car.'

He had a rather ancient automobile which seemed an alternative means of transporting heavy items up the hill.

Emma looked surprised, as the thought of either Maria or Joe, riding on the back of Pippo was something hard to imagine. Neither of them were lightweights, being probably in excess of twelve stone each, and she could hardly suppress her smile as she visualised the scene in her mind.

At that moment Carlo and Paolo arrived in the car with their supplies and took them to the kitchen, returning to join Emma, Joe and the stationary Pippo. Emma thought Pippo was rather quiet; possibly dreading the thought of having to carry either Joe or Maria?

Carlo said to Emma 'Would you like to have a ride?'

'He needs a lot of coaxing just to move,' Joe laughed.

Carlo said 'Well do you want to try? I will lift you on board.'

'I am wearing a skirt, how can I be expected to ride him?' she retorted.

'No problem, you can ride side-saddle like all the ladies do. We can saddle him up' he said.

Emma knew she had to 'bite the bullet' and accept the challenge, as sometimes presented by Carlo, whose sense of humour never faltered. 'Fine, go ahead,' she said.

Carlo knowing full well that Pippo was reluctant to move anywhere and always needed a gentle prodding, was quite confident that Emma would be fortunate even to get him to walk. So the saddle was brought out of the stable and Pippo was made ready, but apparently not particularly happy about it.

He stood quietly as Carlo said to Emma 'I'll give you a hand up.'

He lifted her from the ground and told her to lift one leg up higher on the saddle; to hold the reigns with her left hand; and to hold the saddle with her right, if she felt unsafe.

Suddenly, the animal decided he would take charge and began to trot off at quite a pace, taking everyone by surprise. Pippo, no fool, was delighted to find such a lightweight on his back and headed for the hills.

Carlo, Joe and Paolo, taken by surprise stood for a moment, watching donkey and rider heading off with Emma hanging on to everything for dear life. Suddenly Pippo had a change of plan. He spotted what appeared to be an hors d'oeuvre of some very attractive grass that had sprung up from the unexpected rain of a few days before. Putting the breaks on, he suddenly stopped and, head down, was ready for his feast. This resulted in Emma and her new friend parting company.

As luck would have it, Carlo and Paolo took off after them with Joe puffing and panting a yard or two behind. Carlo, being tall with long legs made it in time to arrive just as Emma was about to take flight and land heavily on the ground. He caught her, but the impact was such that he lost his footing and the pair of them fell to the ground with Carlo landing on his back and Emma rolling over him to land by his side.

For what seemed an age, neither moved as the fall took their breath away.

Paolo leaned over Emma and, concerned, asked 'Are you alright, are you hurt, Emma?'

'I don't think so, just a bit shaken.' She opened her eyes and replied, half sitting up. She then saw Carlo still lying on the ground.

'Carlo, Carlo are you hurt?' He still lay there with no response; worried, she took his arm and again said: 'Carlo are you hurt?'

'Oh please God …' she muttered without ending the sentence.

She looked at Paolo and Joe, who had now arrived at the scene, the urgency and concern in her voice causing Carlo to open first one eye and then with a quizzical expression on his face, the other.

'Have you put on weight, Emma?' he asked, at the same time rubbing his back.

She bit her lip at first, not sure if he was in pain. Gradually she could see it might not be as bad as imagined as he slowly tried to sit up; at the same time trying to keep a straight face.

She now realized he was teasing her. This was the Carlo she knew and with a sigh of relief, she hesitated. What was it that was going through her mind? She couldn't even say the words to herself. What would she have done if he had been injured?

Emma did not want to accept the truth, but she could no longer deny that if anything happened to this man she would be devastated. She just thanked God he was joking and nothing had happened, except maybe a few bruises. Paolo and Joe took his arms and hoisted him upright, then Emma and Paolo linked arms with him whilst they walked back to the house. All of them were now laughing at what must have been the most ridiculous scene.

Joe took Pippo's rope and pulled him away from his gourmet snack, resulting in loud protestations in 'donkey speak'. Joe constantly remonstrated with him and told him he was a very bad boy!

They entered the kitchen where Flora and Maria were preparing breakfast, a trifle later than usual.

'What was all the commotion with Pippo?' Maria asked.

'Oh nothing really. We were just enjoying his company. A new experience for Emma, having never met a live donkey before. Of course it was love at first sight!' Carlo replied, smiling.

With that both Emma and Paolo could not stop laughing and Carlo's nonchalant expression made it worse.

'Well,' said Maria,' by the look of you I thought you must have been rollin' on the ground. Maybe you should clean up a little.'

Having real difficulty not to collapse in convulsions of laughter they hurried off to wash and tidy up. 'Don't be long,' called Maria, with a shrug of her shoulders, which indicated she was not aware of the joke. However, Flora knew that something had set them off and smiled to herself.

After their exciting morning and now fully recovered, they decided to explore the countryside and allow Emma to see the wonderful scenery of the hills which, in places, were almost like mountains. The olive groves and the grape vines were dotted around the hillside, giving way now and again to orange and lemon trees bearing their brilliant coloured fruit, soon to be harvested.

Among the rocky crags above, a variety of trees stood tall, as though they were guardians of the mountains. Emma was told that all kinds of wildlife lived up there.

'What kind of wildlife'? she asked.

'Oh, wolves and wild boar and maybe a wildcat or two,' said Carlo with a serious tone in his voice.

'Emma gasped, 'You are joking.'

'Of course they have a wonderful habitat and are quite safe from people, unless of course the people go hunting.' Carlo replied keeping a straight face. Emma did not reply as she was uncertain if this was another joke and decided not to pursue it any further.

Flora had visited many times before with Carlo, and Paolo, being almost local coming from another village a few miles, away enjoyed showing the beauty of his homeland. They wanted to show everything to Emma as her excitement was so infectious.

Maria and Joe had given Carlo the car for their use, whenever they wished. They drove through a village perched halfway up a mountain, explored a little and then thought it would be fun to go to the beach along the coast where they could have a swim. As they drove through another village Emma noticed straightaway it was so unlike Monte Verde. She could not help noticing that the villagers all wore old clothes and looked scruffy and poor. She was even more surprised to see the children running around without shoes.

She saw a young girl balancing a large vessel on her shoulder as she walked to the fountain in the middle of the Square. It must have been heavy and she wore no shoes either. Emma was quite shocked. Surely they could afford shoes!

She wanted to ask Carlo so many questions, but thought it might be better to wait. She took in the state of the houses, all of which seemed to need work done. There were large cracks in the walls and everything seemed old and in need of repair.

They didn't linger long and passed through the narrow streets out into the countryside, winding their way down towards the coast. They travelled along quite narrow roads that hugged the sides of the mountains and after a while the scenery changed. The mountains dropped away on their right, to give them a view of the bluest sea Emma could ever imagine being real. It was more like a painting. She took a deep breath; this was the most beautiful place on earth.

Arriving at a cove that Carlo knew well, they parked the car under the trees and walked down the little path to the sandy beach. The cove was quite small and private and no one else was there. Carlo told the ladies to change in the cave a few yards along the edge of the beach. They would do so behind a large tree in the other direction.

Emma and Flora changed into the costumes they had bought in London. Emma thought they looked ridiculous and the pair of them could not wait to see what the men looked like.

When they all emerged from there makeshift changing rooms and saw each other they all quickly ran into the sea to hide themselves and to stop laughing. Revealing so much of arms and legs was not for the shy!

Emma could not swim but managed to walk up to her waist holding Flora's hand who could, but decided to save her energy and just enjoy being in the wonderful warm water. Emma loved it, but was a little afraid of going out of her depth. Carlo offered to teach her to swim.

'I have had enough excitement for one day, thank you,' she said.

He laughed and Flora did not press for an explanation, but smiled as she knew she would hear the whole story at some stage.

They paddled and splashed about, the men swimming quite a way out and enjoying the exercise. Flora and Emma lay down and wallowed in the shallows. They decided to dry off in the sun, then headed for a little trattoria that belonged to a friend of Carlo's, for some lunch.

They entered the doorway, which led onto a shady terrace where the tables were arranged to capture the amazing view. Once again Emma turned to the others with a look of sheer delight as the owner came to greet them. He hugged Carlo like a long lost brother, with much laughter, affection, and handshaking with Paolo.

The ladies of course were given a warm and respectable greeting including hand kissing. Emma looked at Flora, wanting to giggle, but somehow controlled it into a smile.

The owner, Tomaso, hurried to and fro as he seated them at a table and announced the day's menu. Evidently there was nothing written down as it only consisted of what was available; the fresh fish of the day fried or grilled. There was different soup, veal prepared *'a la'* this or that; Emma was already lost with the variety.

Naturally there were several kinds of pasta and ravioli with every kind of filling, antipasti of cold meats. The choice went on and on.

At last they made their selections. Emma, knowing she had another dinner that night, declined the pasta and chose fresh fish and salad, which was delicious, followed by home-made ice-cream. Flora had a similar choice, and Emma knowing she had a small appetite, was glad to see her finish her lunch. 'The boys', as she called them, ate a bit of everything and as was to be expected they all looked forward to a siesta when they got back.

'That was a wonderful lunch, Tomaso,' Carlo smiled.

Tomaso, looking very pleased with himself, replied 'So glad you all enjoyed it.'

They all nodded in agreement and thanked him.

However, he would not hear of taking payment, as he was so thrilled that Carlo had come to see him. Emma thought 'what a wonderful gesture' and told Tomaso as they left how much she had enjoyed meeting him, the others adding their sentiments to hers. She did not see Carlo place some paper bills under a plate. He was only too aware that this generosity belied that a living here was not easy and he knew his old friend would not be offended, but grateful that this was done with discretion.

CHAPTER TEN

The Olive Tree

Emma lay down in her room and slept for what seemed hours, but it had actually been just over two. She got up and opened the shutters. The sky had turned to a golden hue, and everything had such a beautiful shade that Emma had never seen anything quite like it. She hurriedly freshened up and dressed herself and went downstairs where Maria greeted her with 'Did you have a nice day, Cara?'

'Oh wonderful,' she said as she kissed Maria's cheek. 'Where is everybody?

'Flora and Paolo must be still resting. We will not wake them as it's still early,' she replied. 'Carlo has gone to his favourite place.'

Emma looked curious 'Where is his favourite place?' she asked.

'Oh it's through the Olive Grove,' was the reply. 'Just keep walking and you will see a small promontory.'

'Oh, please show me where it is,' Emma said, as she walked toward the door.

Maria pointed 'Go past Pippo's stable and when you get to a fork in the path, take the left one and you will see a promontory. He will be there.'

'It sounds very mysterious,' Emma laughed. She had never heard this place mentioned before and was now looking forward to finding out what was so special.

She headed off along the path and passed Pippo's stable, he would have to wait for his good night cuddle. She turned left at the fork and continued walking through the trees until she came out onto what looked like a promontory with a very large olive tree standing alone. She walked nearer; Carlo was sitting on a small wooden bench by the tree. He heard her and turned and beckoned her to join him.

'Sit here Emma and look,' he said, pointing outward.

She walked towards him and sat on the bench by his side looking out toward the sea; followed where he was looking and saw something so beautiful it took her breath away. The sun had turned from gold to a deepening red and it was gently beginning to slide down into the sea, which glistened with the reflection.

Carlo continued to look out at this amazing spectacle of nature.

'When I was a child my mother used to say Mister Sun is going to sleep now, so his brother the Moon can wake and lighten up the sky,' he said and continued to look out toward the horizon.

Emma knew that as he said the words they were one of the most treasured memories in his life.

She gently rested her hand on his arm. 'I understand now why this place means so much to you. It's so beautiful and so special Carlo.'

She paused and said, 'You have never talked about your parents.'

He turned and looked at her. 'They were very adventurous and liked to travel, and after years of being uprooted to one place and another, they found it difficult to settle down. They contemplated going back to Italy, but the times were turbulent and uncertain, so they decided to visit Africa, fell in love with the country, and decided to stay.'

'It's a long way to visit, but maybe one day. It takes two weeks to get there and two to come back and, added to the time needed to stay awhile; it's not possible at the moment. But they come over now and again as they enjoy travelling on a liner. Hopefully one day you will get to meet them.'

Emma looked at him and knew this was something he really looked forward to when it might be possible. She took his arm, saying 'Carlo you must try to visit them one day.'

He sighed and said: 'Perhaps when I retire.'

Emma laughed. 'I think that it might be a long time yet.'

She understood his words, thinking of how he must miss his parents, but understood that he had too much responsibility in his life now.

He turned to face her, no words were needed. She could see in his eyes what this place meant to him and the memories that were so precious. They sat there quietly for some seconds then dusk began to descend.

He said: 'We should head back now before it gets too dark. We don't want anymore mishaps do we? I don't think I could catch you this time; my back could not take it.'

The happy memories were locked away again and laughing and linking her arm in his, they walked through the trees now lit up by the moon.

The branches of the tall olive trees cast weird shadows and Emma was glad that she was not alone. They walked carefully as the trees partly obscured the path.

The moment had passed and he was back to normal. Emma knew that he had allowed her to share something very special with him. She knew that she must never reveal the deepening feelings she held for him and which were growing stronger every day. It wasn't lust. She had never even known what that was and had only read about it in books. This was admiration and so many things she could not put into words and did not even try. It would always be locked away in her heart. Her secret to be cherished always. As long as she could see him nearly every day and share his life, she was content.

They approached the fork in the path and a few yards on they were to pass Pippo's stable.

'We had better be quiet as we pass his stable, as I promised him some treats for his supper,' Emma said.

'Oh well, then we had better tiptoe,' he said, amused, and smiling at her.

As they approached the stable door, they suddenly heard a very loud snore. Carlo looked surprised and saw Emma's clasped hand across her mouth, to suppress a giggle. This eventually grew into uncontrollable laughter, so infectious that Carlo found himself joining her. Neither of them was able to stop.

Emma released herself from his arm and began to run the rest of the way to the kitchen, with Carlo close behind. They burst into the room to see the surprised faces of Maria, Joe and Paolo. Maria's face showed curiosity as to what had caused their laughter. Emma could not stop laughing. When she was able to speak, she said: 'It's Pippo. He snores!'

Maria responded: 'Of course my dear, he is a male, they all snore.'

Joe gave her a glance that showed some desire to respond, but thought better of it.

Emma's devotion to Flora was now so profound; they both were more like sisters. There was a trust and affection that was obvious to all. This was no employer and employee; it was a friendship between two women who enjoyed sharing time together and were able to fill their days discussing everything from their childhoods, which had been so different.

Their shared love of literature, music and the arts, and so many other things they both loved, had brought a great deal of enjoyment of each others company. Flora found it fascinating to hear Emma's life story and likewise Emma loved to hear Flora's.

She was glad that her husband came home and found the atmosphere light-hearted. This took his mind away from the mundane, business and other things: one being Flora's health. With Emma in the house he knew she was in safe hands. This would put his mind at rest and he could escape from the pressures of reality.

The highlight of every day for Emma was when he walked through the door. She began to doubt whether she could ever meet anyone who could compare with him. To Emma he was everything any woman could want in a man. Handsome and wealthy, but this was not what Emma saw. It was his heart, kindness, courage and, something so important to both of them, integrity.

Some might say he had everything, but Emma knew that he didn't. Of course he was wealthy and able to have everything that money could buy. Money was something she had never experienced, but instead he had an ailing wife and a son who was anything but his pride and joy.

He was in a demanding profession which dealt with problems of others and required him to travel. Even when at home he brought business back to the house so that he could attend to some paperwork, before and after supper, which required him to work quite late, after Flora had retired.

Their time in Italy had made London seem far away: business and all the things that had to be dealt with had been left behind. Emma had never seen him so relaxed and happy. Flora, too, although she tired so easily that they sometimes took an opportunity to sit in the shade of the veranda and read or listen to music from Joe's handsome collection of records brought with him from London. They played them on a gramophone, a rather splendid machine which sat on the top of a mahogany cabinet. It had a large brass horn perched on the top with a picture on the side of a dog that appeared to be listening to the music.

Paolo had to return to Rome far too soon and his last few days they all spent together were unforgettable. Emma had really grown fond of Paolo. He was fun and such a gentleman, offering his arm, opening doors and, at times, quite funny. He was nice-looking and seemed to have the qualities that Emma liked so much. However, something was missing as far as any romantic feelings on her part were concerned. For Paolo it was the opposite: he found himself wanting Emma to become something more than a friend. He was too polite to make any advances and hoped that she might give some indication that these would be welcome. He didn't exactly admit this to Flora or Carlo, but the attention he showered on Emma had not gone unnoticed.

When they were alone Flora laughed as she said: 'I think you have an admirer, Emma.'

'Really, who might that be?' she said with a smile. Flora ignored the question and asked: 'Do you like him? I think he will have a very good future. He is very clever and will make a good lawyer.'

'He is charming and I am sure he will do well, but I am not looking for a husband, but thank you for trying to marry me off,' Emma said, unsure of not how serious this conversation was.

Flora replied: 'Oh Emma please do not think that, I would hate to lose you, I was just thinking of you and your future.'

Emma looked at her and regretted that her response may have sounded a little harsh. She took Flora's hand, saying 'I appreciate your intentions and that you were thinking of me, but if this was something I wanted you would be the first to know. I am sure Paolo will make some woman very happy. It isn't anything to do with him; it's me, I don't feel that way about him. So, you see, it wouldn't work. I have to be in love with the man I marry like my mother was with my father. I couldn't settle for anything less.'

'I understand. We won't let you settle for anything less' said Flora as she kissed Emma's cheek.

Emma hoped that the subject would not crop up again, as she did not want to give the impression that she would not consider Paolo: she was sure that he would make a wonderful husband, but not for her. Possibly most young women might jump at the chance, but no one could read what was in her heart.

Flora put her arms around Emma and held her close. 'You will make whoever you decide on a very happy man and a very lucky one.' She smiled and squeezed her arm affectionately.

'Let's join the others. They are probably ready for an aperitif. We won't mention it again.' She laughed and Emma smiled, thinking 'I really hope not'.

The final week had passed so quickly that there was an air of sadness. Paolo had departed and Emma could see he was really sorry to say goodbye.

He kissed her cheek and said, quietly, 'I hope it won't be long before we meet again.' He took her hand and kissed that too and Emma knew his voice was full of sincerity. She was also feeling a little sad. They had enjoyed so much fun and shared some wonderful moments.

He whispered to her: 'I will always be a friend to you Emma, whenever you need one.' She knew he meant it and thanked him with a peck on the cheek. And then he was gone.

They said tearful goodbyes to Maria and Joe and, of course, to Pippo who thoroughly enjoyed all the fuss Emma always made of him. She wasn't quite sure whether this was based on cupboard love due to all the treats she took him, or whether it was genuine love. Whatever it was he seemed to sense that his friend was leaving.

Promises all round were made to come back soon and this intention was truly meant as they reluctantly set off. They were not going to stop off in Rome as Lottie and William were coming to London very soon and Carlo now had to return to business. They caught the train north and changed onto the sleeper to Paris and were back late the next day.

Rosa's greeting was more than enthusiastic; she was tearful and happy all at the same time, as only those of Latin blood seem able to manage. In London autumn had already arrived and the evenings had drawn in, bringing a distinct chill to the air. The house was not cold because Rosa had lit fires in many of the rooms, and the warmth and cosiness was very welcoming to them.

Life resumed to its usual format, Carlo was busier than ever with case books and meetings and often worked late into the night. This was mainly because he would, as always, spend time dining with them, and kept them company for as long as Flora could stay up. This, which Emma felt, was increasingly less than in the past. She seemed to tire more easily and Emma would glance at Carlo and he would know it was time for him to carry her upstairs and sit her down on the bed.

He would kiss her and whisper 'Good night, my darling, sleep well.'

She would just smile at him and answer 'you too' and kiss his cheek.

Emma would then take over and help her put on her nightattire and tuck her into bed. Emma would sit on the armchair next to the bed and read a page or two from a favourite book of poems or a novel until Flora's eyes closed and her breathing became heavy. Emma would always make sure it was the right moment and leave quietly after putting on the small night-light and placing the bell nearby, should Flora wake and need something.

Emma's room was very close and both bedroom doors were left ajar for that purpose. Emma knew that, increasingly, Carlo would sleep in his dressing room adjacent to his study, so as not to disturb Flora. It seemed that this was an understanding between them that was both practical and acceptable. However, Emma wondered if there was another reason, was it too much for a man to lie with his wife, unable to express his love in a physical way due to her health. Memories came flooding back to things that Lottie had mentioned in their very private chats. Emma had found these not only informative, but they had opened up all kinds of questions.

She was not ready for bed yet and went to the library and sat in front of the fire. It was her favourite room in the house, where so often the three of them would enjoy playing cards or listening to records or reading. Emma's thoughts began to dwell on so much that they had shared and how much closer they had become. Those few weeks were so ingrained into her memory. The laughter and the magic of the place, the whole atmosphere of Italy: everything about it had enriched her life beyond anything she could have imagined. And to see Carlo all day, every day, she had begun to know him and understand him better than ever.

Even Flora seemed to have more energy. She wondered whether this place had improved her poor health so that she could once again enjoy her life to the full. Now Emma realized that it must have been a short respite, possibly the clean air, or the food or even just being in such a beautiful place with everyone for whom she felt so much affection. Particularly for being able to spend so much more time with the husband she adored.

She had put all those worries out of her mind whilst in Italy. Now perhaps she had to accept the reality that she could not change things, however much she wanted to. She loved Flora like a sister and to see her health deteriorate was not something she could easily endure.

No, Carlo would always make sure she had the best doctors and the latest medicines and the best care money could buy. With Emma to care for her, they must think positive thoughts.

Emma started to think of the cosy chats that she and Lottie had shared when they had met again and when, quite out of the blue, Lottie had asked her, 'Do you know about the birds and the bees?'

Emma, surprised, answered. 'Well if you mean about men and women and how babies are conceived, I think I know the basics! After all, I did have a brother.'

Lottie laughed. 'I hope you did not learn too much from your brother.'

'Well I did see him without his underwear as he thought it very funny to jump out of the zinc bath we had in front of the range in the kitchen where mother made us bathe. Albert quite naked and, as bold as brass, would just laugh. Of course this was when he was still young,' Emma replied. 'My mother would scold him and tell him to wrap a towel around himself.'

She could always remember wondering how that dangly thing between his legs ever managed to transfer something that made babies.

'Well that's a start. You know what a man's anatomy looks like, but I think you need to know a lot more, my dear,' and she began to give Emma a little 'talk'.

She began, 'Never get involved with a married man. He will promise you the world and when he gets what he wants he will dump you. If you get pregnant, say goodbye to a good life, as it will be one of hardship and sorrow.' Emma would never forget those words.

'Oh, Lottie that would be wrong, I mean if I were married and my husband were to do anything like that, I would never forgive him,' she had said.

'Well, my dear, men are men and they tend to have wandering eyes and it can mean nothing to them.'

'But,' said Emma, 'they must have fallen in love with someone else, or maybe the wife didn't love them anymore.'

Lottie gave a loud tut. 'No it's a pastime with some men and a challenge. And they don't leave their wives,' she added. 'When you find the right one you need to know what men like.'

Emma wondered what was coming next. She had no idea what men liked, except the normal act of procreation, and she didn't know very much about that either.

Lottie pulled her close and began to whisper in her ear. When she had finished Emma was so embarrassed she was speechless. She sat there hardly able to get words out and looked away.

'Well, now you know., Lottie said with a look of amused satisfaction.

Emma looked at her and Lottie, laughing, caused Emma, after the initial shock, also to begin to laugh, until they both were nearly crying.

'That's your first lesson dear; your Lottie will inform you more another time. When you fall in love Emma, it will all come quite naturally.'

Emma couldn't believe Lottie had taken it upon herself to explain the intricacies of love-making, but now having recovered from the initial shock, realized that she had to thank her godmother for wanting to educate her. After all, she was a woman, not a child. Still to be so naïve was ridiculous.

She couldn't help thinking what an amazing woman Lottie was. She was forthright, so blunt, and so knowledgeable about life, and wanted to give Emma the benefit of her experience as her own mother was unable to do so.

She wondered if her mother could have ever been so explicit!

She also remembered her father saying, 'That girl is as tough as old boots, but with a heart of gold,' and Emma knew he was absolutely right.

She wasn't ready to go to bed. Her mind being so active: so much to think about and so many memories. She went to the library and put on a record of classical music. She sat by the fire, just looking at the orange flames and listening to the music that brought back the bitter sweet memories of her childhood. Then her mother and father were both alive and she had imagined they would be there for ever. Nothing in a child's mind could contemplate that life was so transient. Now, so much had happened that she often wondered exactly where her destiny lay.

To her surprise the door opened and Carlo came and sat in the chair opposite her, he smiled. 'Is this a favourite record?' he asked.

'I have so many favourites,' she replied.

He sat and looked into the flames, quiet for a minute or two.

'Such music makes us reminisce, doesn't it? He said.

Emma could not look at him. Many of her memories, always present, began to bring tears to her eyes and she fought to hide them. He leaned towards her, and took her hand and squeezed it without any words spoken. He seemed to understand her pain because of his own which, Emma knew, was so well hidden from the world. It was only moments like this that revealed so much to her about this man who she admired and revered and, yes, loved. She was determined that he would never know her feelings for him.

The tears controlled, but the reality saddened Emma more than he would ever know. She smiled and turned to him.

'Would you like a drink?' she asked.

'Yes, if you join me,' he said.

He chose his usual whisky, which he often called a nightcap. Although sometimes it was not late at night, she always knew the moments when things were worrying him.

'You know me, what will you have?' He smiled.

'Oh, a glass of sherry please,' she replied.

'You sit there. It will be my pleasure to get them,' he said and strode off to the drinks' cabinet. When he returned they had both regained more cheerful thoughts and talked of Italy and how much they had laughed.

'Thank you so much Carlo. It was wonderful,' she said.

'We will go again, don't worry,' he replied.

Emma knew he meant it because she could see the sincerity in his eyes and knew he didn't say what he didn't mean. She also knew that their time in Italy had been as wonderful for him as it was for her and for all of them. He had relaxed and some moments he shared with her were so precious. He had opened a door into everything that was so deeply entrenched in his heart.

He probably had a busy day tomorrow and he would still do some work in his study, so she hinted politely that it was getting late Thanking him again she wished him a good rest. She looked at him and he smiled, for Emma the most beautiful smile she had ever seen on a man; it lit up his face and she wondered how anyone could not want to return it, which, of course, she did before she left the room.

CHAPTER ELEVEN

Christmas

Winter approached and the months dragged by. Carlo seemed busier than ever with so much extra work, leaving Flora and Emma to pursue their own interests. On fine days they would venture out for a short walk or take a trip to Knightsbridge.

Flora, on a good day, did enjoy lunch in Harrods or Fortnum and Mason and of course a little shopping. Never anything too exhausting and only when she could sit and items would be brought to her. The women were similar in stature although Flora seemed to becoming thinner than Emma of late. When Flora liked the look of something, be it a dress or blouse, she would often ask Emma to try it on and model it for her whilst she sat in a comfortable chair. The two women enjoyed this little charade and Flora would quite often buy several outfits, never forgetting to ask Emma's opinion because she seemed to appreciate her taste.

Flora always asked Emma if she would like something she had seen, but Emma always declined the offer; usually making an excuse that it was too extravagant and when would she wear it? The last time she had gratefully accepted were the clothes that she would need in Italy. She had no idea what would be worn there and Flora's advice had been perfect.

The day came when Flora decided she would like to go to Harrods where they could lunch and do a little shopping. Emma enjoyed these outings tremendously, as long as she felt Flora was feeling energetic enough and did not tire herself out. They would take the lift to the ladies' dress department and, Flora being well known as a valued customer, the lady assistant would immediately organise the most comfortable armchair for her, while Emma wandered around the room to inspect everything on show. The assistant would then bring an assortment of the clothes, which she knew would appeal.

She admired a beautiful cream chiffon dress, which Emma thought was the most beautiful dress she had ever seen.

'Oh Flora, it's beautiful.'

'Try it on for me Emma, you know it's less tiring for me,' she said.

'Alright, but it might be too big for you,' she said.

'That doesn't matter it can always be taken in,' she replied.

Emma enjoyed every moment of the opportunity to try on such beautiful clothes, which she could never afford to buy for herself.

The assistant carried the dress into the fitting room and Emma followed her. She handed the dress to Emma and asked: 'Would you like some help madam?

'Well if you can, please, I do not want to damage it,' she replied.

She pulled off her skirt and blouse and stood in her petticoat whilst the assistant put the dress on carefully and fastened the buttons.

'There,' the woman said,' it looks really lovely.'

Emma walked out of the cubicle and Flora, sitting on the chair, was eager to see Emma in the dress. She didn't speak for a second or two. She was so taken aback by the vision that stood before her. Emma looked stunning in the cream chiffon that set off her black hair and her slightly bronzed skin from the sun in Italy.

She smiled: 'Its lovely Emma, yes we will take it,' she said to the assistant. They had their goods packed up. They would be delivered to the house that afternoon.

Both women, having enjoyed themselves, decided they had had enough excitement for one day and, Flora beginning to tire, they took a taxi back to the house. Their shopping arrived a little later and Rosa brought the parcels upstairs and hung them up. Flora decided, as usual, to have a rest as she wanted to be good company at dinner. She always determined to be refreshed for when Carlo arrived home, as this was always the time in their day that they both looked forward to.

These days Flora did not greet him when they heard the key in the door or when it was near the time he would come home. Now she would wait on the terrace in summer or the library in colder weather. This day had been fine, but the evening was cool so a fire had been lit and Flora sat by it. She had put on the Vienna waltz by Strauss. It always made Flora want to dance, although sadly not so much these days. It did seem to liven up the house and, instead, she would encourage Emma to give a few twirls around the room.

Laughing, Emma continued to twhirl her way to the hall just as Carlo entered. As usual he took off his hat and threw it where it landed, usually a bull's eye first time, onto the deer's head. Off came his tie, which was about to be thrown anywhere, when Emma caught it and put it around her neck, knowing that any second his jacket would also fly across the room and hopefully land on the chair. Now Carlo caught hold of Emma and danced the waltz around the hall, whirling her round and round till she was almost giddy and, laughing so much, she cried, 'Carlo stop, stop I am going to fall.'

He stopped. 'Well we don't want that,' he laughed.

Emma thought he must be in good mood. 'So where is my wife?' he asked.

'I am here in the library,' called Flora laughing as she could hear the carry on.

'Have you had a good day, darling?' She smiled at him as he came through the door.

'Well, it wasn't a bad one, so we must be grateful for that,' he said as he approached and gave her a kiss.

She never pressed him about his day and was wise enough to know that when he was ready he would sometimes tell her the events of interest, but nothing that was confidential or sad, as he made light of most of those things.

They would always have their aperitif together with Emma and they would tell him of their activities. Emma thought it must be rather boring for a man to have to listen to their excitement about shopping and all the things that women enjoyed so much, including gossip that would come from bumping into someone or other at lunch.

Sometimes Emma would look at Carlo with amusement. He would nod, making a good effort to look totally absorbed in such trivia. She would find herself wanting to laugh, as by now she knew him well enough to recognize that if anyone had asked him five minutes later to discuss the contents of the conversation, he would be lost. He went on smiling in a benevolent way and would say, 'I am so glad you had such an enjoyable day and I look forward to seeing what I have bought. When will I have the pleasure?'

Both Flora and Emma knew he was joking and, as far as he was concerned, Flora could shop for England, so long as she was happy.

She replied: 'You will have to wait and see when the time is appropriate.'

He raised his eyebrows. 'Oh dear. Then I will have to be patient,' he said, laughing.

The days and weeks seemed to fly by and Christmas approached before they knew it. In years gone by they always arranged large parties, but now Carlo decided to have a smaller gathering as even with all the help in the world entertaining could be exhausting for Flora, and was out of the question. Close friends and family understood this and a quieter gathering was what he had in mind. He wanted to plan a surprise and he set about arranging something that would be exactly that.

Carlo knew that Paolo more than liked Emma and the emotions he felt were mixed. He was thinking of her and how long she would wish to be without love in her life. He fought the need to acknowledge the way he felt about her: he, a married man with a sick wife, had only his integrity to control his growing affection for Emma. It was innocent and built on so much admiration and respect for this woman he had now known for a number of years.

He remembered the day he walked into the Monte Verde tea rooms and saw her. The rather shy young woman who couldn't pronounce Lasagne. So beautiful, so stunning and unworldly, yet so unaware of the stirrings she raised in men.

How could he have ever known what lay ahead? How their lives had become so entwined so closely and how they could read each other.

When she saw him looking at her he would tease her, so as not to reveal the depth of his feelings. She would smile back and then look away shyly. She knew when he was worried or sad, and when he was happy, as if she was his soul mate.

He could talk to her about his concerns for Flora. She would touch his arm as if to say 'I know, I know I can read your heartache.'

'Oh God, he silently asked himself, is it possible to love two women, but in different ways?'

He knew many men would take a mistress, even within their own house, but not him. He would never bring shame into his home. He would not betray Flora or debase Emma. He would give her the opportunity to get to know Paolo and if it was to be that she felt there was a future with him, so be it.

Carlo knew she couldn't find a more worthy young man who had a good future, possibly here in London with his help. And they would always be in each other's lives. He couldn't face the thought of her going away and never seeing her, although he knew, if he had the strength to, it might be the best for everyone. He put all these thoughts out of his mind and set to work to make the necessary arrangements, only having to wait for their confirmation that they were able to come.

He would send wires off to Italy and wait for their replies, asking them to notify him at his office, as it was a surprise for the two women. At least he wouldn't have the miserable Roberto imposing his negative influence on their Christmas. Hopefully, he would spend as little time with them as possible and be off with his friends somewhere else.

But the best laid plans were not to be. Flora had begun to feel more unwell and very tired and more breathless than usual. The cold weather had seemed to make it worse and the London air was not the best for her condition. Both Emma and Carlo tried to hide their concern.

Their Christmas was spent quietly with just a minimum of visitors. Caroline, Flora's sister and her husband James, came up from Devon where they lived in a small cottage by the sea. It was a happy time for Flora and she greatly enjoyed their visit and even seemed to rally a little. Carlo and Emma, with a little assistance from Rosa, dressed the Christmas tree, which had been the largest Carlo could find. Presents, beautifully wrapped were laid around it and placed there secretly to make the most of the surprise on Christmas Eve.

It was a mixed tradition in the house, as in Italy, that it was Christmas Eve when the main celebrations and presents were exchanged. Here in England, Christmas Day was the big celebration, so Carlo declared that both days should be equally honoured.

Emma loved the way he made everyone happy with the double opportunity to enjoy two special days instead of one.

It was Christmas Eve when they opened their gifts. Emma had bought an embroidered shawl for Flora, which she had found in a shop in Chelsea. It was quite beautiful and Flora was delighted. For Carlo she had found a silk tie and matching pocket kerchief in blue. She had never returned his red one as she couldn't part with it. Her excuse, with apologies, was that she kept forgetting to launder it. He would laugh and tell her not to worry and that she should keep it.

They all exchanged gifts for each other and when the last parcel was read out with her name and handed to her from Flora, Emma was so excited and could not help wondering what it could be.

She hurriedly undid the ribbon and the wrapping paper and inside concealed in blue tissue paper, was her surprise. She unwrapped the contents, her excitement growing with every second.

With the last bit of tissue removed Emma couldn't believe her eyes. The soft cream chiffon dress lay beautifully folded.

Tears welled in her eyes. She tried desperately to hold them back. It was the most beautiful dress she had ever seen; the one she had tried on for Flora in Harrods, and now it was her Christmas present. She went and threw her arms around Flora and kissed her cheek.

'Oh Flora thank you so much,' she was only just able to speak the words.

Flora hugged her back. 'It will look far better on you my dear friend,' she said smiling.

Then Carlo said: 'What about me? I paid for it you know,' giving her one of his quizzical looks. She knew of course he had, but he was joking as he did so often with her.

'Oh Carlo thank you, thank you so much.' He smiled.

She wanted so much to kiss and hug him, but she felt if she did, she would never want to let him go. Instead she felt a little foolish when he said 'Well, I don't think Flora will mind if you give me a hug.'

With that everyone laughed and Emma very politely gave him a little hug.

'That's better,' he said laughing. 'We will all wait to see you model it tomorrow: Christmas Day.' They all smiled in agreement. Of course she did and they all agreed how lovely she looked. For Emma it was a wonderful moment she would never forget.

It was decided that as soon as the weather became warmer it would be a good idea for Flora to visit Caroline and James. The sea air in Devon might help Flora's health. Carlo agreed and would consult the doctor. Luckily Caroline had been a nurse during the war and had helped wounded soldiers recuperate. It was then that she met James, who was a doctor. The two of them fell in love and after the war they had married and gone to live by the sea.

So when spring came early, with very sunny days, James and Caroline took Flora back to their seaside cottage. It was decided that she should stay a few weeks. Carlo would visit a few days here and there and bring her back when she wished. There were not enough bedrooms for Emma to go and it was not necessary since Flora would be in safe hands. Flora and Carlo suggested Emma should have a little holiday. Flora was sorry Emma couldn't come with her, but said that she deserved a chance to do whatever she wanted, all expenses paid.

'Do the things you enjoy and maybe, if Lottie is here and I believe she intended a visit around now, you can have time to enjoy yourselves.'

'Oh Flora, I shall miss you,' Emma said, and she meant it.

She might find it hard to know what to do without Flora to care for, and whose company she enjoyed. Carlo would be busy catching up with business and would probably be away some of the time.

She would have to be content with Rosa's company, she thought laughingly. They could discuss food and what to cook, as well as the world's problems; a great pastime for her. She and Rosa got on very well and she believed that God had sent Emma to them for a purpose. Full of all the old superstitions believed everything that happened was always for a reason. She would say this to herself, and to anyone who would listen, crossing herself at the same time.

'When I was left a widow at nineteen, He gave me the chance to have another life, and gave me the opportunity to look after Carlo,' she would say proudly.

This was usually to Emma, who would listen and agree because it was what Rosa needed. In return Emma had made a friend for life and was always remembered in Rosa's prayers.

The day arrived when the three of them departed for Devon. They would take the journey slowly and, if necessary, stay in a hotel. There were

115

some lovely villages on the way. The weather was fine and so they did just that.

Carlo had to travel for a few days. He was to be back later in the week so Emma felt like a fish out of water as there was not much to do. She could always occupy herself reading, listening to music or taking walks in the park; but when she learned Lottie was due in London the next day, she knew that the two of them would spend as much time together as possible. This was always their plan and particularly if William was tied up in meetings, their purpose for being in London.

She met Rosa in the kitchen seeming a little upset, 'What's the matter Rosa, you look worried?'

'Oh, Miss Emma, it's my sister, she is unwell and alone,' she said. With the sobs, and her strong Italian accent, Emma could hardly understand her.

'Which sister, Rosa, where is she?' Emma asked.

'It's Louisa, she lives in St Albans, and it's too far to just hop on the bus,' she said, amidst the sobs.

'Look, there is no need for you to be here, Rosa. Go to your sister and stay a day or two until she feels better. I am sure Carlo won't mind. It will be fine,' she said as she put her arms around Rosa's shoulders and gave her a little squeeze.

What Emma didn't know was that Rosa had taken a telephone call from Robert's college, which with one thing and another had left her in a confused state. Something about Robert being in trouble again and not wanting to be the bearer of bad news thought it would all come out soon enough. She did not want to worry anyone at this time, as it would no doubt be dealt with in due course.

'You are sure Miss Emma? I don't know if I should,' she stuttered between sniffs.

'Of course I am sure, now go and pack a bag and I will call a taxi cab to take you to the station.'

She smiled as she gave her a gentle shove in the direction of her room and went to Carlo's study where he had told her there was some money, should it be needed. She took sufficient for the train fare and the taxi and some for Rosa's needs. She telephoned for the taxi and within minutes Rosa appeared with a bag packed with a change of clothes and all that was necessary for a few days' stay.

When the taxi arrived Emma sent Rosa off with wishes to her sister for a speedy recovery. She told her not to worry about anything and to stay as long as she was needed. With that Rosa, of course still tearful and full of gratitude to Emma, was sent on her way.

Emma said: 'Try to let me know how your sister is and when you will return.'

It was unlikely Louisa had a telephone, but those that did have the luxury might be kind enough to oblige in the circumstances. Carlo would be back this evening and she was sure that he would say she had done the right thing in the situation. He was leaving for Devon in the morning to spend the weekend with Flora.

He had already told Emma she should have time to spend with Lottie and to enjoy herself; go out to lunch or tea or, of course, go shopping – the way to every woman's heart it seemed. She busied herself with tidying here and there, then freshened up and put a little rouge on her cheeks, brushed her hair and made herself presentable for his homecoming.

CHAPTER TWELVE

The Malocchio: 'The Evil Eye'

It was earlier than usual when she heard the front door open and close. She walked to the stairs and looking down to the hall she saw his coat lying on the chair, but no sign of Carlo. This was so unusual; she had never known him not to call a greeting, even when he had a bad day, always making his arrival known. Somehow she felt something was wrong. She hurried down the stairs. A feeling of dread filled her that was it about Flora. Maybe she had taken a turn for the worse.

Emma had this sinking feeling in her stomach and was afraid. She knew by heart his habit of walking into the library and going to the mahogany drink's cabinet, and she would hurry to get there first. Smiling, she would lift the whisky or the aperitif bottle and depending on which choice was made, she would know what kind of day he had had.

Whisky usually meant not a good one and an aperitif a good sign, which always made her laugh. But tonight there was nothing as usual; no grand entrance or even a greeting.

She entered the library and found him sitting on the couch with his head in his hands, his tie undone and lying loosely on his chest. She stood silent for a moment too afraid to ask him what was wrong; she had never seen him like this before. He looked at her and stood up and she could see in his eyes the anguish he felt inside. Emma instinctively went to him and gently placed her hands on his arms. After a few seconds she asked what had happened, dreading the answer, afraid it was something to do with Flora's health.

'Carlo what is it?' He could hardly find the words as he sighed and answered. 'Oh, Emma,' he paused a moment and looking in her eyes said: 'Its Robert, he has been sent down from his college.'

Emma didn't know what that meant, but said nothing, the relief she felt was momentary when he said: 'It means expelled, thrown out.' Emma did not know whether to be relieved or not, it wasn't Flora, but with his next words the reality was brought home with a crash.

'He seems to have gone missing for several days; the college tried to contact me at the office and was told I was away.'

Emma felt his pain, his dilemma. The last thing that Flora needed was this news.

She placed her arms around him to comfort him, as you would a child. She wanted to hold him to her to take the pain away. They stood there for a moment then he pulled her close to him and rested his head on her shoulder.

'What did he do that was so bad?' she asked.

'Whoring around in the town, getting drunk; bringing the college into disrepute and, if that is not bad enough, being caught in flagrante with one of the lecturer's daughters. I don't know what to do, oh God, Emma, how do I tell her?' he said.

She waited a second and said softly: 'Perhaps you should wait. He will come home and have to tell his mother himself. It might be easier for her if he is here.'

They still stood close and now she became aware that she was in his arms and was surprised at this closeness, so unexpected, only his cotton shirt and her blouse separating them. She could feel the warmth of his body. Aware of the scent of the cologne he wore, her legs began to feel weak and afraid to move; they stood that way for what seemed an eternity, but was only a matter of a minute or two.

Neither spoke, but something had been awakened within her whole being: it was the longing she had for him without even realizing that the fire of desire had been lit inside her.

Silently she asked: 'Oh God, help me please.'

He stroked her hair and she knew that they were on the brink beyond which there was no return. Nothing had prepared them for this awakening of the passion that had lain dormant so long for both of them.

Now, his world crashing down around him, he was lost and it was she who had to find the strength to pull away from him.

The words Lottie had spoken in her little talk were coming true: those warning her about the dangers of falling for married men.

'You will know when the dragon awakes and breathes the fire of desire into you and nothing in the world matters except being with him.'

On reflection Emma began to wonder if there was something deeper in the warning about being in love with a married man. Had there been anything in his behaviour that would have given concern to Lottie. Was there a danger of anything more than friendship between her and Carlo? Yes he was handsome and rich and would have no trouble in enjoying the convenience of having a beautiful young woman as his mistress on his doorstep. But Lottie didn't know him as she did and, fortunately, nothing more was mentioned along those lines.

Now it was she who wanted to taste his lips, feel him caress her and let her drown in the ecstasy of him taking her beyond this world; where nothing mattered except this moment of being in his arms. Her heart pounded and she felt she was falling further and further into the abyss. She knew, by the way he held her so tight and stroked her hair, that it was the same for him.

Was all the bantering and teasing just a shield to hide his feelings? She had never really known, but now she knew the need they both felt was born from something much deeper than some moment of lust. He had integrity, and principles. He would never bring shame into his home or betray Flora; this had prevented him from taking advantage of this situation.

Neither of them could have betrayed Flora. She was more than her employer; she was her friend almost a sister-and she knew that neither she nor Carlo could ever live with the guilt.

Again she pleaded silently to God to help her regain the courage she needed to step back from his arms. She recalled the words Carlo had once said to her. 'We must play by the rules or suffer the consequences,' and she knew he lived by those rules as best he could.

Quite suddenly she began to feel that God had answered her prayers and had given her the strength to act on those words. Carlo gently pulled away from her as he whispered 'Forgive me, Emma.' His voice was so quiet, so gentle, she couldn't stop the tears that filled her eyes. He gently placed her at arm's length.

She answered 'For what?'

He replied 'For burdening you with all this.'

She looked at him. This man for whom she had so much love, so much admiration.

'Do you think that I could live in this house, being treated like one of the family, and not feel your pain? You have so much courage, compassion, and integrity. No one will take that away from you.'

She meant those words from the bottom of her heart and knew whatever happened she would rather die than bring shame and heartache to this house.

He was silent; he looked at her with eyes that said a million things that words could not. She fought to hide her tears and put her hand in the pocket of her skirt and took out the red kerchief she had never been able to part with.

He took it from her and said: 'You still have it,' as he gently wiped away her tears.

She nodded. 'I kept meaning to give it back to you.'

She could see his eyes were moist and knew he was fighting to hold back his own tears. He took hold of her hands tightly and raised them to his lips. She knew now he loved her and she loved him even more for preventing what could have brought so much pain to all of them. He could have made love to her and she could not have stopped him. This made him rise even more in her esteem.

Just so long as she could be near to him and know that he felt deeply enough for her to prevent the terrible consequences of their moment of passion. They both knew it could never have been once; stealing moments to be together and hiding their feelings until, so desperate to be together, suspicions would be raised. Finally, Flora and Rosa would notice. No, neither of them could live this lie; the very thought of it would destroy all of them.

Taking his arm she said: 'I think we need a drink.'

He replied softly: 'I think you're right.' He put his arm around her shoulders and they walked to the drinks' cabinet.

'What will you have?' he asked.

'A whisky,' she replied

He looked surprised and said: 'But you don't drink whisky.'

She gave him a little smile. 'Tonight I do.'

'Drink it slowly then,' he said, also smiling.

They sat opposite each other in two armchairs. He lifted his glass to her and she returned the gesture.

He looked exhausted. 'Carlo you must get some rest, don't let Flora see you so tired and worried, she will know something is wrong.'

'Don't worry, I am leaving very early in the morning so please do not get up.' He rose slowly from his chair. He seemed reluctant in some way to leave her. 'I will be back after the weekend, maybe with Flora, but we will have to see how she feels.'

He walked over to her and took both her hands in his and, holding them tightly, he said: 'Thank you Emma.'

She looked at him. 'For what?' she murmured.

'For being you.'

He turned to go and facing her again said: 'Please don't ever leave,' with such a look that Emma wanted to just hold him once more.

She replied: 'Perhaps it would be better if I did.' She knew it would be fatal to go to him. Instead she looked back.

'I will never leave until you tell me to.'

'That will be never.' He wanted to add: 'I don't know how I could live without you,' but stopped himself.

Emma gave him one more smile and wished him a good journey and asked him to give her love to Flora.

She bit her lip to prevent revealing the emotion she was trying so hard to hide. Turning away she said: 'I will get you some breakfast.'

'No thank you, I will get something on the train. You have a good rest and enjoy a few days with Lottie. Go shopping, take her to lunch, there is money in my study drawer,' he said.

He always told her the same thing if he was going away in case either Flora or she needed anything. But apart from the money she gave Rosa, she never took any for herself.

She didn't need anything: it was all here: just so long as he was.

She hardly had to spend anything on herself. She only had to mention she might need something and it was hers. He turned back and said: 'Telephone if you need anything. Caroline's number is in the top drawer'.

She smiled. 'Yes I know. Get some sleep Carlo.' She looked back at him one more time before they parted; now realising she loved him more than life itself.

Emma woke a little later than usual the next morning. She had felt drained. At first she was unable to sleep, her mind full of what had transpired. She wondered if he had felt her longing to keep him in her arms forever. Eventually she fell asleep not knowing the answer.

She got up and looked through the window. The sky was blue and the sun was shining. It made her feel better; she must get him out of her mind and stop remembering the feelings that had been so difficult to control.

Lottie had arrived the previous day and they had planned to have dinner this evening. She really needed to see Lottie and clear her brain of everything. She should try to make the most of having the house to herself, but she didn't really want the house to herself. She missed Flora and, most of all, she would miss Carlo.

Why was life so complicated, so painful, and why did she have to fall in love with him? It wasn't planned, and she didn't even know when it had begun. Maybe it was the first time she met him, but even more likely it was when she got to know the man.

It took a long time before sleep took her on some strange and mysterious journey, full of odd people who for the most part were unrecognisable. It was with relief, when she awoke, to find it wasn't real and that other things took precedent. She washed and dressed and put on her best frock: the cream chiffon the one they had given her at Christmas knowing she looked her best wearing it. Carlo had paid for it and to her it was the most precious thing she had in her wardrobe. Doing her hair in the style he always admired, swept up at the side with the back loose and a decorative comb to secure it. The comb was another gift that he had brought back from one of his trips. At first she had worried that Flora would not approve of Carlo always bringing something for back for her, but it was Flora who would always tell him to remember Emma too.

The telephone rang and she ran to answer it.

'Hello Emma.' She recognized the voice, it was Lottie, 'Are you ready for Davis to collect you? We can decide where we want to go when you get here.'

'Emma, so happy to hear her voice replied, 'Yes I am ready.'

Lottie said Davis would be there in minutes and true to her word he was. The door bell rang and Davis greeted her and escorted her to the Rolls. This was always an excitement for Emma, as Davis was always chirpy and full of the latest news.

Their day was as wonderful as ever. When Lottie was in London, they went to Knightsbridge and then to Piccadilly and Fortnum and Mason, and a new restaurant that Lottie had discovered and wanted to try. When shopped and fed they returned to Cheyne Walk, where they collapsed, surrounded by shopping bags mostly with gifts for other people. Lottie loved to buy for all and sundry. There had also been a list from William, who hated shopping and left this duty to his wife.

Emma and Lottie played a game on these occasions, sneaking off to a counter with some excuse to purchase something or other, but really it was a gift for each other.

Emma would also buy a gift for Carlo and a silk scarf for Flora who loved them. Too tired to do much more than to rest and talk, they would later dine at their leisure.

Their enjoyment was being in each other's company. As usual Lottie always was full of stories of their time abroad. These were told with all the talent of an orator, or maybe an actress, for which Emma always thought Lottie was a natural.

Sarah was the housekeeper but, being an excellent cook, would enjoy preparing something light and tasty for them. This would was always be accompanied by an appropriate wine.

After an evening with Lottie she always felt renewed. They laughed so much and life seemed to take on a different hue. It was getting late when Emma said she thought it was time to go home.

Lottie said: 'Why don't you stay?'

But Emma said she wanted to change her clothes and be there in case anyone telephoned. It was better if they met up the next day as had been planned.

Davis dropped Emma back at the house and waited whilst she unlocked the front door and entered the house. He then wished her 'good night' and said he would see her the next day.

Emma felt light-hearted. Lottie's company always had that affect on her: she was so natural and amusing and they could talk about anything, although Emma did not mention what had transpired the night before. She could not bear to explain anything as she still wasn't sure how.

This was something so precious between her and Carlo and she was not ready to reveal, even to Lottie, the very thing she had been warned about. How would she understand? It was better to lock their secret away. Nothing wrong had happened and it would not: she vowed that it would not.

She went to her room and took off her dress. She laid it over the back of the chair in her dressing room and put on her house dress. It was a beautiful flowing gown made from a soft silky material that wrapped around and tied in the front. Another gift from Flora who insisted that she didn't have to wear some frumpy dressing gown, especially in summer when the nights were warm.

She decided to bathe before going to bed and went to her adjoining bathroom. Another unexpected and wonderful thing that Carlo had arranged for her and all of them was to have the latest plumbing. This had all been carried out while they were in Italy. The water was warm and inviting, she took off the house dress and laid it on the chair nearby and climbed into the bath. She lay there enjoying the warmth and the fragrance of the perfumed salts Flora had given her. She closed her eyes rubbed the soap into lather all over her skin letting the water run until all the soap had gone.

Feeling tired after their busy, yet enjoyable day, she hoped she would be able to sleep well. She stepped out of the bath, and took a towel from the rail and wrapped herself in it humming as she dried herself in its soft fluffiness. She then applied the cream that Flora had suggested was an excellent balm for the skin and which had come from some exotic place far away.

Feeling refreshed and ready for bed, she put her gown back on and walked into the bedroom. The light was dim, but something drew her attention to the far side of the room by the door. Something had moved and Emma's, heart began to race.

A figure came out of the shadows. It was tall like Carlo, but it couldn't be, he would never walk into her bedroom unannounced. The figure spoke.

'Hello Emma.'

She stood rooted to the floor, her eyes trying to accustom to the darkened room. No, surely it couldn't be, but her worst fears were confirmed: it was Robert!

She tried to control herself from showing her anxiety. She sensed it would be better to try to look unafraid.

'What are you doing here Robert? Get out of my room.' she said as calmly as she could.

He had a smirk on his face. 'It's not your room Emma, this is my house and I can go where I like.' The look on his face frightened her. She answered: 'It's not your house, it's your parent's house, and I live here with their permission,' she retorted.

He ignored her words and said: 'I thought you would be glad to have company: a young man to give you attention and comfort.'

'What are you talking about? Have you been drinking?' she asked.

She could see him half swaying and slurring his words.

He lurched toward her. 'I am going to show you what a good time a young man can give you, Emma.'

His mouth uttering words that were alien to her, she was afraid as he moved ever nearer to her. She tried to step aside, but, drunk or not he was too quick and powerful for her to avoid him. He had the physique of his father, but there the resemblance ended. He looked nothing like him. His hair was fair and mousy and he had cold blue eyes that had a look in them that frightened her.

Suddenly, he sprung forward. Emma was taken by surprise at his speed as he grabbed the gown and pulled it open revealing her nakedness. Recovering from the shock, she screamed at him.

'Stop Robert. Are you mad? You will regret this.' Her voice betrayed her as she tried to brave herself out of this terrifying ordeal.

He moved quickly, picked her up and threw her onto the bed.

Every second that passed she tried more desperately to free herself from him, afraid that he was going to rape her or even beat her.

Then to her surprise, he began to kiss her neck and moving slowly down her body she realised that this was not exactly his aim, which was to arouse her.

This was what his ego needed, and, as the realization of his intentions had became more and more obvious, Emma fought him until she ached, but he, with his strength, was determined to achieve his goal.

The tears now free falling as he did things to her that she had never dreamed of. She hated him but her body had a mind of its own. He had loosened his trousers and they were around his knees. He had managed this manoeuvre whilst holding her hands above her head. He was very adept and experienced for his twenty odd years. Emma sobbed. She was so ashamed as her body responded to his touch. She now knew what it felt like to go beyond the point of no return. She cried as she tried to fight him, but as much as he forced himself on her, she was no longer able to find the strength to struggle anymore. Then the moment came when it seemed the world had stopped and it was not Robert's name she screamed, it was Carlo's.

She knew she had ruined it for him. She laughed hysterically as she saw the expression of fury on his face. So terrible, it was enough for Emma to know that he would now try to hurt her. He had already raised his hand ready to strike her as he pulled himself up away from her. Then suddenly, she saw her chance to free herself from this vile creature. She lifted her knees as high as she could and with both feet together she aimed them as hard as she could into his crotch. Unable to move for a few seconds she was totally fascinated by the reaction it had achieved. She watched as his eyes rolled to the back of his head, and at the same time letting out a blood-curdling scream.

His trousers still at half-mast, his furious tirade began.

'You bitch, you f…. bitch,' but the words of profanity faded as Robert's terrible screams of agony preceded them, as he fell backwards onto the floor.

Now Emma realised this was her chance and with as much strength as she could muster, got up from the other side of the bed. As quickly as her sore and aching body would allow, she rushed to the dressing table a few feet away. Opening the top drawer, she took out her mother's dressmaking scissors that were kept there.

127

Robert, swearing and groaning, lay holding himself between his legs. Emma stood towering over him and lifting the scissors in both hands brought them down into the fleshy part of his arm. This produced another scream as, at the same time, he tried to hold with one hand his wounded arm, out of which the blood ran freely.

'I am going to kill you,' Emma screamed, as she raised both her arms again and stabbed him as viciously as she could.

He pleaded with her to stop. He knew that she was totally out of control and might carry out her threat. All inebriation gone, he was faced with the consequences of his actions. The bravado had now completely left him.

He whimpered: 'Stop Emma, please stop, I am sorry.' But now she was a different woman, wild and crazed with anger.

'You're sorry, you're sorry! You filthy wretch. You have ruined my life. Do you know what you have done; you have brought shame to this house. I thought you loved your mother but this could kill her. As for your father, he might kill you.' She could hardly get the words out for sobbing.

'But you and my father,' he sobbed. Only now could she see everything. He had thought she was Carlo's mistress, so twisted and jealous and damaged that he had dreamt up a reason to ruin everything, without thinking what it would do to his mother and father. Only now faced with the truth, the terrible reality had begun to sink in, and Roberto was afraid.

He dragged himself across the floor leaving a trail of blood behind. He was still unable to stand up properly, whilst Emma walked behind him her arm was still raised, with the scissors, ready to plunge into him again.

He reached the landing and, half crawling, dragged himself to the edge of the stairs trying to grab hold of the banister. Falling part of the way he managed to reach the bottom of the stairs.

'Get out, Get out!' she screamed, wanting to kick him, but without anything on her feet she would achieve nothing but possibly a broken toe.

Robert needed no encouragement to escape and still holding himself in his most vulnerable spot, half limped and half crawled, towards the front door.

Emma opened it and seeing his coat on the chair, she threw it out after him. He half stumbled and fell down the steps. Gathering up his coat, he took off down the street pulling up his trousers as he went.

Slamming the front door, she locked it. Only now the full realisation of what had happened began to hit her.

She rushed into the library and poured a whisky. She knocked it back nearly choking, but hoping to kill the pain and the heartache. Then she collapsed on the couch in tears, with the sobs engulfing her whole body. Now all she wanted was oblivion; to curl up and die. Still sobbing uncontrollably, she buried her head into a cushion trying to take the pain away.

After a while she poured another whisky, also knocking it back, hoping that it would make her so drunk she would pass out. But nothing helped. She wanted to rid herself of him and hurried up the stairs to her bathroom and ran the water that now was only just warm. It didn't matter, she had to clean herself and remove every trace of him from her body.

Letting the water cascade over her, she took the soap and covered every part of her with lather in an effort to make her feel cleaner, but removing the horror and the shame was impossible. Emma knew it would stay with her forever.

She tried to start thinking straight but the most terrible thing of all was that she knew she could no longer stay in this house.

It was late but she had to phone for help. She dried herself as quickly as she could and went into Flora's bedroom, where there was the nearest telephone and dialled a number. It rang the other end five or six times before it was answered by Sarah. When Emma heard her voice she could hardly speak, for sobbing.

'Hello, who is it?'

Emma trying to control her voice, answered: 'It's me Emma, please get Lottie.' But Lottie had heard the phone ringing and hurried to relieve Sarah from what must be something urgent as it was after midnight.

She heard Sarah say 'Emma' and then Lottie said 'Hello' into the handset.

'What is it Emma?' Knowing deep down this was some kind of an emergency for her to be phoning this time of night. Emma tried hard to be coherent and managed to mumble. 'Please come. Something terrible has happened.'

Lottie did not ask questions. Time enough to ask later. All she knew was that she had to get to Emma as quickly as she could.

129

CHAPTER THIRTEEN

Heartache

'Are you alone Emma?'
Emma replied 'Yes.'

With that Lottie, without even asking what had happened, was not going to waste time. She knew that something terrible had occurred because of the stress in her voice. The quicker she got to Emma, the better; there would be time for explanations then.

'I will be there in ten minutes. Lock the doors and answer to no one.'

'Yes,' sobbed Emma.

Lottie called Sarah to get Davis and the car and to dress herself as quickly as possible as they had to go to Carlo's house right away. Davis knew better than to ask questions and said he would get the car immediately.

True to her word, they arrived almost to the minute as the houses were only a few streets from each other. Emma, now dressed in the first thing she could find, was waiting near the door. After Lottie made her presence known, the door was opened and they entered the hallway. Lottie indicated to them to wait in the library and ushered Emma, who she was now almost carrying, to the drawing room.

Sitting down on the couch next to her and, cuddling her close, whispered 'What is it my darling, what has happened? It wasn't...?'

She never ended the sentence because she knew it could be nothing to do with Carlo. That was impossible. He was in Devon with Flora and, in any case she knew he would never harm Emma. In fact in her hearts he had always feared the opposite was more likely. She knew there was something very special between them, knowing them both so well. Whatever it was she was convinced it was nothing to do with Carlo.

'Tell me my darling, what has happened?'

Emma turned her tearful face to Lottie and tried to speak. Lottie knew this was not the time or place to get the full story, but she had to get something out of Emma in order to deal with whatever had caused this distress, aware that something really bad had taken place. Holding Emma close, she comforted her until she was able to explain something of what had occurred. Lottie waited until she was able to speak.

'I was raped by Robert.' She could hardly say the name for the sobs that were unstoppable.

'Oh my God,' said Lottie, almost in tears herself. Totally shocked, she was hardly able to believe that such a thing could have happened, here, in this house. The repercussions were already flooding her head. Now was not the time for questions and could make things worse for Emma. The main thing was to get her out of this house and think of what could be done later.

Still holding Emma in her arms she said: 'Come, we will go to my house. I will get Sarah and Davis to put some things in a bag that you might need. Is anyone here tomorrow?'

Emma shook her head. 'No, Rosa won't be back for a few days and Carlo, after the weekend,' she sobbed.

'Alright, we will come tomorrow and collect whatever else you need.'

With that she left Emma for two minutes and instructed Sarah and Davis to go and put some essentials in a bag as quickly as possible and put them in the car. Emma was in no fit state to oversee anything and Sarah, as a woman, knew what was needed. Within half an hour they left the house and drove back to Cheyne Walk.

Lottie knew that Emma was in such a state of shock that it was important to get her to calm down before she could get any proper explanation of what had led up to this dreadful event.

Lottie beckoned Sarah. 'Get some whisky in a tumbler. I need to calm her. She is in no fit state to answer questions.'

Sarah nodded and headed off to get the whisky. Lottie cuddled Emma and rocked her like a baby. She was trying to think how it could have

131

happened. Her patience was rewarded when after a sip or two of the whisky; she looked at Lottie with tearful eyes

'Please, Lottie, what I tell you, you must not tell anyone. Please promise me. It's very important.' The tears started again.

'My darling, you know I would never make a promise to you without keeping it: whoever and whatever it is about.' She kissed her cheek and felt the pain that Emma was in; her confusion, her desperation, and waited until she was ready to speak. The whisky seemed to have helped a little to obliterate the pain that was enveloping her whole being.

Now a little calmer Emma said 'When I arrived back at the house, I decided to have a bath. I was so happy. I had enjoyed our day together, and I put on my robe and as I walked into the bedroom, I was suddenly aware of a movement in the shadows near the door.'

Reliving everything again was proving more difficult than she could ever have imagined. She managed to utter his name and relate what had happened.

Lottie, herself now in tears, said: 'The bastard, the dirty bastard.'

Holding Emma now tighter than ever, they clung together in the despair of the heartache they shared.

Emma, finding it hard to speak between sobs, said: 'But Lottie it's not only about me: it's Flora. This could kill her.' Hesitating for a second she added, 'It's what Carlo would do to him. There is no love lost between them. I am so afraid what will happen. I have to go away Lottie, I can't go back. They must never find out.'

Lottie knew only too well that however they were to overcome what lay ahead was only the beginning of a nightmare for all concerned. The prospect of explaining Emma's sudden departure from the people she loved would be difficult. She and William would be the first port of call for the whereabouts of Emma. And what of Robert? Would he think of facing Emma, who, as far as he knew would still be in the house. The whole situation did not bear thinking of. Nothing could be achieved tonight.

The main thing was to get Emma to sleep and think of how to deal with things tomorrow.

She knew she would find it hard to sleep herself. Having made a promise to Emma, she would have to convince her that it was vital for William, too, to know the truth. As a diplomat he was an expert in depended keeping confidences of national importance, and was not the one to worry about.

However, Emma was not to be faced with a dilemma about this aspect until she was able to deal with it. William was likely to be late home from his meeting at the Foreign Office, as important issues needed to be discussed. Lottie, deciding to sleep with Emma, left a note for William saying, as Emma was not well, she was staying with her in the guest room.

Next morning Lottie woke early and eased herself from the bed, so as not to wake Emma, still sound asleep. She wanted to get Emma's things from the house as soon as possible, in case someone returned earlier than expected. She got herself ready and dressed in some slacks that were all the fashion, and a jumper.

She hurried downstairs and found Sarah up and about. She had already told Davis to get the Rolls ready, with some empty cases and a large trunk for Emma's possessions. Lottie thought a lot of Sarah; she seemed to be able to predict what was needed without being given instructions.

Doris had finally retired and Sarah, who had been in service since she was young was recommended to replace her as Sir James Cavanaugh's housekeeper. She had been ideal for the post and had looked after him well.

When Sir James died, Davis, having found the woman of his dreams, asked Sarah to marry him. She also had found love with Davis. Now they were both irreplaceable for Lottie and William, who perceived them as a real blessing.

They drove the few streets to the Villarni house and parked outside. Lottie knocked at the door, just in case anyone had returned earlier than expected. No one came to the door so Lottie put Emma's key in the lock and entered. The house was empty and slightly dark, so unlike the house she had visited so often.

There was an atmosphere that she couldn't describe. An air of sadness or was it her imagination? There was no longer the light and laughter that had been there in the past.

She asked Davis to take up the empty cases and they started packing. They emptied the cupboards and drawers and wrapped all the breakables inside the clothes to protect them. Sarah stripped the bed linen, which held evidence of what that happened. Quite a lot of blood had splashed not only on the sheets but on the floor.

She asked Sarah to fold the sheets and send them to the laundry, as they used the same company and they should be returned to this house. Hopefully Rosa would think that Emma had sent them before she left.

Lottie also noticed that the rug by the side of the bed had stains, too. She went to the bathroom and brought a piece of wet cloth and soap and began to try and clean the marks. Some came off, but not completely. There was nothing that could be done so they just had to hope that the remaining stains would not be noticed. They looked everywhere before going downstairs to see if there were any other items that may have belonged to Emma, but nothing was apparent so they locked up and returned home.

Lottie told Davis to take everything up to the bedroom, next to Emma's, so that she could go through everything and decide what she needed and what could be stored.

Emma was now awake and feeling terrible. Not only her body, but her head and her heart ached. Lottie found her sitting on the bed without much desire to move. She placed her arms around her.

'I know what will help, a nice warm bath with lots of special herbs that are from the Orient, famous for all aches and pains of the body.'

Emma looked at her with soulful eyes and wanted to say that it was not just her body that hurt, it was also her heart.

She had been plagued with wondering what she could possibly do or say to Carlo and Flora in a letter, as her reason for running away. Then the terrible thought flooded her brain: he may think it was because of the other night when she had found herself in his arms.

'Oh God,' he might think that she was upset or afraid of what had happened and whether it could happen again. He took the blame by saying he didn't want to burden her with his problems. But she was the one who had felt herself drowning in his arms, not knowing how to control her emotions. If God had not listened to her plea for help, they may have got to the point of no return.

She started to feel tearful again. Just the memory of the moments she spent in his arms, knowing it had been unplanned and innocent. Now, the worst thing in the world was she could never see him or Flora again.

What would Flora do without her friend and companion? What reason could there be for Emma to run away and not say goodbye?

Lottie held her close and found it hard to control her own tears. She knew she had to be the one who stayed in control. She had to talk to Emma as there was not a lot of time before Carlo would return to London. Something had to be arranged because Emma was right: Carlo would be certain that, as Lottie was so close to Emma, she would know where she was and why she had gone.

'Emma, darling, we must talk. Can you tell me why Robert did what he did? I know you found him strange and that he showed his dislike for you. Even he and Carlo did not get along, yet Flora seemed to be oblivious to anything negative about him.'

Emma, now trying hard to stop her sobs, hesitated and said in a whisper, 'He thought I was Carlo's mistress, I don't know why.'

Lottie thought she knew why. Carlo and Emma always seemed to play jokes on each other and seemed to delight in each others company. Robert, so much absent from the house with boarding school and university, was unable to see that their affection for each other was nothing untoward.

Lottie had once read a book on Greek mythology about Oedipus's love for his mother, and had always thought Robert rather an odd young man with a rather unpleasant disposition. Perhaps he was confused and jealous of Carlo, whose looks and personality were so different to his. He did not resemble Carlo apart from his height and build. As for looks and personality, there was no comparison. Lottie thought if ever there was a cuckoo in the nest, it was Robert!

There were times when Lottie herself had concerns that Emma might find herself out of her depth, and in a situation that could only lead to misery for all concerned. But Carlo seemed to have integrity and, whatever he felt for Emma, she believed he would never bring shame into his home, or be able to live with the ensuing guilt.

Flora, a very quiet and elegant lady, but wise in many ways, knew that the light-hearted bantering was good for the atmosphere in the house. She wanted her husband to come home to a house full of laughter and happiness, and not to be worried and always concerned about her health.

His business world was full of demands: not only on his time and expertise, but the inevitable emotional draining that was part of his profession.

Emma had brought something to their lives: a special quality of empathy and kindness that made Flora regard her as a sister. Carlo could go about his business and know that his wife could not be in better hands. Lottie was also aware of the genuineness of their relationship. It was apparent to anyone who entered their home.

She had deliberately given Emma that little talk, hoping the light-hearted, although a fairly explicit, chat had the significance intended.

Lottie realized that Emma's life experience had been lacking in that department and that her beloved friend, Molly, had not been there to advise on the perils awaiting a young, innocent woman.

It was her place, as godmother, to be there, to inform and guide where possible. Her love for Emma was deep and she had taken the role of the nearest thing to a mother. Having their own child was the one thing that had been missing for her and William. Still, she was philosophical about it and had so much to be thankful for. Not everything we want can be obtained. She had married the man of her dreams and now she had to try to repay back her good fortune. Maybe it had been her role in life to be there for Emma as much as possible. Now the tragedy that had occurred meant some speedy decisions must be made.

Emma had been quiet and thoughtful. Still hesitant when she looked Lottie in the eye, and speaking slowly, she said: 'The night before something happened. It was unplanned and took Carlo and me by surprise.'

She told Lottie how events had led to finding herself in his arms and the effect it had on her, and that she somehow knew that they had both found themselves between heaven and hell.

'I prayed to God to help me, Lottie. I had lost all sense of anything except being close to him, not able to move away.'

'Suddenly, I don't know how, but I think God heard my prayer and Carlo gently released me. When he looked at me, Lottie, I could read so much in his eyes and knew without words what I believed was in his heart.'

The memory had brought back tears and Lottie knew that what she had feared had nearly happened. The outcome made her so proud of Carlo and Emma for their strength, but she knew in her heart that if Emma had stayed in that house it would only be a matter of time before love overcame all; an outcome that could bring misery for all concerned.

'Emma, we need to decide what you would like to do. William is now acting First Secretary and his reason for being here is for meetings with the prime minister and senior officials. There is this Hitler chap strutting all over the place, and causing concerns to everyone. Also Mussolini gaining power in Italy and William has to meet many other people in diplomatic circles. The poor man is tired out.'

Lottie paused and continued: 'If I were in Italy you could stay with us, but nothing is certain at the moment as to when we will return.'

Emma replied: 'Thank you Lottie, but I think I want to go to Maria and Joe for a bit. I know they will want me to be there, but I will not say I am coming, as I will have to make them promise not to mention anything to anyone. I know when they hear what happened they will keep it quiet.'

Lottie was worried. 'Are you sure it's the right decision?' she asked, 'Carlo would find out. He may go there for business.'

Emma responded quickly. 'No, he will not leave England, Flora is too unwell, and, in any case, Joe is now taking care of business there. Once I am gone I could leave a note saying something regarding family, who suddenly required me to help. He may not believe it, but it might lead him away from the truth.'

Lottie realized that they needed to sort out a plan. In fact, according to William's conversation, there may be a need to travel to see various big wigs on diplomatic issues and she hoped that she could accompany him. She needed to explain everything to him and persuade Emma that to confide in him as it would be quite safe and he would be very helpful. She had to do so very quickly, as much depended on the success of Emma's plan.

'Now, Emma, you must go through the things you want to take. Everything else can be stored here safely. I will arrange everything. We will book you on the train to Paris. You know the procedure, as you have been before, so that will make things easier. I will book your night sleeper train to Rome. You will have your private compartment and when you arrive there will be someone to meet you and get you to Monte Verde. So don't worry about anything.'

Emma hugged Lottie, 'I will miss you so much. I do hope when you get back to Rome I will be able to see you.'

'Of course, my darling, when things settle you can come with us and stay, hopefully.'

Emma kissed her godmother on the cheek and said 'Thank you Lottie, what would I do without you?'

'Now if you feel a little better, it would be a good idea to go through your possessions and take what you need. If there is anything else required, it can always come over later. Travel light as you will need the lightest clothes for summer, which you have already. Warm things we can arrange later and all your precious possessions will be quite safe here.'

Emma agreed it was the most sensible thing to do. She knew she was right and didn't feel the need to drag trunks and a lot of heavy luggage with her, just the right clothes her small precious bits and pieces and some photos: those she would never part with.

Most precious of all were the smaller items that Carlo and Flora had given her. Particularly the things that he had brought back for her: combs for her hair, her crystal clock and other items that would not take up too much room. It didn't take too long, although choosing between different items was the difficult part. She reminded herself that her belongings were safe and sound until she could retrieve them in the future.

After having chosen and laid everything ready to pack she went downstairs and joined Lottie, who had been busy sorting out travel arrangements for her.

'It's possible for you to leave tomorrow afternoon, which will get you to Paris in time to catch the night sleeper. It could work out quite convenient, Emma, as you would arrive the next day in Rome, then you will be met and arrangements will have been made for the journey to Monte Verde.

'Now, what about something to eat?'

Emma, at last beginning to feel a little better, realized that she had not eaten for twenty-four hours and that, too, she had to accept that what was done could not be undone. Unless she died from heartache, she must do whatever was necessary to protect the people she loved more than anything in the world.

CHAPTER FOURTEEN

Carlo

Emma sat in the train's private compartment that Lottie had arranged for her, staring out of the window at the passing French countryside, but seeing nothing. The pain in her head was nothing to that in her heart. She contemplated ending it all, as there seemed nothing that could she could do to take away the reality of what had happened. There were no easy answers on how to prevent the on-going sorrow for the people she loved so much. She realized only too well that Carlo might think it was his fault that she had left. Flora might think that she had run off with someone, which he would not understand either. Even the culprit, the awful Robert, might be a suspect, although it must have been obvious to Flora that Emma had never shown the slightest interest in him. In fact quite the opposite.

Maria and Joe would be in shock and sorrow and her wonderful Lottie would be devastated. She knew the consequence of her doing such a thing was getting herself rid of the pain at the cost of those she loved who were left to live with their heartache. Could she be such a coward? She knew the answer to that. It would have been worse than them all knowing the truth. She would have to find the courage to go on and deal with whatever destiny had planned for her.

Exhausted, she fell asleep, and when she woke the sky outside had turned dark and, for the first time in hours, she felt hungry and thirsty. She opened the door of the compartment and saw the attendant coming along the corridor to inform the passengers that dinner would be served in the restaurant car. She asked him if she could have her choice served in her own compartment as she felt unwell.

'Of course, Signorina,' he said kindly, handing her the menu and telling her he would call back in a few minutes for her order.

She wasn't really very hungry, but the pains in her empty stomach were an additional thing for her to bear and so she selected a light meal of chicken and vegetables, and red wine which she knew would help her sleep. The wine did help and the chugging of the train and the pure exhaustion of the last few days had helped her to sleep better than she expected.

The next morning the mountains of the Pyrenees began to appear through the window and Emma started to feel a little better and noticed the snow on the peaks and the valleys of green pine. The constant tunnels were never ending and, when at last they began to descend into Italy, the memories flooded back of her last visit and the journey that had been so wonderful.

So far there had been no hitches and, arriving in Rome, a message came by hand that the train would be going on to Naples and she would be met there. Arrangements had been made for her continuing journey to Monte Verde. Emma blessed Lottie. She could never have done all this on her own, in her state of mind. Everything was planned so well. The journey had been good for her, helping her get control of her emotions and find the courage to go on. As promised, a chauffeured car was waiting for her and she was driven to Monte Verde.

Emma was not disappointed in her welcome from Maria and Joe. Although shocked at what had occurred, they nevertheless took Emma into their lives, as welcome as the first time they had met her. They were protective and sworn to secrecy of her whereabouts. They didn't press too much at the beginning, realizing this was one of the worst experiences a woman could suffer; and so much worse when in the circumstances, when the culprit was in their own family. Emma was family to them and, unfortunately, so was Robert!

They didn't bombard her with questions, realizing the need to be diplomatic. Things would be explained in due course when Emma was ready. Obviously there had been enquiries as to whether she had been seen by anyone, but Lottie had been able to put them off the scent with some story to appease curiosity.

As time went by Emma began to feel a little stronger, but nevertheless still heartbroken by what had happened to her. She buried herself in her new life and the company of Maria and Joe. Their warmth and affection made Emma feel so loved that she began to smile again, until something happened to remind her.

There was a certain amount of secrecy regarding her presence and very few were aware of her being there with them. The one saving grace for her sanity was the surprise that had given her a new lease of life. Maria said one morning after breakfast: 'You know, Emma, you have not been to see Pippo.' Emma gasped.

'Oh my darling Pippo, I was so wrapped up in everything, how could I forget him?' She smiled and this was the first real glimpse of the old Emma since she had arrived.

'I am going now, Maria,' she said.

'Finish your coffee first' Maria said as she laughed.

'No, I must see him right away or he will never forgive me.'

Maria thought 'Why did I not remind her before? I think we might be on the right road when she sees the surprise.'

Emma rushed out of the kitchen along the path to Pippo's stable. It was only a short walk to his summer stable; the winter one was adjacent to the house, it was closer, more sheltered and warmer.

The stable door was open, Emma entered and then nothing could have surprised her more as lying down next to him in the straw was the most beautiful silver coated donkey washing his face She stood for a moment in her tracks just able to mutter.

'Oh, you are so beautiful.'

Just then Maria came up beside her.

'That's Pippo's wife. She only arrived the other day. We have to give her a name, perhaps you could think of one.'

Emma thought that by the look of it they were already in love! Emma threw her arms around Maria's neck and gave her a kiss.

'Yes, thank you. I will think of a name. A beautiful name.'

Maria thanked God, maybe now with something to love and bring her back to life everything would be alright in time.

After a few months had passed Emma began to feel unwell. She noticed she had got a little fat, thinking it was the pasta and Maria's cooking that were to blame, until she started to feel nausea in the morning. This all seemed to coincide with other symptoms. Her monthly cycle had stopped and the awful truth became apparent that she was pregnant. She cried herself to sleep that night and asked her Maker: 'Will I never be free of this horrible creature? What am I to do?'

She knew now that she had to tell Maria and Joe: there was no way that she could hide the truth.

At first they were shocked and then Maria, cuddling her, said: 'Listen darlin', we going to have a baby in the house.'

Looking at things from the positive perspective, for Emma there were none. Maria tried to help her accept the reality that it was not the baby's fault; but even Maria's acceptance of the situation did not help. Emma was still distraught and the thought of having Robert's baby horrified her.

Dreadful thoughts kept running through her mind, which she sometimes felt were evil. Perhaps if she threw herself down the stairs or took some strange concoction known to the local women, she could abort it. Once again the whole episode came back to haunt her and ruin her life, she suspected for ever.

These horrible thoughts still invaded her mind until the sheer exhaustion of trying to forget made her feel sure she would never be able to put the past behind her. If it hadn't been for Maria and Joe she knew she couldn't go on. But, as with everything in life, time began to change the depth of the pain inside her and she realized that she had to accept although may never be able to forget.

Gradually, from somewhere, she found the courage to busy herself as much as possible, and, with the love and affection she received from Maria and Joe, she found the strength she never thought would be possible.

She was nearly three months pregnant and began to show the presence of the new life within her. In fact Emma was surprised just how obvious her pregnancy showed. She even began to be curious about the baby's sex: would it be a boy or a girl? Maria was sure it was a girl.

Emma was surprised. Although Maria had never had a child, she seemed endowed with considerable knowledge about the way different positions showed the way boys and girls were carried.

She would smile and say 'We have to think about names. I am sure he or she will be beautiful like you. Emma.'

'Will it be an Italian name?' she said, smiling.

'We can think of some beautiful names darlin'' said Maria, eager to get

Emma thinking positively. She tried to be more cheerful and found herself beginning to remember all the lovely Italian names she had heard.

Then reality returned and the thought that it could be a boy, brought back the fears that had never really left her. Maria would quietly remind her that this little life growing inside her was an innocent baby and one that carried the Villarni genes. 'Just forget about its father,' she would say. In fact Maria's enthusiasm made Emma laugh a lot and did help to take her mind off the reality of the situation.

CHAPTER 15

Paolo

Rome was stiflingly hot in August, as usual, and Paolo looked forward to the break when the city closed down. He could take the whole month to go home and enjoy the cooler breeze of the Mediterranean and the hills that gave some relief from the heat. He would call in at his sister Gabriella and her husband Dimitrio and collect his old car, which was for driving to their house in the hills, and enjoying visiting friends and family. He looked forward to passing the time swimming, eating and glorying in the beauty of the terrain. His thoughts turned to Emma and the last time he had enjoyed their holiday together.

Spending time with Emma he had found himself becoming totally infatuated or maybe much more. Could he dare to admit, even to himself, that he was falling in love with her? She was always friendly. They laughed a lot together and she seemed to enjoy his company, but he did not dare to give her any indication of what was in his heart.

He would visit Joe and Maria and maybe they would know if Carlo could get away again and visit them.

He was doing well in the partnership Fratelli Donati Studio Legali, which seemed to have been the mainstay not only the Villarni family, but its relatives for several generations.

He had progressed faster than he could have imagined. This was helped by the eldest partner having health problems. The workload had necessitated assistance to deal with their many clients. Paolo was ambitious and determined to get ahead. This opportunity had suddenly given his position a boost. His one concern was that the Donatis seemed to be a little too well connected to the political leaders who seemed to becoming more and more powerful. Mussolini was changing the political arena beyond recognition and not to everyone's liking. Paolo was no Fascist and kept his views to himself. However, there was always the risk that he might be asked to participate in some political activity and this worried him considerably. He was not happy to see his beloved Italy changing in a way that was not, in his opinion, for the good. Of course the poor were still poor, and the richer were even richer, but to see uniforms and marching in the streets was not his idea of progress. At least, here in the south away from the city, life still went on with a slower pace and politics seemed to have passed these sleepy villages by. He knew that Mussolini and his cronies were not a popular item on their menu!

He also planned to spend a few days with his sister Gabriella and her husband Dimitrio. They had a reasonable lifestyle considering any reasonable income was fortunate in these times,. Their wine distribution business had provided a better standard of living than most: the wine from the popular Villarni estate was considered to be excellent.

He and his sister had inherited their old farm house from their parents. It was in the hills above their village, not far from Monte Verde. They would go there when opportunity allowed, particularly in the hottest months of the summer, at weekends.

Dimitrio was a good handyman and did a fine job keeping the house clean and habitable. Gradually, when they could afford to do so with Paolo's help, they would modernise it step by step.

They kept his old car in good condition and found it invaluable for escaping to the beauty of the countryside, and their precious retreat, when they could. Paolo loved the opportunity to spend his holiday time there and did his share of the jobs that were needed. He found this enjoyable after spending his time in an office.

After an affectionate few days with them, he headed off to Santa Alina, the name of their house. It was close to the road which rose sharply up the mountain and before long it came into view.

Every time Paolo came back fond memories flooded his heart with happiness at the recollection of his childhood with his parents and sister. He sighed. Although they did not have much money, they somehow managed one way or another, and he and Gaby never went without anything. He knew now that it was Carlo who had been giving a helping hand with his education and the introduction to the Donati brothers' law firm.

He decided the next day he would go and visit his aunt Maria and uncle Joe. The Villa Rosa was only a kilometre or so higher in the hills above the village of Monte Verde and he could hardly wait to hear all the news. Of course he was hoping that Carlo would bring Flora and Emma back for another holiday, but he had heard that Flora was not so well. Also the political situation might not be ideal. This was something that he sensed with a kind of foreboding, which was now becoming a concern.

He pulled up at the side of the Villa Rosa and stepped out of the car. As he closed the door he looked up and saw a figure of a woman, who seemed to be hurrying through the side door to the house. No, it couldn't be…but it looked like Emma. Paolo hurried, almost running, after her; had she seen him, was she playing a joke and hiding, later to jump out on him? He smiled to himself; how wonderful if they had planned a surprise.

He ran into the kitchen, but it was empty, no one there. He laughed to himself; she must be hiding-and everyone must be in on it. Maria suddenly appeared and greeted him. Somehow she seemed nervous as she kissed and cuddled him with words of delight and affection as always. But there was something not quite the same in her greeting, almost a holding back from her usual exuberance.

He said: 'Alright, where is Emma and everyone? They can all come out now.'

Maria found it hard to respond. In fact she seemed speechless and bit her lip. He started to ask her questions; he now realized something was not right and at that moment he stopped in his tracks.

Emma walked into the room. She had been next door and realized she could not leave Maria to deal with lying and pretending this was or wasn't a joke. The look on Emma's face was one of distress and he could see she was near to tears. He then noticed her shape, the bump now obvious, and he rushed toward her and took her in his arms.

'Emma,' but he couldn't find the words, he wanted so much to ask her what had happened, but just held her tight.

Maria got up from the chair she had needed to sit on, when everything became too much for her, and left the room. She knew instinctively they needed to be alone for Emma to explain or not. It was up to her to say what she felt was needed in this situation.

When at last Emma gained enough courage, she began to explain what had happened, without naming the culprit.

Paolo was in deep shock and unable to speak, his mind full of all sorts of things. Surely this was not Carlo's child she was carrying? He had always known in his heart that the feelings they had for each other went deep, but somehow he couldn't believe that this was anything to do with Carlo, but he could never be certain.

There was nothing that seemed to indicate anything untoward in their relationship and it had always seemed quite innocent and, at times, jokey. Paolo just could not believe that it was anything else. He knew Carlo was a man of principle. Surely he would never compromise the women in his life, or himself; but had he weakened and, in a moment, succumbed to the inevitable?

Emma looked at him and said: 'I know what you may be thinking'.

He took her hand and waited for her to speak; he didn't want to say the name.

She said: 'It wasn't Carlo. I was raped.' He gasped, unable to take in her words.

'My poor, dearest friend,' he said as he brought her closer into his arms. 'What are you going to do? Why did you come here? Flora and Carlo would have looked after you and never have let you leave.'

'Please, Paolo, you must never tell them I am here. They must never know,' she sobbed. 'Please, please promise me you won't tell them.'

Paolo didn't understand anything. He knew that of all the people in the world, they would never let her go. They loved her too much and, whatever the outcome, she would be cared for. It was a complete mystery, but he assured her that he would keep her secret.

'Emma what are you going to do? You can't hide away forever. 'Listen to me, marry me, I will look after you and the baby. You will not want for anything, we can live in Rome and no-one will know unless you wish it.'

She looked at him, unable to find the right words to tell him how much she appreciated his kindness.

'Oh Paolo you are the most wonderful man: a true friend. I could never have wished for such a friend and it's because I value your friendship so very much that I could not accept your offer. I would not make you happy and you would resent me and I couldn't stand losing you like that.'

He looked at her with tears that glistening in his eyes and said 'You still love him, don't you?'

She didn't answer for a moment, unable to find the right response. Then could only say 'Who?'

He replied softly 'Carlo.'

'Why did you say that?

He looked at her. 'The way you were together, the way your eyes lit up when he came into the room. When he saw you he came alive; all the teasing and bantering was a way to hide what was in both of your hearts. I know he would never bring shame or degrade you, Emma, or hurt Flora. Whatever has happened he would have looked after you.'

Emma kissed his cheek and said 'You are the most valued friend I could wish for. Whoever gets you as a husband will be a very lucky woman.'

She squeezed his hand and he kissed hers. Both of them found the moment difficult to deal with, their emotions too near the surface.

She could never tell him it was Robert. No one must know. The repercussions were too terrible to imagine.

They sat quietly and somehow got through the difficult moments. He didn't press her further, knowing that it was only in time that she would reveal the whole story, if circumstances made it necessary.

Now it was too painful and he desperately wanted to offer the comfort and kindness that he felt in his heart. He knew he was in love with her and, whatever had happened, she was here and maybe in time she would feel differently. He knew that she had suffered something so awful to run away from the people she cared for so deeply, and who cared for her.

Paolo was puzzled, trying to put the pieces together. He realized that the culprit must be someone known to Carlo and Flora, otherwise the obvious police procedures would have been carried out; but this seemed to be something that had to remain hidden from the truth. His thoughts were distracted as Maria now returned and offered them some home-made lemon cordial, believing that perhaps it might help to change the intensity of the situation and lighten the atmosphere. She hoped it would help Emma to take her mind off everything and, hopefully, that Paolo would help her achieve that.

Maria thought the world of her nephew and nothing would make her happier than if these two people found love together. It would be a happy ending to this sad story.

'Oh Mia Donna, I pray you will help them,' Maria said silently.

Paolo had to go to Naples to carry out some business for the law firm. There was talk of opening another branch of the business there and a possibility for him to transfer there, perhaps eventually becoming a junior partner, as his abilities were highly regarded.

He hoped this might happen. Nothing would please him more than to be close to his sister and her husband. If Emma was to be in Monte Verde, what could be better? He told her he would be back at the weekend and if she would like he would take her for a ride and show her some new places she had not seen before. She was not to worry, as no-one would know her. Maria was delighted, believing it would help to lift the dark cloud that hung over them. She said that it would be a good idea and she would prepare lunch or a picnic, whichever they preferred. This was a perfect opportunity for Emma to stop grieving and slowly find some peace and happiness again.

The next day Paolo left early and drove to the station, deciding to take the train as it was faster than driving and he could read the papers he was taking. He parked his car at the side entrance, ready for his return in a day or two. Normally, a few days in Naples were enjoyable and a chance to catch up with old friends after his day's work was ended. However, now his plan was to get through the necessary business as quickly as possible and get back to Monte Verde.

It still took three days as the paperwork and the necessary acceptance of the firm's business associates had to be done with professional caution. Paolo was prepared that a certain amount of socialising was required. As he was representing Fratelli Donati, these future business associates were to be given every encouragement to recognize the professional attitude of their representative, and particularly that of a possible new partner.

At last Paolo, satisfied that his mission had been accomplished, caught the train back to Sorrento. He knew he should really call in to see his sister Gaby, and decided to make a fleeting visit. He arrived at the station and headed outside to where he had parked his car. As he did so he heard raised voices coming from the other end of the street, where passengers were dropped off, or picked up, by the old taxis. There was always at least one that still eked a meagre living from those who needed transport.

Someone was shouting in Neapolitan dialect, another in English, with a bit of Italian thrown in. This attracted Paolo's attention. He could see two men were arguing about the fare. What took Paolo's attention was the younger man, whose poor knowledge of the Italian language was mixed with English expletives, and who looked uncannily familiar. He wasn't sure as it had been several years since he had seen this younger man. He looked slightly older than he remembered and yet he was becoming more and more certain that this was someone he knew. Yes. He was sure it was Roberto. His face was contorted with anger, which brought memories back to Paolo of the moody, unpleasant young man he remembered. Yes, it was Roberto.

He decided he was not going to intervene, although more than surprised at seeing him. He wondered what on earth he was doing here and had he been at Monte Verde? Millions of things were running through his head. He could not change his plans and follow and see where Roberto was headed. It seemed obvious to him that he was going to the train station, but Paolo could not spend time waiting for the outcome. Neither did he feel inclined to as he had to hurry if he was to pay a quick visit to his sister.

All he knew was that this did not seem to be a good omen and his head was trying to put some sense to what he had witnessed. It had left him puzzled.

He couldn't believe that Carlo would have sent his son here on business or for anything else: he knew well this father and son relationship was anything but close or trusting. He resisted the invitation to stay for dinner, much to Gaby's disappointment, but he promised that he would return another day soon and enjoy her cooking, which seemed to appease her disappointment. He drove the car up into the hills of Campania. Always awe-inspiring, the beauty and the scent of the herbs and flowers filled his senses and almost took his mind off the worrying incident he had just witnessed.

He stopped off at his house, needing to freshen up and change into a cool shirt and cotton trousers. Not forgetting a quick shave and a splash of cologne, he left business papers and his travelling bag in his makeshift office, got into his car, with a perfume he had bought for Emma, and headed up the mountain to Monte Verde.

CHAPTER SIXTEEN

Emma

Emma really enjoyed Paolo's company and she missed him already. He had helped her to regain some semblance of hope that she might be able to forget her terrible ordeal. She was only sorry that her feelings for him were only as a valued friend. She was not in love with him and never would be.

Yes, some might think that she should take the opportunity to marry a man who loved her so much that he would take on another man's child; make her respectable in the eyes of the world and give her a comfortable life. He was now on the road to being a successful lawyer and would be able to provide for her and her child in times when so many were poor and had nothing. She knew that he would try everything to make her happy, but she also knew she would not be able to give him back the happiness he deserved, and she would never be able to use him in that way.

She let her thoughts drift for a while as she sat in the garden contemplating everything. It was such a beautiful day; she tried to keep her thoughts on more positive things. A slight breeze swayed the trees.

She had learned that this sometimes meant that rain might come, but, at present she enjoyed the moment and returned to reading her book.

Her attention was suddenly directed to a figure walking towards her from the side of the house. Emma's heart froze.

'No, it couldn't be.' As the figure approached the dread in her heart caused her to feel faint. 'Oh God, no, please no.'

Emma cried out, 'Maria, Joe!' but they were nowhere that they could hear her.

The figure spoke 'Emma, please listen to me.'

Robert stopped a few feet away from her and seeing her stand up he could see she was pregnant. He could hardly believe what he was seeing, but knowing only too well that this must be with his child. He approached her, but she backed away, almost hysterical.

'Emma, please forgive me, I am sorry, marry me and I will make it up to you, I was jealous. I loved you, but I was too young and stupid to be able to deal with it, always thinking you were my father's mistress.'

She screamed at him, 'I don't care what you thought; you have ruined my life and your parents.' Go away, I should have killed you.'

Now unable to control herself she became so distraught that the screaming and crying brought Maria and Joe rushing into the garden.

Maria, now as distraught as Emma, was screaming 'bastardo, bastardo,' and other words that described her disgust and even hate for him.

Joe now faced him, full of anger that he could not control.

'Get out of here, never come back or I will get a gun and kill you,' he swore, comparing him to a piece of faeces. Robert, his eyes streaming, hurried away, they hoped for ever.

Emma now felt terrible, pains had begun to envelop her body, she could hardly breathe and then she fainted, fortunately landing on the grass. Everything was in a turmoil. Maria and Joe were afraid of what this had done to Emma. She was not the fainting kind and they immediately knew they had to call for help.

Paolo parked in the usual place at the side of the house, now so keen to see Emma and ask the inevitable question about the young man at the station. He gave a little knock at the kitchen door, the usual place he would find someone. But the kitchen was empty. He called politely in the hallway entrance, but there was no response.

Wondering where everyone could be, he ventured further into the house, where he could now hear voices coming from the floor above. He couldn't quite make out what was being said, but somehow he thought the voices were a mixture of female and male. There was unmistakenly a sob which he was sure was from Maria, and could no longer resist hurrying up the stairs.

The door to Emma's room was open and at a glance, he could see her lying in bed, with both Maria and Joe and a third man attending her. He knocked gently at the door, they all turned towards him.

He said 'Oh Zia, Zio forgive me, I could not help over-hearing. What's happened?'

He could hardly hold back the fear in his heart. Maria took his arm. 'She has lost the baby,' she said sobbing uncontrollably.

Joe stood looking rather helpless, trying to comfort her. It was obvious the other man was the doctor from Avellino. Paolo had seen him once before and remembered his name was Dottore Mezzini.

He spoke, addressing them all, but with a particular look at Paolo.

'Let her rest. I have given her some medication and a sedative, sleep will help. Emotional shock may have been to blame or stress of some kind.'

Looking over the rim of his glasses and, now observing Paolo's deep concern, he continued. 'She is a strong healthy young woman and she should be fine. She must stay in bed for a few days and keep off her feet and do nothing strenuous. I will ask Signora Pallini, the midwife, to call every day.'

With that he placed some bottles of medicine on the side table, put on his hat and patting Paolo on the shoulder said, with a smile, 'She will be fine.'

Paolo, by this time had leaned over the semi-conscious Emma and was holding her hand to his lips. The doctor departed.

Maria and Joe, somewhat surprised, could not help smiling, realising that Dr Mezzini, on witnessing this demonstration of concern and affection, had obviously taken it for granted that Paolo was the man in her life and maybe a lover's spat had something to do with it.

Physically, Emma recovered very well and within a week or two seemed to be feeling a lot better, but mentally the shock of seeing Robert again, here in Monte Verde, was something that she had found hard to come to terms with. How did he find her and did Carlo and Flora know what happened? Had he gone home? Somehow Emma didn't think he had. Surely Lottie would have told her. There had been rumours and, from what Lottie had said, it seemed that he never did go back home; too afraid of the truth coming out.

Lottie had been a provider of news she received when in London, although Emma often wondered if everything had been censored by her to prevent further distress. She would visit Emma whenever she could, as she and William had always made time to come to Monte Verde when time allowed.

Lottie tried hard to keep anything unpleasant from Emma; her excuse was that they only had time for fleeting meetings with Carlo and Flora, and avoided what was only to plain to see; the gradual deterioration in Flora's health. She did mention that Flora's sister had come to stay and was looking after her until they found a suitable companion, most likely with nursing experience, always avoiding discussing Emma's sudden departure. Lottie could see that even mentioning Carlo and Flora would bring tears to her eyes, and she would change the subject as diplomatically as she could.

The month of August flew by so quickly that Emma knew Paolo would have to return to Rome and, although she was not in love with him, she had begun to depend on his friendship and, in many ways wished she could feel differently. But it wasn't there and she knew there was only room for one: for the man so deeply entrenched in her heart, and who she could never forget.

One thing that might bring Paolo back to Campania sooner than later, was the news that the new office in Naples seemed to be looking positive. Also there was another option, with Sorrento becoming another possibility, which for Paolo, was even better.

He was also likely to be offered the post of a junior partner as he was so well thought of by the brothers Donati.

So, when it came to their last dinner before leaving, which had been prepared with all his favourite dishes by Maria, it was with a slight sadness for them all. When the evening was over Paolo promised Emma that, if he had any say in it, he would definitely take up the opportunity to work in the Sorrento office.

He would then be able to see her often, possibly every weekend, and maybe she would enjoy the big city, where she had a fleeting visit when they were all here on holiday two years before.

He had never given up the hope that, with time, perhaps Emma would begin to feel something deeper than friendship. He now loved her more than ever. He wanted to protect her and be there for her always. Obviously, he would do his best to provide for her and help her to forget Carlo and the past, and was certain he could make her happy.

The months flew by and life went on very much the same in the mountains of Campania. When the grape harvest came it was a time of celebration, as was the picking of the olives.

Emma by then had recovered her strength and participated in the harvesting. She found treading the grapes in the large vats amazingly enjoyable. They laughed and sang and Emma found herself feeling the squishy red liquid under her feet very liberating.

In the evening they were exhausted and hungry. After a hearty dinner of homemade pasta, and a few glasses of last year's wine, they went to their beds, sleeping well, and looking forward to the next day. The physical activity had helped Emma to forget things for a while, anyway.

The political situation had not affected them here, but there was a certain amount of concern in the country. They were always anxious to hear the news; Emma, in particular, worried about Carlo. Perhaps no news was good news as she tried to keep busy with the many pastimes she had learned from Maria, an expert knitter, who also made beautiful lace work that she never had the time for in London.

When the colder weather arrived the house was warmed with wood from the trees that thickly covered the hills all around them. It had been collected and left to dry during the summer months and now filled the whole house with cosy comfort.

The only thing that was beginning to cause some concern was the news that the political situation in big cities like Milan and Rome was becoming worrying.

Paolo had come back several times to prepare the new office and he gave them news of how things had changed, with the Blackshirts marching in the streets and broadcasts from Mussolini. He also told them about the role Italy was taking in the world arena.

Emma was glad that she was here in Monte Verde, which seemed a world away from what was going on in the cities. Paolo did not reveal how concerned he was with the already growing threat to England and Mussolini's dithering between whose alliance he would choose: Churchill or Hitler.

He was glad that he was soon to be in the south, which he felt would be less caught up with politics. This was more obvious in Rome where there was an atmosphere that was hard to define; where the pro-Mussolini faction was convinced that all his promises would bring about new beginnings for Italy. The hope of a better life with more opportunities and more affluence: a nation that had a future that was good for everyone.

Paolo wondered whether this would extend to the poor south. He kept his doubts and his opinions to himself as he already realized that it was a wise man who did not voice opinions when they could have serious repercussions..

News was sometimes slow, but not the bad news that England had declared war on Germany. It was 3rd September 1939 and suddenly everything seemed to be put on hold. Not all the day-to-day things, as they had to be attended to. Harvesting the fruit was always enjoyable and always a good reason to celebrate. Nevertheless, the news seemed to overshadow the usual gaiety of the occasion.

The years Maria and Joe had spent in England were precious; Emma feared the unknown repercussions on Carlo, Lottie and William. What was going to happen to everyone? Her heart began to ache again with the worry.

The winter had seemed long, but now Emma and Paolo saw quite a lot of each other and although, as far as he was concerned, nothing more had developed romantically between them, he was a patient man. Just being with her, when the opportunity arose, was something that he looked forward to; so it was for Emma.

It seemed that the best information they could obtain regarding the war was on the wireless, as they were sometimes able to tune into the BBC. But Emma had begun to ply more detailed information from Paolo on what was happening with the war and its effect on England. He always seemed well-informed of the situation: his office was kept up to date by the senior partners in Rome.

She could always rely on him to cheer her up. She was sure that he avoided anything that might upset her, which of course he did.

They always laughed a lot and both Maria and Joe were happy that, in this worrying time, they avoided showing the fears that were under the surface for everyone. Always trying to put on a smile, while saying 'Que sera, sera,' 'what will be, will be.'

When spring came, they had a lot to do and Emma enjoyed in occupying herself in the work for the preparation of the food they grew. Also the vines and the olive trees, particularly the old tree on the promontory, which she visited quite often. She hugged that tree and talked to it, telling it how much she loved it, and how much she knew Carlo loved it. She was sure it understood and absorbed the love she gave, because it seemed to thrive, grow stronger, and taller and produce its fruit in abundance.

She went at the same time everyday when the weather was fine, to watch the sunset. She remembered the time when she and Carlo had become so close. The memories were so sweet, yet so sad. When the pain became too much she would hurry back to the house and put the memory into the place in her heart, where it would stay for ever. Now added to her worries was what the effect of the war was having on London.

The day came when Emma could hardly believe she had been at Monte Verde for over a year and a half. It seemed a lifetime, yet it was more like yesterday when she recalled so much of the past. She wanted to know about Flora and, of course, Carlo. In some ways she hated thinking as everything then came back to haunt her, making the pain in her heart excruciating. She tried to move her thoughts on to more positive things. How lucky she was to have wonderful people like Maria, Joe, and Paolo, who had helped her through so much. Then the day came that brought heartache again back into her life.

A letter had come and Maria was in the kitchen with tears in her eyes. She had tried to hide her face from Emma as she entered the room, but Emma knew that something had happened to cause her distress. Something Maria was having difficulty hiding. Emma put her arms around her and held her close. She waited, not saying anything. She had an awful feeling that the letter she held in her hand had bad news, and was the reason for the tears that Maria could not hide.

Emma gently guided her to a chair and said softly: 'What is it Maria? Don't be afraid to tell me, is it bad news?'

Maria knew she had to tell Emma, but was unable to because the tears were falling down her cheeks. Emma hugged her tight and began to dread what it was that had caused this lovely, warm, kind woman so much difficulty in coming out with an explanation. Emma had a feeling it was because the news would affect her.

'Please tell me, is it Carlo?'

'No', hesitated Maria, 'it's Flora. She has died.' Emma broke down and the pair of them hugged each other as the tears flowed.

CHAPTER SEVENTEEN

May 1940

The funeral over. Friends and family gathered at the hotel where Carlo had arranged for the wake to be held. It was the usual custom to hold the wake at the house, but it was something he could not face. Neither could he bear to stay long and make polite conversation. He excused himself as quickly as was possible. He was empty inside: everything that had been meaningful in his life had gone. He needed to be alone and drown his sorrows in the only way he could think of.

He sat in his study. The whisky bottle nearly empty on the desk in front of him. Rosa was not much comfort as she was hardly able to talk sense while crying and sobbing. Carlo told her to go and rest and not to bother with preparing dinner for him, as he was not hungry. He just wanted oblivion and not to have to think. The only way he was able to achieve this was to drown the pain in whisky.

He went into the library and sat in his favourite armchair, wanting desperately to close his eyes, when the doorbell rang. There was no way he would answer it. Whoever was there was very persistent and rang the bell again and again. At last Rosa answered the door. Carlo heard mumbling of voices outside the room, and then the door opened.

It was Lottie. She said nothing, but quietly came towards him. He had not even said goodbye to her and William and, for that, he would apologise later. He had merely excused himself and left. Lottie placed her arm around his shoulder.

'Carlo, I know this is a difficult moment to intrude on your grief, but I have something here that I must give to you.' He didn't look up and Lottie was not sure if he had taken in her words. She bent down and touched his shoulder hoping she could reach him.

'It's very important, Carlo, please let me do what I promised.'

He was hardly taking in the words. He shook his head trying to make sense of what Lottie was saying.

'Forgive me, Lottie, let me just try to think straight.'

'Carlo, there are some letters here that Flora entrusted me to give you after…' She hesitated. 'She wanted you to read them in the order they are in. They will explain everything. Read them while you are alone and after, when you are ready, you know where we live.'

His mind, still fuzzy, was wondering when and why had Flora given her letters to open after she was gone.

She bent down, kissed his forehead and walked back to the door, with one further glance at Carlo's puzzled expression. She somehow knew that, after the pain of today, the contents of the letters would first give him more heartache but, after reading them they might help to make him want to live again.

Determined to sober up, he went to the little closet off his study and splashed his face with water, hoping the coldness would help him regain some semblance of sobriety. He sat down at his desk and opened the large envelope that Lottie had given him. The first letter was marked one. He opened it and began to read.

My Darling Carlo,

You have been the most wonderful husband any woman could have wished for; you have been kind, generous, never complaining that I have not been able to be the healthy wife that a man needs. Your compassion and understanding are such that my love for you has made me try to avoid bringing you more pain. Therefore, when you read this letter, I hope you will understand why I kept the contents from you. I knew it would only give you more heartache, a dilemma that would make things worse at a time when nothing would have been achieved by adding to the already heavy burden you carry.

I know where Emma is. When you read the next letter everything will be made clear about why she left. It was for our happiness, Carlo. She sacrificed her happiness for us, even though she knew it was not easy for us not to know the reason, but it was better than the truth.

Go to her Carlo. She is in Italy with Maria and Joe. I know if there is one person in this world who will help you to find happiness again, it's her. You have my blessing my darling. Your loving wife.

Flora

Carlo put the letter down; he could no longer read any more as his eyes were flooded with tears. He wiped them away, now anxious to be able to read the other two letters. The next envelope was marked 'two'. He opened it and he began to read:

Dear Mother and Father

If you are reading this letter it's because I am no longer on this earth. I was the reason Emma ran away. I returned to the house when father was away with you in Devon. I was drunk and came back to the house, which was empty. I went to my room and after a while I heard Emma returning home. She went to her room and I heard her run a bath and I hid in the corner of her bedroom. When she came out I raped her. I didn't mean to force her; I thought I could make her want me instead of my father. I thought she was father's mistress, but I was so wrong! I realised too late she was a virgin. She fought me and stabbed me with scissors and I thought she was going to kill me. She managed to drive me away, and I knew then I could never come home again.

By chance I met one of the boys from the village near Monte Verde who mentioned there was a woman staying at the Villa Rosa. She had beautiful blue eyes and a foreign accent, and was helping with the grape harvest. I immediately went to Italy and found her there with Maria and Joe. She was pregnant with my child and I begged her to marry me, but she screamed abuse at me and I had to leave. I heard that she was so distressed she lost the baby. I wanted to die, there was nothing left for me and I knew I could never return. So I joined the army and left this letter in my kit, as many men do, to be sent to their family if they are killed. I could not go to my Maker without telling you the truth. I know you will never be able to forgive me, but I still pray that you can.

Your loving son Roberto.

The third envelope was a telegram and a letter. The first containing a very simple message. It read as follows:

It is my painful duty to inform you that a report has been received from the War Office notifying the death of Captain Robert Villarni, which occurred on the 12 May 1940 on the battlefield whilst defending his men.

I am to express the sympathy and regret of the Army Council. Signed by the Officer in Charge of Records.

The other letter in this envelope was from his commanding officer. It was a letter of condolence, which said that it had been recommended that Captain Robert Villarni be awarded the Distinguished Service Order for bravery in defending his men in the line of duty.

It was signed by Lt Colonel Jonathan Mainwright.

Carlo placed his head in his hands. He was drained of everything and only able to sob until there was not a tear left in him. Now exhausted, physically and mentally, he fell asleep for several hours.

It was dusk when he awoke but he was still unable to absorb everything that he had read. Finally, slowly, everything began to sink in, but it took several hours before he began to formulate what he must do.

He decided he had to see Lottie and William, if they were available, because he needed to know so much more. He had to get over today, and his wife's funeral and yet she had left him a message from beyond the grave.

She had told him to go to Emma. Perhaps she had some foresight that he may need help. No longer able to rest, or leave things for another day, he decided that it would be better not to waste time just thinking, but to go and see William whilst he could. Carlo was aware his reason for being in London was the meetings with the Prime Minister and the War Cabinet.

William had not even been able to confide his fears to Lottie, but had made her return to England for the time being, as things were so uncertain. If they went badly the last thing he wanted was to have to worry about getting her home safely. It would be his responsibility to organise the exit plans for the embassy staff and their safe evacuation. That would be enough to keep him busy.

Lottie, although not knowing everything about the political situation and how precarious things were, was aware of the uncertainty.

This made her have concerns about Emma, who would not have the opportunity to know just how dangerous things might turn out to be. She knew, without even asking, that William would do everything he could to help Carlo. He would have to warn him that to go to Italy now would have real dangers.

They had for many years been close friends and William was aware that Carlo held dual nationality. This meant that when he was in England he was subject to British laws. When in Italy the same criteria applied, and he would be treated as an Italian citizen.

Conscription had been in force since the First World War, and every man and boy who could walk would be in danger of being packed off to a unit somewhere, or even worse, in Carlo's case, be arrested as a spy.

Carlo now made the effort to freshen himself and called to Rosa to make some strong black coffee, and, yes, a piece of her chocolate cake to give him some energy. She brightened up immediately; so glad to see him better and seemingly with a purpose, as he had changed his clothes to something less formal than the black suit.

After the coffee and cake he headed off on foot to the Cavanaughs which was only a ten minute walk away. He knew the exercise would be good for him. The evening was quite warm for late May, and it was a good opportunity to help clear his head. It was obvious they were expecting him and, with warm greetings, ushered him into their favourite room, which also happened to be their library.

The house was magnificent and had been in the family for generations. Lottie had brought a few up-to-date things and he wondered where she had acquired the art of interior design. It was tasteful with just the right amount of art and objects d'art. The address at Cheyne Walk had always been regarded as one of the best in London, and Lottie had done it proud.

Carlo declined a drink, saying he was still recovering from his over-indulgence of earlier. They sat down on the comfortable soft chairs and William began to address the situation.

'Well, my friend, I expect you want to go to Italy, but before you answer I have to go into certain facts. As you know, I am not at liberty to go into details of the government's plans. However, what I can tell you is we are in uncertain waters and, as things stand at the moment, if you were to enter Italy as Carlo Villarni it would be extremely dangerous. Your family name is well-known and, as an Italian who has spent most of his life in England, you could be interned and, at worst, suspected of being a spy.'

'I know the dangers,' Carlo replied. William leaving Carlo in no doubt that what he guessed he was about to undertake, continued:. 'On the other hand you could immediately be enscripted to the army, which would not help Emma. The other factor is that if Mussolini goes with Hitler and war is declared between England and Italy, all hell will break loose and you both could be in danger. The next difficulty is now we are at war with Germany, getting back to England is not easy and I cannot say how or what the best way would be at this time.'

'Of course, whichever way things go, there are people who will do what they can to get you home. However, I will be truthful, Carlo. I know if I was in your shoes and it was Lottie, I would also risk everything to get her home.'

William stood up, went to Carlo and put his arm around his shoulders and smiled.

'Well?' William asked.

Carlo, smiling, replied: 'You know my answer.'

'Well, then, there is no way you can go rushing off without what I hope to be able to do. You must have some papers in a different name, and also for Emma.

'It will take a day or two, but I have the connections and will arrange it. I also think I can get you out to Italy but, if things hit the fan, I cannot hope to get you out the way we came in, because it will be a sudden departure and all hands on the wheel so to speak! However, there are already some connections we have who will try to help. This is not anything I can guarantee now, but you will know when the time comes.'

'How can I ever thank you enough?' said Carlo. 'I hope this is not compromising you in any way.'

William smiled. 'You know that old saying, 'it's who you know, not what you know. I may have to convince the powers that be that you are doing a little work for the British government, being fluent in both languages and having a mother who is the daughter of Lord Davenport. You know how the old school tie works?'

'Plus of course, I will add that I have known you for twenty years and you went to Oxford.'

They both laughed began to devise a plan on how to get things moving.

Carlo turned to Lottie: 'May I ask you something? Did you know what was in the letters?'

'Yes, Carlo, Flora thought I should know how important it was for you to know the truth and to have the information that was in them.

'It was also in case, for any reason, they did not reach you, I would be able to tell you myself. Please forgive me, Carlo, but if you had known the truth earlier, Emma's sacrifice would have been for nothing.'

He took Lottie in his arms and hugged her unable to speak for a moment or two. With difficulty in controlling the emotion he felt, he looked at William and said: 'May I kiss your wife? How can I ever thank her for her integrity and strength in keeping the promise she made to Emma?'

William nodded, smiling, as Carlo kissed Lottie's cheek. She stood back from him and said: 'You look after my god-daughter'

Carlo replied: 'With my life.'

He turned back, as he had one more question and hesitated for a 'Has she found...?' But he did not have time to complete the sentence because Lottie replied 'No, just a very good friend, there is only one man in her heart and he is here in front of me.'

Carlo now regained some resolve that, come what may, he must go to Italy. He could only think of getting to Emma and bringing her home. Somehow he got through the next few days while William used every possible route to the connections he knew to enable him to acquire the correct and vital paperwork. It was also necessary to get papers for Emma. She would be safer as an Italian citizen.

On arriving back at the house he was a different person. Rosa had been waiting for his return, anxious as always for his wellbeing, particularly since the awful events that had consumed his life seemed to come and one after another. But the moment that Carlo came through the door that evening, he was a different man.

He smiled at her and said: 'Rosa, get my small satchel travel bag ready and pack two changes of clothes for warm weather.'

She looked at him with surprise, but did as he asked, sure that she would know his plans at some point. Being astute, she already suspected that if he was going somewhere warm and his whole demeanour was so cheerful that the destination was not difficult to guess. Now concerned about feeding him, she knew the answer to help him get back to his old self was his favourite: Lasagne!

CHAPTER EIGHTEEN

Destiny

It was two days later that William called Carlo and said that he had the necessary documents and that they should meet and discuss everything down to the last detail. He had achieved far more than he at first thought possible. He had a passport and other papers for Carlo in the name of Vincenzo Travinni and for Emma, as his wife.

William had managed to get Carlo on board the diplomatic plane carrying them both to Rome, where William was due to return. He had convinced 'the powers that be' that Carlo's role was to be an undercover special envoy to gather information on the situation in the south of Italy; to find who the people to know were and who to avoid in the region. Being able to speak the language and knowing the region was invaluable and, with such a good recommendation from William, everything was arranged.

He had already made arrangements for Carlo to get to Monte Verde, but from there he would be on his own and, depending on the situation regarding Mussolini's plans, he may have to find his own way back. Nevertheless, there were certain contingency plans that he could rely on to help him, with contacts who would be as helpful as possible.

Carlo had to memorise these as nothing could be written down in case of being caught. He understood his situation might become precarious, but with his knowledge of the area, the people and the possible dangers he was determined to carry out his mission.

Within hours William phoned and asked Carlo to be ready to leave the next morning. Davis would collect him and they would travel together to the private airport used by diplomats.

It was later in the afternoon when they arrived in Rome and were collected from the airport by the embassy chauffeur and driven into the city. It was decided that Carlo should be dropped off in a quiet street near the station, as it should be less likely that he would be noticed, and could avoid being seen leaving the embassy.

Carlo knew that now he was on his own and thanked God that he had changed into the discreet clothing that made him look like any other local Italian man of indiscriminate appearance, going south. He could speak the Neapolitan dialect like a native and from now he would become Vincenzo Travinni.

The journey was long and changes had to be made onto the special train that went via Vesuvius. When at last he arrived in Sorrento he was to be met and taken on to Monte Verde and the Villa Rosa. He was to wait after alighting from the train and sit on the bench outside the station entrance until a man approached who would greet him by his new name.

He had fallen asleep on the last leg of the journey. There had been so much that had happened and sleep had been hard to achieve; but the chugging of the train had at last brought him to the point where his overtired mind and body had surrendered to the oblivion of sleep.

This uncertain state of unconsciousness brought vivid dreams so confusing and unpleasant, that waking up was a relief.

He now had to face the ordeal of the unknown, beginning with meeting this stranger who was to take him on the next leg, which for him would be the most important part of his journey.

He arrived in the station and pondered on what the man who was to meet him would look like. It was a matter of minutes before all was to be revealed. A young man approached him and said: 'Vincenzo, mio amico, come sta!'

Carlo was taken aback and almost unable to respond. The last person he expected to be the person to meet him was Paolo, who immediately hugged him and, taking his bag with an arm around his shoulders, they walked to a car parked a few yards away. Meantime, Paolo began talking to him in dialect, to which Carlo replied. Paolo indicated to wait until they reached the car to begin their conversation when he would explain everything to Carlo. They drove out of the city and onto the coast road.

Paolo said: 'I know you have much to ask me, Carlo, and I have much to tell you before we reach Emma.' He paused, 'I suggest we stop briefly at my house where you can freshen up and I will fill you in with everything you want to know.'

He smiled as he added: 'Everything is fine, Emma knows nothing.'

Carlo waited until they were in the car when he said quietly: 'Who is the person I have to thank for you to be the one to meet me?

Paolo smiled and whispered, 'Lottie.'

Of course, he should have known that Lottie knew everything. Who else would Emma have gone to in her hour of need? Who else could have got her to the other people who loved her and that she loved in return, and to receive the help that she needed so badly?'

Lottie had always been recognised as a brilliant actress. She had been able to pull off the transformation of a young cockney maid to become Lady Cavanaugh, which would have been impossible for most people, and something that he could never have envisaged. Yet she had done so, and, with the love for her godchild, had been able to hide the truth so convincingly.

Carlo had forgotten that the deep love she held for her best friend's child was so strong. He believed she would put her life on the line for Emma, as would he.

She had no choice but to pretend she knew nothing of Emma's whereabouts and he didn't blame her, as he respected her loyalty. If he had known the truth, nothing but disaster for all would have been achieved and Emma's sacrifice would have been for nothing.

They spoke when they got into the car: for Carlo there was so much to catch up on. 'What is London like now? Paolo asked.

He had heard about the bombing and wanted to know how the people were coping. He told Carlo that he was compelled to be involved with the Fascists. The reason that was he had to choose between being drafted into the army, unable to do anything to help the resistance, of which he was a member, or to appear to be part of the regime. If possible he would not be required to be involved actively, as this would mean leaving the Donati brothers without their much-needed junior partner in Sorrento. This proved to be the best bit of luck that could have happened, as he was just to be on the inside and hopefully have access to crucial information for the allies. He hoped that he would be able to pass on anything relevant to the growing resistance movement on the anti-fascists who were now on his own doorstep.

He explained to Carlo that there was already a small band of these groups in the area, and that they would be very helpful to all, when the time came.

'While I have to play along, fortunately the Donati's do not want to lose their new young partner. They make sure I am employed in very low-profile activities with the black shirts.' he grinned.

Carlo smiled at him. 'Try to keep it that way or we may have to kidnap you and take you with us.'

They arrived at Paolo's house. Although Carlo was very anxious to get to the Villa Rosa and see Emma, he knew he needed to hear what Paolo deemed necessary for him to know, and also to have a change of clothes from the few he had in his satchel. The weather was still hot for the time of year. He felt the heat, as it had been some time since he had been in Italy.

Paolo offered him a drink of fruit juice, which was very much appreciated, but not, however, without him asking 'Nothing stronger I suppose?' Paolo smiled. 'Later my friend,' Carlo replied as he changed his clothes. Then they sat down and Paolo explained much of what he was anxious to know.

He said: 'I never told Emma I knew who the person was, and why she had run away. When I saw Robert at the station, it all just seemed to add up, and, when she had the miscarriage, then I knew for sure. One day I arrived to visit Emma and Lottie was there. Obviously it was a little awkward, but I told her not to worry as I had promised I would never reveal where Emma was. When I knew that it was Robert, I understood everything and my heart ached for her. I told her a long time ago I would always be her friend and I had the opportunity to prove it, even though she told me she didn't love me in the way that would make me happy. She said I would resent her and she would lose a very valued friend. What could I do? I then accepted defeat Carlo, and now I will prove it and help you both to get back to England.'

Carlo hesitated a second, he knew how much he owed Paolo, who was in love with Emma but respected her and her honesty. He hugged the young man and, trying hard to hide the emotion so near the surface, thanked him several times.

Paolo said: 'You are a lucky man Carlo, to have a woman love you so much that she would give up everything for you and Flora's happiness.'

Carlo replied: 'I will spend the rest of my life trying to make up for it. Now we must go, I cannot wait to see her.'

They finished discussing everything that Paolo thought was necessary at this time, and he promised to set to work on looking into all possibilities of what would be the best and safest route for their departure. One thing that did concern Carlo was that they were making all these plans without knowing what Emma wanted. Carlo prayed that Lottie was right and that she would want to leave with him. What if she felt that she wanted to stay with Maria and Joe?

Well, it was no good worrying about that now. He would know soon enough.

They set off up the mountains and parked the car near the house. Paolo got out of the car and said: 'Go in. It's your moment to speak to her.'

Carlo nodded his head and entered through the kitchen door at the back of the house. It was the way that everyone who was family or friend entered. Maria, as usual, was busy preparing food for their dinner. Glancing up and nearly dropping the plate she was holding, she crossed herself and mumbled 'Carlo, Carlo!'

She could not find more words: the surprise and happiness overwhelming her. She wanted to ask him how he had got there and so many other things. He hugged her and, no longer able to think of anything other than seeing Emma, he dropped his bag and asked the tearful Maria to unpack it for him.

He asked: 'Where is she?' Maria, still struggling to speak, whispered 'At the olive tree, it's nearly sun-set; you know how she loves it there.'

He gave her a kiss on her cheek and left her with tears of joy in her eyes. He rushed through the door into the pathway outside as Paolo began to walk toward the house. He looked at Carlo with a questioning look that didn't really need answering.

Carlo smiled and said: 'At the Olive Tree.' Paolo nodded and walked towards the house.

Carlo walked quickly through the olive grove, his heart pounding, and at last he stopped close to the tree. She was sitting on the bench that his father had built and where his mother had brought him so many years before, when he was a child. He recalled what now seemed so long ago, when he and Emma had sat together, and the moment he realised that she meant so much to him. In her, he had found his soul mate who had given him joy and laughter, whose empathy and compassion had brought Flora the help and love of a rare kind, even between sisters.

He stood looking at her for a minute before she glanced towards him and then stood up. She was unable to speak and for a moment she had a look of disbelief on her face. Then the reality brought the tears that were beyond her control. He walked to where she stood and took her in his arms and said as gently as he could: 'Emma, I know, and I love you.'

He pulled her even tighter into his arms and whispered, 'Is it too late?'

She looked at him. 'Never too late...'

He took her face in his hands and said: 'My darling Emma, let me wipe those tears away.'

He then realised he did not have anything to use, and she saw that he had forgotten he had no jacket or pockets. She put her hand in her skirt pocket and pulled out the red kerchief.

He smiled, took it and gently dried the tears.

'You still have it.' She nodded and he kissed her lips and she returned his kisses with the unsuppressed passion that had never been possible before.

They stood awhile drinking in the moment that had been so long awaited, but he knew he had to find the words to explain everything and how he had found her.

Emma spoke first. 'When I heard Flora had died, I felt so guilty, Carlo. Who would care for her? Was it my fault that she had deteriorated?'

'No Emma, there is a lot I must tell you. I know how close you were to Flora; you know she loved you as you did her, but now I know why you went away, you did it for us, at first I thought it was ...' He hesitated for a second and added, 'because of me, that last night.'

She could see how guilty he must have felt as he looked into her eyes. 'I could never forgive myself and have never stopped suffering guilt for that moment when we were so close.' He stopped speaking.

'Oh Carlo, you know it wasn't, I could never have left you and Flora, but we both knew it would have been something we could never have lived with. The guilt would have destroyed both of us, but you took the blame and it made me love you more than ever.'

He held her close, lost for the words that were in his heart.

'I love you so much, Emma, and have done for a long time. You brought so much happiness to us.'

He stopped for a second or two then he added, 'But perhaps it was for the best, how long could we have gone on pretending?'

She knew he was speaking the truth; could they have gone on hiding their feelings? They would never know.

He continued: 'If Flora had known the truth, what a terrible thing Robert had done, I don't know what would have happened; it would have been so terrible for her. I can't begin to think how she would have been able to live with the truth. And if I had known I think I would have wanted to kill him.

He stopped, and then slowly said: 'She left some letters that I feel are important for you to read. One is from Robert sent on by the War Office when he was killed. It's very important for you to know that Flora told me to go and find you and that you were with Maria and Joe.' He paused.

She wrote, *if there was anyone in the world that would help me find happiness it was with you, and gave us her blessing.*

He held her tightly in his arms and let her sob the pain away until she was able to accept that there was nothing that could be undone, that God and destiny had decided everything from the beginning. They stayed until the sun went down, talked and held each other, afraid that this moment was not real. There was so much to say and when he felt it possible to tell her the most important thing of all.

'Emma, I have come to take you home, we cannot stay in Italy, things are unstable with what is happening with Mussolini and which way he will go. It could be very dangerous.' She looked at him with concern.

'But Maria and Joe?'

He replied: 'They will be fine they are Italian and far away from the city. As long as they do not get involved with politics they will be safe here in the hills, and believe me there are many who we already know have joined together to form a resistance. But for you and me its different. I will explain everything to you later, Emma, I will make it up to you; I will never let you out of my life as long as I live.'

She looked at him unable to speak, but just held him until his lips again found hers.

They slowly walked back to the house to find the news had reached Joe, and now Maria had decided to organise a surprise. She hoped that what she had planned would not be unwelcome, but this had to be done. No more waiting as these were dangerous times and every moment was precious for Emma and Carlo who must be united together in the eyes of God and the world, and she was determined to make sure that would happen.

She had taken Carlo's bag to his room and began to hang up the few items inside and as she emptied the contents, she noticed the blue tissue paper that lay folded at the bottom, protecting what she thought was slightly unusual in a man's case, particularly with so little room for non-essentials. Carefully, unwrapping the folds, the soft cream chiffon material revealed itself. She lifted it out gently and holding it up could see it was the most beautiful dress she had ever seen. It must have been put away carefully in the tissue for it had a fragrance still lingering. It seemed familiar and the realisation soon came to her that it had an owner and it was Emma.

She put it on a hanger to let any creases fall and laid the tissue paper over its top.

She knew now what she must do. She hurried back downstairs to the hallway and picked up the phone, dialling a number she knew by heart.

'Vito,' Father Vittorio answered.

'Yes its Maria, what are you doing?' she asked her brother who had been the village priest for many years, after Father Di Marco had retired.

'Since you are asking, I am sitting down drinking a glass of wine with my feet up after an exhausting day: two funerals, a baptism; and a wedding,' he replied. Even thinking about it raised his blood pressure. A screaming child all the way through the baptism with the lungs of Caruso was the first event of the day: Then a wedding where the father of the bride, who had drowned his sorrows in something far more powerful than holy water, decided to plant a punch on his pregnant daughter's intended, causing an unexpected catastrophe.

The last straw was the funeral, when the widow of the deceased fainted after an hysterical outburst during the funeral service.

Now his sister's nonsensical demands about a wedding. She must be having some kind of brainstorm expecting a wedding ceremony at night and not in his church! 'Has the world gone mad?' he was about to exclaim!

'Well, you must make another wedding' replied Maria.

'I suggest you phone tomorrow and, whoever is getting married, we can put a day in the book, he replied.

'No it must be tonight before the baby comes' she answered

'What baby, what are you talking about Maria, have you been drinking?' Maria tutted and continued with her determined demands for her brother's attendance this night.

'You must do it here. God will not forgive you if you don't.'

Maria thought Vito was about to explode, who, now certain his sister was going through some kind of mental aberration, answered trying to control himself: 'I only do weddings in God's house.'

But Maria, determined, said: 'You told me God is everywhere, your house, my house, everybody's house. Do you think he cares when the circumstances are so urgent?'

Vito, now about to hang up, stopped as Maria said: 'Alright who do you owe the new church roof to, whose father paid for water, electricity and provided work for Monte Verde, who paid for the school?'

Father Vito now replied, 'Giancarlo, but he is with his Maker'

'Well his son is not,' answered Maria.

'But Carlo is married to Flora.'

Maria replied quietly 'She is now with God and I know he wants you to help him now, as he has also kept up the promise he made and continued the benevolence his father started.'

Father Vittorio was quiet. He was beaten and he knew it, and now understood what he must do.

'What time?' he asked, submissively.

Maria, content she had achieved her goal, replied 'Seven o'clock, and you will have a dinner to remember,'

Vito was convinced by the added temptation, as Maria's cooking was not to be missed and far better than his housekeeper's.

'Don't forget your vestments,' she added, just to annoy him. The remark received a grunt. Honestly, as if he would. He said 'You forget that this ever happened, or the bishop may defrock me!'

'You had better forget it too or you may find yourself in more trouble than the bishop,' she retorted.

The happy couple returned to the house, Maria and Joe beaming with happiness at seeing the smiling faces of Emma and Carlo. And Maria more than ever pleased at what she had organized. She had unpacked Carlo's bag for him, and if she hadn't, she pondered, why had he asked her to deal with it? Maybe it's what he had planned. But Maria's knowledge of men was that they are inclined to procrastinate and there were times when a woman must decisions for them!

Maria, in her heart, thought this was a sign from above, as Carlo had brought Emma's most treasured dress, perfect for her wedding. Did he intend it? Well, if he didn't, she was sure the surprise would be most welcome.

As soon as they had a proper greeting and talked about so much in a short time, Maria said to Emma, 'We have a guest tonight and a special surprise.' Emma laughed 'Another surprise!'

'Yes, now why don't you go and prepare yourselves for our celebration dinner. You and Carlo are in the blue room, but Emma, you are in the rose room, for now.'

Carlo looked surprised that they would be given separate rooms. After all they had been through, surely a little departure from tradition was called for.

'Now Carlo don't give me that look, all will be well', she laughed, 'let Emma get ready without your interruptions. What is another few hours, um?'

Everyone laughed and guessed there was something afoot. Emma kissed Maria and Joe and, of course Carlo, and went to her room. It was the room she had slept in when they came on holiday, but with a difference; there hanging up on the front of the wardrobe was her dress. She couldn't help crying. He had brought it, even in these circumstances. She had been brokenhearted when she discovered that it had been left behind. It was probably still at the house, forgotten in the rush to empty her belongings.

Now it was here and what more appropriate for this, their rejoicing at being together again. This time, God willing, for as long as they lived.

She bathed and did her hair the way she used to; the way he liked it. For the first time in more than a year or two she put on a little rouge on her cheeks and some perfume that had been a gift from Paolo, who had acquired her favourite by asking Maria.

Looking in the mirror one more time and pleased with the result, she made her way downstairs. Everyone waiting for her to appear. Carlo too had been persuaded to wait for her there with everyone else.

They were silent, but smiling, he spoke first. 'You look so beautiful, Emma.'

'It's the dress,' she laughed.

'No,' he said, 'it's you that makes the dress.'

Everyone nodded their agreement.

'Now,' Maria said 'We have a special guest tonight who has come to carry out a ceremony that I believe should seal the happiness of the most deserving of couples. Of course if it's not they can change their minds.' She laughed. Carlo had wondered if something was going on that seemed out of the usual. And, as for Father Vito being invited so quickly, well?

Now Paolo had arrived and Maria and Joe spoke in unison. Joe taking over, said: 'Carlo have you the right intentions toward Emma?'

Carlo laughed and replied, 'Yes, quite a few.'

They all laughed but he now realised that this had been a cue, and turning to Emma said: 'Will you marry me Emma?'

She now looked at him and half smiling and full of emotion said 'Yes! Oh yes!' and Carlo took her in his arms and kissed her.

'Right' said Father Vito, wanting to get on with it, 'Let's begin, I am getting hungry.'

Much amused, and in agreement for they wanted the celebrations to begin, they went out onto the terrace, which Joe had quickly decorated with flowers and some bunting, along with the table ready for the celebration. Joe gave Emma away, Maria was maid of honour, and Paolo was best man. The evening was perfect, warm and pleasant and in no time at all Emma Grey had become Signora Villarni.

The wedding breakfast could not have been better; Maria had excelled herself and now Carlo looked at Emma and smiled, 'You must be tired.'

She smiled at him knowing that this was a hint for them to excuse themselves from their guests. 'You must be, too, after all that travelling,' she replied.

Paolo, taking the hint added, 'I think it's all that wonderful food and wine, its time I made a move. What about you Father Vito?'

The priest being passed caring would have been quite happy to sit there for some considerable time and was quite oblivious to the polite hint for the newly-weds to be alone.

Maria gave him a nudge and, winking, added 'Yes, Vito you look all in. I suggest Paolo gives you a ride back home and you can have your car delivered tomorrow morning.'

He looked slightly disappointed that the party was about to end, but finally took the hint. Thanking Maria and Joe for a wonderful evening and giving the happy couple a parting blessing he accompanied Paolo to his car.

Paolo had never been a big consumer of alcohol and had taken it slowly, realising that it was very important that nothing untoward occurred in the travelling arrangements, that could cause problems for any of them. His position as a lawyer and now a member of 'The Party' could cause un-imaginable complications.

Everyone wished them a safe journey home and Carlo whispered a quiet thank you to his friend with, as was the custom, a gentle hug. Paolo smiled and whispered with a big grin on his face, 'Sleep well, see you tomorrow.' He got into the car and departed the one and a half kilometres down the hill to the village.

Carlo turned to Maria and Joe. 'How can I ever thank you both?' He gave Maria a kiss on her cheek and an affectionate embrace for Joe. Emma did the same and, feeling emotional, could hardly find the words to express her feelings. Maria smiling, and possibly remembering her wedding night, said: 'Off you go... sleep late and God bless you both.' Her eyes shone with the glistening of a tear.

Carlo stopped at the door to their bedroom. He smiled: 'I am supposed to carry you over the threshold, am I not?'

Emma, laughing, replied: 'Better not, remember your back. Not a good time to injure yourself!'

He opened the door and, almost carrying her inside, closed it quickly and took her in his arms with an unmistakable grin that she could see in the half light from the moon that lit up the room.

He smiled. 'Don't worry about my back, Signora Villarni.'

Emma laughed. 'You haven't changed, have you?'

'Never will,' he replied, with that look she knew so well.

She looked at him. 'Please promise me that you won't.'

'I promise,' he said taking her into his arms and kissing her again and again to make up for all the time they had been apart, and for the love that had survived more pain and heartache than could ever have been deserved.

They took Maria at her word and slept late and, even after waking, Emma, due to a call of nature, carefully freed herself from the still sleeping Carlo's arms. She looked down at his face and thought just how much she loved him.

He was still the most handsome man she had ever set eyes on. Their need for each other had been so strong and sleep was postponed until the excitement and the events of the day, not to mention, the best wine, had taken their toll. Both laughing, they realized that this wasn't a hotel and they had to respect that their hosts would expect them to make an appearance well before lunchtime, which wasn't too far away.

Emma decided now she was awake she may as well bathe and do something with her hair. She thought Carlo's father must have been a very clever man. When he had the house modernised, he tried to make it as practical as possible. Each large bedroom had a small dressing room with a sink and, eventually, when Carlo had inherited the house, he had installed the latest plumbing available.

He had invested a great deal of money in many directions, not only modernising the house with everything available, but wherever possible adding the luxuries they had in the house in Chelsea; some of it a very expensive investment. Much had been a fairly recent renovation for when Maria and Joe returned to Italy.

After all, they had lived in England for twenty years and had been used to proper plumbing, a rare find in these villages.

Apart from the Villa Rosa, Carlo had continued to honour his father's promise by continuing to pay for the many works that were needed to improve the lives of the village of Monte Verde.

After she was satisfied with her appearance she opened the door. Carlo was sitting up in bed and beckoned her to join him.

She smiled. 'So you are awake.'

He pulled her to him, 'Yes, very, you didn't need to fix your hair,' he laughed as he pulled her into his arms. Now they would be late for lunch!

Suddenly, there was a frantic knocking at the door. They both looked at each other, was it that late?

Carlo said: 'Go to the bathroom Emma and I will see what is so important.' A voice that was obviously Paolo's answered. 'So sorry Carlo, it's an emergency!'

He put on a dressing gown that obviously belonged to Joe, as it was as big as a tent and too short. Nevertheless he was decent and opened the door to a worried-looking Paolo.

'Bad news. War has been declared between England and Italy. You and Emma must leave tonight. It's all arranged. I will tell you all when you are ready.'

Carlo told Emma to get ready and pack what was essential while he bathed so they would be ready to go later.

Emma, now worried, hurried to get her things together. They then dressed in the usual plain attire of the country folk and went downstairs, Emma felt a little shy and was not sure how the conversation would go.

However, she need not have worried as it was confined to the necessary plans that would be for their eventual departure. The very subject brought a sad and woeful expression to Maria's face.

For Emma the last eighteen months with them had given her back a life that was bearable and, with the close friendship of Paolo, the thought of leaving them was causing confusion in her emotions. But she knew that there was no choice. Carlo had made it clear that they had to leave, not only for themselves. If they were discovered here everyone connected to them could also be in danger. For the moment she must put any negative thoughts aside and pray that everything would be alright.

CHAPTER NINETEEN

The 3rd of June 1940

Lunch had been delayed slightly because Paolo had been summoned to the office in Sorrento for something that was apparently urgent. He had called by very early to tell Maria he could be late and, therefore, perhaps they should not wait on account of him. Maria of course had somehow had a premonition that lunch may finish up as an early dinner. She told him not to worry and to arrive when he could.

Emma and Carlo, relieved to hear that they had not inconvenienced anyone, after some coffee and fresh bread and marmalade. a speciality of Maria's of course, decided to take a quick walk on a small path up to the top of the hill behind the house. Emma expressed certain anxiousness as it looked rather steep, but Carlo, smiling, said: 'Don't worry, I will take you through a secret path that's hidden from the road. I promise you will love the view. I want you to have a wonderful memory of this place to keep until we return. And we will, my darling.'

They set off, with Carlo holding her hand, and, as promised after a short climb that was easier than it looked, they walked along a flatter piece of rock and, behind a small clump of trees, they came upon the entrance to a cave that was completely hidden from view.

Emma, genuinely surprised, said: 'Well, what a hiding place. How exciting, I bet you found this when you were a boy.'

Carlo laughed. 'Of course.'

'Who knows it's here?' she asked.

'No-one. My secret hideaway.'

'We can make love here, no-one will find us.' He gave her one of his looks that she could never quite tell if he was joking or not.

'Better not, the ground looks a bit uncomfortable', she said looking for some clue as to whether this was a joke or not.

Carlo grinned 'We haven't really got time, if last night was an example, have we?'

She knew he was joking. 'Of course, you are quite right, sir, nothing so important should be hurried.' Both laughing, they continued further into the cave which began to rise slowly upward.

They arrived at another opening and found themselves at the top of the mountain. Emma, now a little breathless, found herself looking over the bay and the bluest sea imaginable.

'Oh Carlo, it's so beautiful,' she said looking at him.

'Yes, This is the other side of the mountain overlooking a different bay, its called the Dui Golfi, in English the Two Gulfs; one side is Versuvius and the other the Bay of Salerno.'

They stood together his arm around her. 'Remember this place, this day, and I promise we will come back, Emma.'

She could see what looked like a tear and knew she was the only person in the world to whom he could ever show how much this place, this country, meant to him.

Of course she understood, this was his birthplace and his love of both Italy and England was deeply engraved in his heart. Now they were at war, it was breaking.

Their last few hours with Joe and Maria were to be spent with overtones of sadness, but joy as well, as now they knew that, with God's blessing, they could get away before things got really dangerous. All they wanted was for Carlo and Emma to be safe and have a happy life together after everything that had happened.

Paolo drove as fast as he could, anxious to get back to the Villa Rosa as quickly as possible. He had left the office in a turmoil, the staff running about not knowing what to do. The news of war between Italy and England had filtered through to them. It was something that no-one had really believed would happen. Paolo made the excuse that he had important legal issues to deal with and, in the circumstances; perhaps it would be advisable to close the office early. He realised very little work would be done and that everyone should go home to their families as no-one, at this point, had any idea what would happen next or how it would change their lives.

Naturally, there were those who had been taken up by the rhetoric of Mussolini and were of the belief that in joining Hitler, they would be the victors. Their might together could win a new powerful union in the world and defeat the enemies of the Third Reich and their Il Duce. And which would make Italy great again.

Paolo said nothing, careful to avoid any comment that could be interpreted as him being for or against this devastating news. He sent everybody home, gathered up his papers and locked the office door.

He knew, of course, questions might be asked as to why he had taken this decision, but he felt convinced that his senior partners would have more pressing things to deal with than to worry about his decision to close the office early.

He arrived back at the house and entered the kitchen, where both Maria and Joe were busy occupied with preparing what looked like their combined lunch and dinner, presuming that everyone would be hungry. Maria turned towards Paolo smiling, 'Ciao caro,' giving him a little kiss on the cheek.

He looked at her face and could see she had not taken the news too well.

He said: 'Zia, don't worry, everything will be alright.'

She looked at him with a questioning expression. 'I know I have to think positively', she said, with a little sniff.'

He looked at both Maria and Joe.

'I know Emma has been here long enough for you to want her to stay forever and now you feel afraid she will not come back; but I am sure God didn't bring her here, and then join her and Carlo together, after all they have been through, not to protect them. Just keep praying Zia.'

She smiled at him and said 'I know it's for the best and that Carlo and Emma must leave tonight.'

He didn't need to fill in the details. The fewer people who knew, the less dangerous for everyone, should anything go wrong. The tears filled her eyes and Joe hurried to her side and held her tightly in his arms. He was as distressed as his wife, but trying to keep from showing his feelings by keeping a brave hold on his emotions.

The last thing in the world they wanted was this. They had never really believed it would happen. Surely their leader would not drag them into another war, with the country where they had lived happily for so long?

The terrible realisation began to sink in that Emma and Carlo were in danger and their escaping to England was more complicated and dangerous than ever. Their trust in their nephew gave them courage to accept that there was no other choice. They would count the days until they heard that Carlo and Emma had arrived back in England safe and sound.

Carlo and Emma, holding each other's hand, laughing and enjoying every second together, stopped at Pippo and Gigi's stable. Yes, that's the name Emma decided to call Pippo's bride.

'Look Carlo. They are like us, totally in love.'

They are grooming each other with such enthusiasm. There was no mistaking what this pretty little donkey had done for Pippo. They went inside, gave them a cuddle and stroked their long silky ears. The donkeys seemed to revel in, and gave little noises of approval.

Emma told them that they would return as soon as possible. She gave them both a kiss and quickly departed before their goodbyes proved too painful.

Deciding that they really must not delay Maria's cooking plans any longer, they approached the house and saw Paolo's car parked in its usual place. He had returned quickly for their last few hours together. He would deliver them safely to the beach after dark, and see them safely on board a fishing vessel.

Trying not to let their departure be as sad as they were feeling, Carlo and Emma entered the kitchen. They could tell immediately by Maria's face that told a story in itself. She was still crying and wiping her eyes with a handkerchief, Joe still comforting her.

'Alright, our worst fears have happened but we must remain positive. Let's hope this war will be over quickly,' he said.

They all nodded. Maria crossed herself and tried to put the gloom she felt aside for the sake of the others.

Paolo, taking Carlo aside, said 'I got here as quickly as I could this morning. When I got to the office the phone went mad. Evidently word got through that war could be declared anytime and, within half an hour the news was confirmed.

'Tomaso's brother is sailing tonight and you will leave with them on the tide from the beach we go to. You must travel light, but take something warm for the journey. They will take you to Sicily, and then his cousin will take you to Malta. There you will be met and arrangements for your journey to England planned. I will try to contact William and tell him where you are.'

Emma turned to Carlo. She wanted to say something, but the words did not come, they didn't need to. They both knew what this meant because William had already warned Carlo that, if this happened suddenly, it would not be possible to get them both back to Rome safely, and in time for the necessary evacuation of everyone in the embassy.

Paolo spoke up. 'I had already made a contingency plan in case of this happening. It's out of the question that both of you would be able to get very far by road.'

Carlo said: 'Whatever decisions have to be made, we will be together. No matter what, I have our papers and, come what may, we will have to face it together.'

Emma looked at her husband and knew that he would stand by his words. She put her arms around him and he held her close and murmured: 'Don't worry Emma, we will find a way. I am sure there are those who will help us. There are other means to leave Italy other then by road.'

Paolo agreed. 'You know how much Tomaso loves you, Carlo; he is no Fascist. In fact very few are here in Monte Verde.

'His brother, Mario, is a fisherman and sails as far as Sicily for the best fish. I went to see him and hinted that I may need his help in something that could be risky. Without naming names, I said that there was someone who means a lot to him who may need his help, as his life could be in danger. Tomaso said 'I won't press you to tell me now, but you know Paolo, I have known you since you were a little boy. If someone we know is in danger and is dear to you, they must be close to me and it goes without question that I will do all could to help.' I thanked him and said 'that at this moment it was not necessary, but if it is I will let him know.'

Each was aware that this was no light-hearted promise. Everyone tried not to look so glum and was quiet, waiting for more information on what lay ahead. Whatever it was they all knew it would have to be implemented sooner rather than later. Much later was not on the agenda as the escape had to be done by sea and tonight.

It was now no longer possible to feel the elation and happiness that had filled everybody's hearts. Their joy of seeing these two people, who had been through so much heartache, now joined together, had been uppermost in their minds. However, destiny had brought them another difficulty to overcome, and, this time, it could be life-threatening.

For Emma and Carlo, the main thing was they were together. That knowledge gave them the resolve to face what ever fate threw at them and they would trust in God to guide them through it.

They sat silently until at last Maria said: 'No-one has eaten for hours, and you cannot think straight hungry'.

This brought a lighter tone to the atmosphere. Maria was always thinking of her flock's need for sustenance. She got everyone moving, although food was the last thing they had been thinking about. Finally, it was served with the realization that it could be sometime before they would eat again.

As usual, excellent antipasto was followed by baby chicken and zucchini in tomato sauce. This was, naturally, accompanied by red wine from their vineyard. This helped to make them relax. It could be their last meal at the Villa Rosa for who knows when!

The food and wine seemed to have done the trick. It had lightened the atmosphere, when Paolo broke the news that they would have to go as soon as there was little moonlight and the sea was calm. They would leave from the local beach where they had swum when they were all on holiday. They could only take necessary items that were light and easy to carry. Making sure they had some warm and comfortable clothing for the night at sea.

'Don't worry,' Paolo spoke assuring them he would know when the sea conditions and the moon were at their best. They should prepare themselves for a speedy departure.

There was not too much time to prepare for their departure. Having eaten enough to line their stomachs they packed the few necessary things that were easy to carry. Emma's dress had to be left behind.

Maria said: 'Don't worry I will put it away safely for when you return.'

There were more tears from both women. Still holding each other tight, they found it difficult to leave each other's arms. In turn the men saved their good-byes to the last. They left Monte Verde.

Paolo's car drove them down the dark mountain road to the beach where on so many occasions they had enjoyed their swims. This most private of coves held so many memories for all of them. Fortunately there were no other vehicles on the road and within ten minutes they had arrived. Paolo parked his car amid the trees where it could not be seen from the road.

There was little moonlight and when they got used to the darkness, they carefully walked along the side of the beach where the rowing boat was to pick them up to take them to the larger vessel.

Paolo told them to take off their shoes, ready to walk through the shallow water to the small boat. It was there, waiting for them in a little inlet where the water was deep enough for them to get aboard from the rocky out-crop without getting too wet. They had to wade through water on the way, but it was not deep. Emma had tucked her skirt above her knees and Carlo rolled up his trouser leg.

Now the most painful moment had arrived they hugged and kissed each other. Even the men tried hard to hide their feelings. Emma was really tearful to have to say good-bye to Paolo, to whom she owed so much. Carlo hugged his cousin and Emma knew, without even looking, that this moment was the hardest for all of them to deal with. They were helped into the boat and went swiftly away into the darkness.

The fishing boat was quite large and they were guided down below to a cabin that had been made as comfortable as possible for them. It was evident that the accommodation was very basic, for it was difficult, with all the will in the world, to make it other than as clean and comfortable as possible. Emma and Carlo realised that Mario had given them his own cabin and they were both grateful for somewhere to rest and, hopefully, get some sleep.

Emma did not know how she would be able to deal with a rough sea and just hoped that she would not get sea-sick. They were fortunate that it was currently fairly calm, but when they got out to deeper water this might change.

Tomaso's brother suggested some herbal tea and hoped they would sleep through the journey to Sicily. This could take several hours depending on the sea conditions.

Towards the open water the visibility had deteriorated. In one sense this was helpful to keep them less visible to any other shipping; on the other hand it made the going slower and hampered them getting to the island as quickly as possible. Later they were given a warm drink of coffee and there was no mistaking something a little stronger in it.

Emma looked at Carlo, still unable to believe what had happened in a matter of only three days. Here she was with the man she loved more than life, and now his wife and, with God's help, going home together. She prayed now and begged Him to keep them safe. Thanking Him over and over again, she at last fell asleep.

Emma had been encouraged by Mario, their skipper, to have a few more swigs of an unknown beverage, which turned out to be rum. It certainly did the trick and she cuddled Carlo, in the bunk that was meant for one. He had also circumbed to the effects of a swig or two of the elixir, letting their dreams take over. They had been encouraged to rest. If there was anything untoward occurring they would be aroused immediately.

It was still dark when they arrived in a small cove. Somehow word had gone well ahead as, waiting for them, were two men dressed in fishermen's clothing. A small boat, which had been waiting in the shallows, had come to meet them.

They were lowered very carefully over the side of the bigger vessel, and without too much difficulty, found themselves being rowed swiftly to the shore. Much to their surprise it had started to rain and their helpers smiled, saying: 'Its good: less people to see us.'

They then began to speak in what sounded to Emma an even more un-intelligible dialect than Neapolitan. It was quite beyond her comprehension, although Carlo seemed to cope with it.

They hurried along a path towards some buildings in the distance, but as they got nearer they turned off into a dark alley. They approached a door set in the old wall, which must have stood there for hundreds of years, and were quickly ushered inside a tall house with closed shutters.

They followed the two men and found themselves in an enclosed courtyard, with several doors leading off, and were guided towards one. Entering a passageway, they continued until finally entering the last door and found themselves in a large room, which served as a kitchen with a large wooden table and several chairs, where they were to sit.

The smell of something wonderful cooking filled the air. A pasta sauce was simmering on the stove. Emma and Carlo looked at each other with delight as it had been many hours since their final meal with Maria, Joe and Paolo and they were now two very hungry people.

Their hosts told them to eat well as they would be leaving before long. This was just a quick stop before the next leg of their journey which would begin in an hour or so, when their next boat would take them to Malta, and, please God, well on the way for them to get home.

They had time to digest their much-appreciated food and, thanking their hosts for everything, they were led back down the passage again to the courtyard.

Slowly, Mario opened the old door and carefully glanced up and down the street. It was still raining and now Emma and Carlo, dressed in borrowed Fishermen's' waterproofs and hats, looked like any of the men getting ready to take their boats out to sea for the night's fishing. There was no-one about and they strolled towards the jetty. Arriving within minutes, they quickly climbed aboard and, with enormous relief, took off their waterproofs and headed for the interior of the ship.

Once again they were introduced to one of Mario's relatives. They no longer knew who was related to whom, it was just the usual thing in these parts. Nearly everyone was related to each other in some way or another. All that mattered was that they were family and that meant everything.

CHAPTER TWENTY

The Santa Teresa

They pulled up anchor in no time and were on their way into the blackness, which now seemed a bit intimidating. Being unable to see anything, Emma went below. Once again they had been given a cabin. This boat was larger than the previous one as the men sometimes went to sea for several days. The waters between Sicily and Malta were deep and fruitful and the men took advantage of being able to take home a big catch.

So far their adventure had been without danger and Emma prayed that God would help them reach safety. This part of the journey was long, and the sea rougher and Emma decided she would try to sleep as the swell was not so noticeable when she lay down. Carlo went up on deck to speak with the men and to discuss what plans were being put in place for them when they arrived.

The wind had really picked up and the ship was rolling side to side, Carlo could cope fairly well with the sea, but he was worried about Emma. So keeping the conversation fairly brief with the skipper, whose name was Toni, he was told that when they docked, Malta, being in British hands, arrangements had been made for him and Emma to be taken ashore to meet their next aid for further arrangements.

It seemed to Carlo that Paolo had been busy communicating with William, for however else would this be so well organised? He also knew only too well how much he owed to Paolo, who was risking his own life in helping to get him and Emma back to England

He went down to the cabin and found Emma sleeping and was hopeful that the sea would not get rougher and wake her. For someone not used to the rolling and swaying from side to side of the ship, it could be quite nauseating.

They had been sailing for several hours and it seemed the weather had worsened and visibility was bad.

Suddenly there was a loud knocking on the cabin door. Toni stood there and said quietly, 'There is a light off the starboard, can't tell who at this distance.'

Carlo knew their host was a little concerned.

'I suggest that if they come near to us, you and the Signora go to the hold. It smells a bit, but it's better to hold your nose there than anything worse!

Carlo knew what he meant. There had always been a risk that German ships could be in the area and if they were suspicious of anything that did not look as though it were just a fishing boat, they could be in trouble. England and France, already at war with the Germans, were aware that the enemy had submarines and gunboats roaming everywhere in the waters all over the Mediterranean and Tyrrhenian seas.

The one good thing was that the Santa Maria flew the Italian flag and was less likely to attract unwanted attention. However, Toni knew where the Germans were concerned, one should never be too confident about anything. His family had suffered in the First World War; for him, as with many Italians, the new threat was like a bad memory coming back to haunt him.

As the skipper, he left as quickly as he came and headed for the bridge shouting orders as he went. The crew went about their business preparing nets and securing ropes in the heavy sea. All looking as if this was a fishing vessel, and about to secure a good catch.

Carlo woke Emma and, in the easiest way he could manage, told her of their situation. The last thing he wanted to do was to frighten her unnecessarily, but at the same time he had to warn her there were certain precautions to be taken. They realized that, if the ship was boarded and searched, all would be lost if they were found without a plausible reason for them being there.

Emma said: 'I have an idea. See that big cushion? Let's stuff it in my dress. It will make me look very pregnant and I will lie on the bunk feeling very sick and you can say that the baby wasn't expected yet. We hope to get to land as quickly as possible, maybe an island nearby.'

Carlo looked at his wife. 'You know you are brilliant, my darling. Maybe you are pregnant, we don't know do we'? he smiled.

Emma looked at him and said, 'No, we don't do we!' grinning coyly,

'You had better ask Toni to kit you out like a fisherman's wife and give him the good news!' Carlo said.

'No, I think just a big jumper, a bucket by the bed and a damp cloth over my brow.'

He gave her a quick kiss. 'Brilliant,' he said and hurried out of the cabin door.

Carlo told Toni the plan and that both he and Emma had Italian ID with them, so that was fortunate. Toni was only given false names for their own safety and they were not asked to explain anything about themselves, thankfully.

He had told Emma, if the worst came to the worst and they were confronted with the enemy, she needn't speak, just moan and he would do the talking in dialect to her and she was just to acknowledge.

She looked at him, already the most awful thoughts flooding her head. She had found the love of her life again and now in only hours they could both die. All she could think of was that if they were killed she wanted them both to go together; she could never survive losing Carlo again.

He pulled her close. 'Stay calm Emma and play your part and we will be alright. We have to be just ordinary Italians on a visit and delayed because of the weather,' he assured her as confidently as he could. He gave her a kiss again and, as he turned back to the door he gave her one quick smile and headed back to the deck.

Their worst fears came about as the boat approached them. Neither Toni nor his men could identify the vessel properly, but there was something about its appearance that didn't ring true. Due to the bad visibility, and because of the rain, it was impossible at this stage to identify.

The vessel gradually came closer and eventually alongside, flooding the deck with search lights. They could see that although it was meant to look like another fishing vessel it wasn't and was too fast. Toni's suspicions were correct, as now they could see what appeared to be guns. Both Carlo and the skipper looked at each other acknowledging this looked like their enemy, and that now everything depended on their innocent behaviour, which hopefully would get them out of trouble!

They attached ropes to the Santa Teresa and four men came aboard led by what could not be mistaken as the commanding officer. They carried guns and were in the uniform of the German Navy.

Toni put on a friendly attitude and greeted the man in dialect. He was the kind that immediately let you know he was in command: arrogant and inclined to shout.

Everything depended on their acting naturally. The one thing that could help them was that they were reasonably confident that this man was not familiar with the Italian dialect the crew would use. Pretending they were unable to understand German was vital. Carlo did have a little knowledge of the German language and enough to catch the gist of what was being said.

However, they would never suspect that these peasant fishermen would understand anything they were saying. Carlo stood on the deck with the others waiting for the next move.

The officer shouted in German. Carlo knew he was asking where they were going and what and who was on board. He looked at the skipper, and testing the water of the German's knowledge of their dialect, said: 'Tell him we are fishing, and that in this unpleasant weather, the fish don't run.'

Toni, catching on said to the German officer in his Sicilian dialect: 'How nice to meet our allies and, yes, we are doing our duty and catching the fresh fish for our people and our friends.'

Toni took the Germans hand and shook it, whilst still gabbling on about how Il Duce and his friend Hitler would together win the war.

The German officer, now showing some impatience from this sudden flow of a language from Mars, and not understanding a word, was only able to recognise the names of the Fuhrer and Il Duce. Then, Toni deciding to play the scene to the hilt gave the man a salute.

Of course the situation was not funny in any sense of the word and this German could have taken this response unkindly. However, giving Toni a long look, which screamed impatience, he made a gesture in sign language, showing he wanted to inspect below.

This was even more comical as the German made a gesture pointing downstairs with hands at the side of his face to indicate sleeping quarters. The three of them trooped downstairs. One of the Germans stood on the deck, whilst the other two were sent off to look around and search the ship.

The officer shouted back at them: 'Go and look in the hold.'

Carlo almost crossed himself about their change of plan not to hide down there.

When he first came aboard the smell of fish was overwhelming, but surprisingly now it hadn't seemed so bad and he had got used to it. Approaching the cabin the smell somehow seemed stronger, which was not the case before.

He walked behind Toni, touched his shoulder and gestured by touching the side of his nose with his finger and pulling a face.

Toni turned round and winked, with that typical Italian gesture of pointing his finger into his cheek. The meaning of which was to say he had done something artful.

Of course then Carlo knew he had deliberately thrown something fishy down there. It was unpleasant, but he could not help thinking this man was clever.

They approached a couple of small empty cabins and went on to where Emma was. The officer opened the door and was instantly surprised to see a woman laying there on the bunk moaning. He threw up his hands and in German shouted: 'What is this, why is a woman here?'

Carlo stepped forward and said 'Mia Moglia' and patted his stomach and uttered 'bambini.'

The German started asking questions, which Carlo understood perfectly. But he rattled off a reply in dialect that they were going to visit a relative, got off course and then decided to fish anyway and now the weather was bad.

The stench of the fishy smell had now permeated into the German's nostrils and enough was enough. All he wanted now was to get off this 'schizer' vessel. He ran up the stairs and headed toward the rear of the ship, when a shout from the other two members of his crew emerged from the hold and halted him in his tracks. Carlo wondered what had happened and why he was now hurrying toward them.

In very fast German, they were shouting very excitedly-something about guns. He told one of the men who accompanied him to wait there while he and the other man went with him. Carlo, who had understood too well the German word for 'guns', realised that a whole new and worse scenario was about to take place.

The German officer's mind was racing, asking why there were guns on a fishing boat? What exactly were they up to besides fishing or was that just to hide their real purpose? And exactly what had they found?

He glanced at Toni who looked down, which was enough for Carlo to know there was something he had not been aware of when getting on this boat. Just who was these 'fishermen?

They were left with the German, who had a gun in his hand.

At that moment Emma was aware that something had happened and with all the shouting knew that the 'something' was not good. She had left the cabin and walked quietly toward the narrow stairs up to the deck. As she put her head above the top of the steps she came face to face with a gun.

Both she and the German were surprised, which gave Toni the opportunity to bring his hand up and strike the man in his throat. He went down like a ton of bricks, choking, and collapsed on the floor.

Carlo quickly took Emma's arm and rushed her back towards the cabin.

'Go and hide. They must not see you. We have to catch them all by surprise and you are in danger my darling quickly.' He gently ushered her down the narrow steps.

Emma looked at him with so much concern, afraid of the worst; she had just found him and was she about to lose him? She bit her lip and hid the fear as much as she could. He grabbed her hand and whispered 'Wait for me, I will come for you.' He blew her a kiss and rushed back to the top of the stairs.

Toni now with the gun in his hand turned to Carlo and said in perfect English

'Well, my friend, one down, three or more to go.'

Carlo was lost for words for a second and shook his head with surprise, 'You're English!'

'No. As Italian as you, but brought up in England and there lie's my loyalty. You, my friend, are very important to someone, so this lot have to go.'

With that he threw the, now dead, German over the side.

'Quick, let's take them by surprise as they come up from the hold.'

Carlo nodded; he then grabbed the gun and a large piece of wood from the side of the deck and gave it to Toni. They ran and hid behind the entrance to the hold where they could not be seen by anyone coming up from below.

'Get ready,' he gestured to Carlo. 'I will clout one and you the other.'

Carlo nodded and within seconds the first head appeared. Toni waited until the commanding officer, who was in front, was nearly at the top whilst the other two men were just behind him and about halfway up.

He hit the first man hard on the head, who fell backwards onto the second man, who then fell onto the third, but not before Carlo had knocked the second one senseless back down the steps, where the three of them lay on top of one another at the bottom.

'To get their weapons, we have to deal with whoever is still on their boat. They will know by now something's amiss.'

Carlo looked at Toni. 'Who are your men? he asked.

'You don't want to know,' he smiled.

'Well, not now anyway, but whoever you are, we owe you our lives,' he said, patting Toni on the back.

'Don't thank us yet, we have one more job to do!'

With that he gestured to keep his head down and to follow him. They went to the other side of the boat and ducked low, hidden by the ropes and equipment that was piled high. Now, at the other end of the vessel they could see a sailor standing close to the bridge of the German boat and being joined by several others.

The visibility had deteriorated, and although they were quite close, the swell of the sea had both vessels bobbing up and down, making it worse.

Toni winked at Carlo. 'Thank God we didn't fire any guns, let's get them over here one by one.'

Carlo knew what had to come next. He knew it was 'them or us,' so with his best efforts to sound in authority, shouted in German hoping he had got his grammar right.

'We have found some guns. We have prisoners and we need you to help get them aboard. We have them here in the hold.'

The man on the cruiser shouted he would be over right away. He needed to secure the boat. He was in charge, as they also heard him address the others. This of course was worrying as they were not sure how many there were. But obviously they had to deal with all of them as no-one could be left on their boat.

Carlo translated for Toni the bad news that it seemed there had been more than four men aboard who they would have to deal with. Sure enough the fifth man climbed over and headed toward the rear of the ship. Whilst he held the rail to descend the steps, Toni quickly went up behind him and struck him on the back of his head with the gun and he went down like a sack of potatoes.

Carlo said: 'You don't muck around, do you!

Toni sighed. 'Can't afford to, do you know what they would have done to us, given the chance?'

Carlo shook his head.

'Beaten us till senseless and then put a bullet in our brains if they had got no information out of us. And with your wife, my friend …' He didn't finish the sentence.

'We must get the others somehow; get these bodies onto their boat and then sink it. Then no trace, and no retribution.'

Fortunately for them, there was a drop the other side of the rail into their boat. The other men now climbing across from their vessel wondering what was happening to their comrades.

They took a deep breath knowing that no one could be left on the German vessel and all of them had to be dealt with.

Carlo said: 'Perhaps I should shout through the loud hailer that every man was needed, and to secure their boat so they can assist with the prisoners.'

Toni paused and, with a loud sigh, agreed this seemed the best option. At least his voice would be slightly distorted and, in German, ought to be convincing enough. Carlo picked up the loud hailer and shouted what seemed like a command to be obeyed. Sure enough two more men appeared, one busy seeing to the ropes that were attached securing the two boats alongside each other. He, unaware that this was a trap, hurriedly climbed aboard the Santa Teresa.

Not noticing Toni and Carlo, who were slightly obscured by the top of the open hatch, they hurried to their destiny: heavy metal bars across the back of their heads. Carlo had never considered killing anyone in his life, but this was war and nothing would prevent him from protecting Emma, What Toni had revealed would not be anything but a brutal end to all of them.

He now realised that Toni and his crew were definitely not just fisherman, but professionally trained men in the art of killing, like soldiers. Of course that was exactly who they were. He just hoped that they could all finish this horrifying experience alive.

Having despatched the last of the enemy, the rest of the crew came out from their positions where they had been placed for the strategy needed, if things had gone wrong. They swiftly removed the dead bodies and returned them to the now empty cruiser, which was then fired on. Having swamped the decks in fuel oil, it went up like an incendiary. It burned and sunk to the bottom of the Tyrrhenian Sea.

'I can say thank you for saving our lives and it won't be forgotten. You are a brave man,' Carlo said, shaking his hand.

'You're not bad yourself, Signor Travinni,' Toni replied with a grin.

Carlo thanked God Emma had stayed hidden; he did not want her to witness what had transpired. It was something that had to be done, but it was not something to be witnessed if it could be avoided. Of course he had to tell her. She took it well and expressed her thanks to Toni and the crew.

'How can we ever thank you? You risked your lives for us.' She was almost tearful with emotion. 'God bless you all.'

Toni took her hand to his lips, a typical Italian gesture of respect and politeness.

'You were very brave and kept your head, Madam.' He reverted to English manners and form of address. 'I think everyone could do with a tot or two. All agreed?'

A rousing cheer went up from everyone and an assortment of alcohol, but mostly rum, went round the group. All were now eager to celebrate their success, which was followed by a prayer thanking God for their lives and asking forgiveness for what they had to do. They raised their glasses and said in unison: 'For King and Country.'

They headed for Valetta, which was now only thirty nautical miles to safety, as this was British territory, and their task was to deliver their two passengers safely to their destination. Whoever they were was not revealed in case of being captured. All Toni knew was that they were to be protected at all costs and maybe, one day, he would find out.

Arriving in the small straights that led toward the city of Valetta, they gathered to say their goodbyes. Emma, although a little tearful, smiled and thanked them all for risking their lives.

To Toni she gave a hug and said: 'We can never thank you enough, please God take care of you.'

Carlo shook Toni's hand and then as Italians do, they hugged each other like brothers. Emma turned back and waved and said 'Be safe.'

'And you too,' they all shouted as Emma and Carlo departed.

They learned much later that the crew were part of the newly-formed commando sea forces that Winston Churchill had created and who became so important in their role in helping win the war that followed.

When they alighted from their boat they were at a landing stage and there to meet them was a man in uniform. He marched straight to them and introduced himself 'I am Commander John Simpson. I am here representing the Governor, Sir Maurice Bonham-Carter, who is unable to greet you in the present circumstances, but who welcomes you to Malta and would like you to be his guest at the Residency. It may not be for very long, as we hope to get you both safely on a plane to England as quickly as possible. Things look as though they may deteriorate very quickly.'

Both Emma and Carlo thanked him and were now so glad to be on dry land after their unexpected adventure which could have so nearly caused their demise.

They were driven to the governor's residence, where they were made very welcome and given the opportunity to freshen up before dinner.

Carlo and Emma both looked at each other and, smiling, knew that there was only one person that had been able to have arranged all this.

The both said together, 'William, egged on by Lottie.'

Emma said: 'We have so much to thank them for, Carlo.'

'So very much, Emma,' he replied, taking her in his arms and kissing her.

They felt relief after all they had been through and now hoped that there were to be no similar experiences and that going home to England would be soon.

It came surprisingly faster than they had expected. They went for dinner with their host, the deputy governor, who was amazed at their story and their apparent resilience after such a terrifying ordeal. Carlo was able to tell him of all the help they had received in escaping from Italy and said they were very much looking forward to going home.

'Well, you will no doubt be glad to hear you will be leaving tonight, so I will not be able to offer you room and board,' he laughed.

Both Emma and Carlo were so glad at the news and thanked him for their wonderful reception and hospitality. He said: 'Just give my love to Blighty.'

They both promised to do so.

A few hours later they were taken to the airfield where an RAF plane was parked on the runway. They were escorted to the steps and found themselves greeted by the crew of a bomber bound for England with a few other diplomatic staff, who were being recalled.

Both exhausted, they fell asleep and were woken when they had arrived on British soil. They were overjoyed to see Lottie and William waiting there to greet them. They owed William so much, as it was obvious that he had arranged their rescue through his connections in high places.

Emma looked at Carlo and with tears of relief and happiness.

'Oh, Carlo at last we are home.'

'Yes, our home, have you missed it?'

'You most of all,' she said.

She couldn't mistake the shine in his eyes, as he took her in his arms,

'Promise you will never leave me again then,' he whispered.

She looked at him. 'Never, as long as I live.'

CHAPTER TWENTY ONE

1960 The Epilogue

Emma, refreshed after her swim, lay down on the sun lounger. It was late afternoon and the sun was still warm, but the light had changed to that soft golden hue that made everything so beautiful. She sighed as she wallowed in the moment of bliss, so absorbed in her thoughts and thanking God for everything that He had given her. She had to smile as the memories of the years that had passed so happily, came flooding back.

The Villa Rosa was now the most beautiful exclusive hotel in Campania and the most popular, with what some regarded the most amazing view imaginable.

A voice spoke to her and she looked up, 'Scusi, Signora, your apperativo is here, it's 5.30.'

A young man stood there smiling at her. He was tall and very handsome, with those beautiful brown eyes that seemed to speak volumes. His dark wavy hair completed the picture.

He spoke: 'You look lovely today and you have caught the sun.'

Emma laughed. 'Are you flirting with me, young man?'

He laughed and shrugged his shoulders.

'Well, why not? We Italians always appreciate a beautiful woman.'

He began speaking at first in the local Neapolitan dialect, which Emma understood as she had been so long in Italy in the past. He spoke again, but now in perfect educated Italian. She was about to reply when aware that someone was behind her, she felt strong arms around her shoulders.

A familiar voice said 'You should go and try your luck on that pretty blonde over there, and leave your mother and me to enjoy our anniversary.'

Carlo laughed as he looked at his son. It was like looking in the mirror at himself as a young man of nineteen. His son was certainly a danger to all young women!

Taking Emma's hand, he said: 'It's nearly time, my darling.'

She stood up and gave him a kiss before they began to walk hand in hand round the pool to the little promontory where their beloved olive tree still stood. Carlo told her it could have been there for hundreds of years and could have seen it all before.

'Look Emma,' and they watched the red glow of the sun slowly sinking into the sea.

'Do you remember that story that my mother used to tell me when I was little, about the sun going to sleep so that his brother the moon could come and light up the sky?'

'Of course, how could I ever forget it?' she said softly.

She stood looking back at the tree and she could have sworn that she could see a face in its gnarled old bark that seemed to smile.

She whispered, 'I love you tree,' and blew it a kiss. She was now more certain than ever that it understood every word.

Carlo said: 'And I love you too, and the olive tree.' He smiled knowing how much it meant to both of them. They sat on the old bench and watched the rich gold of the sun turning red as it sunk slowly into the Mediterranean.

So many years had passed since that day when he had found her again; here where they now stood, but it was still like yesterday as he took her into his arms and kissed her with as much passion as that first time, when at last destiny had brought them back together and, this time, for good.

Memories began to flood back when he recalled Flora was right with the message she left for him in his desperate hours, that Emma would give him back a purpose to life. Had she realised all along that a special bond had grown between them?

But he had always remembered the advice his father had received from Father di Marco. 'Always play by the rules, or suffer the consequences!' They had done so.

He took her hand. 'We had better go back and get ready for the party, there could be a few surprises in store,' he said, smiling.

Emma laughed, she knew the people she loved the most in the world would have been invited: Lottie, William, Paolo and his wife and, with Maria and Joe now in charge of arrangements, everything would be perfect. They would all be together with their son Gianni, who was the greatest blessing of all, and everything they could have ever wished for.

About the Author

Andria Lawrence began modelling, mostly photographic work, at the age of eighteen, after being spotted by an agent while working as a temporary receptionist for a fashion house.

Later, after joining another well-known agent, she was invited to join the cast of a light-hearted TV weekly series of comedy sketches, in which different well-known actors played the central character.

Drama and comedy shows saw Andria working with many of the great stars, not least Morecambe and Wise, Michael Bentine and Dick Emery in 'A Square World'. She also appeared in a number of TV commercials; and it was in one of them, for Tavern Keg Beer, that she was spotted by Roy Skeggs of Hammer Films. As a result, her acting career took off, with parts in *On The Buses, Love Thy Neighbour, Man About The House*, and *Countess Dracula*.

She had always wanted to write but, until recently, time and circumstances always seemed to prevent it. *The Olive Tree* is her first novel.